Also by Colin Cotterill

The Coroner's Lunch
Thirty-Three Teeth
Disco for the Departed
Anarchy and Old Dogs
Curse of the Pogo Stick

THE MERRY MISOGYNIST

Colin Cotterill

Quercus

First published in Great Britain in 2009 by Quercus
This paperback edition published in 2010 by

Quercus
21 Bloomsbury Square
London
WC1A 2NS

A CIP catalogue record for this book is available
from the British Library

ISBN 978 1 84916 196 1

10 9 8 7 6 5 4 3 2 1

Printed and bound in Great Britain by Clays Ltd, St Ives plc

To my wife, Jessi, who rescued me from misogynous ways and turned me into a big soft thing.

To Anjan, Valérie, David, Lizzie, Dad, Tony, Kay, Martina, Dr Pongruk, and Bounlan for their invaluable help and to Ethel Appleyard, who did me the great favour of producing me.

Long overdue thanks to Richard Curtis and Laura Hruska for launching and subsequently suffering me.

Aaaaand, a special thanks to all of you who have been helping with the Books for Laos project (www.colincotterill.com).

FORM A223-79Q

ATTENTION: Judge Haeng Somboun
C/O: Department of Justice,
People's Democratic Republic of Laos

FROM: Dr Siri Paiboun

RE: National Coroner

DATE: 13/6/1976

RESUME:

1904 Plus or minus a year - years didn't have such clear boundaries in those days. Born in Khamuan Province, purportedly to Hmong parents. I don't recall it myself.

1908 Whisked off to live with a wicked aunt.

1914 Dumped in a temple in Savanaketh and left to the will of the Lord Buddha.

1920 Graduate from the temple high school. No great feat.

1921 Buddha investment pays off: shipped to Paris by kindly French sponsor intent on making something of me. The French make me start high school all over again just to prove it wasn't a fluke the first time.

1928 Enrol at Ancienne Medical School.

1931 Meet and marry Bouasawan in Paris and join the Communist Party for a lark.

1934 Begin internship at Hotel Dieu Hospital. Decide I might want to become a doctor after all.

1939 Return to Laos.

1940 Frolic in the jungles of Laos and Vietnam. Reassemble broken soldiers and avoid bombs.

1975 Come to Vientiane hoping for a peaceful retirement.

1976 Kidnapped by the Party and appointed national coroner. (I often weep at the thought of the great honour bestowed upon me.)

Sincerely,

Dr Siri Paiboun

CONTENTS

1

FIVE DEAD WIVES

By the time the calendar pages had flipped around to 1978, Vientiane, the capital of the People's Democratic Republic of Laos, had become a dour place to live. The fun had been squeezed out of it like the hard-to-come-by juice of a durian. It was flat and colourless and starting to feel sorry for itself.

The novice socialist administration that had ousted the six-hundred-year-old monarchy was starting to realize its résumé didn't match the job description. In the two years since taking over the country the prime minister had survived four assassination attempts. The army was moonlighting in timber exports and Pathet Lao troops were black-marketing petrol. A new class had been added to those sent to the north for re-education: corrupt socialist officials.

The numbers told the tale. The per-capita income was less than ninety US dollars, and over a hundred thousand people had already fled the city to try their luck in the Thai refugee camps across the Mekong. Eighty-five per cent of those remaining in the country were subsistence farmers yet for the first time in its history Laos had resorted to importing rice. An unprecedented drought the previous year had resulted in the Department of Agriculture's predicting a famine for '78. It appeared even the Lord Buddha had deserted his flock. Decrees had been passed limiting private commerce but that hadn't made a lot of difference as there was hardly any money to spend. The five hundred million dollars pumped into the city by the US imperialists during the Vietnam War had well and truly dried up. The expressions on the faces of the people who lived in the quiet capital city advertised the city's joylessness. In fact, on March 11 of that year, there were only two truly happy men in the entire country.

One was seventy-three, soon to be seventy-four-year-old Dr Siri Paiboun, the national coroner. It was astounding that a man so ancient, with so much bad karma tallied up against him, had been able to find any joy at all. Two years earlier, his dream of retirement had been bullied out of him and he had been designated the country's only medical examiner. It was the nadir of a lifetime of unfortunate decisions: decades of trying to understand his own Communist Party, decades of marriage to a woman too focused on revolution to start the family he craved, decades of putting together soldiers broken from the countless battles of a never-ending civil war. What was one more unwanted job after a litany such as that?

But then, as if by a belated good fate, widower Siri had been reunited with Madame Daeng, the freedom fighter, still pretty at sixty-six, still carrying a torch for her silver-haired doctor. The couple had tumbled head over heels in love and, just two months earlier, they had married. The honeymoon showed no signs of abating and the smile hadn't left the coroner's lips since.

The other truly happy person on that steamy March day was the man who some knew as Phan. He'd just done away with his fifth wife and, as usual, nobody was any the wiser. How could a man not be overjoyed at such success?

'Are you Dr Siri?'

'Yes.'

'Dr Siri Paiboun?'

'Yes.'

'The coroner?'

'Three out of three; you win a coconut.'

'You have to come with me.'

Siri stood at the foot of the stairs that led to the upper floor of Madame Daeng's noodle shop on Fa Ngum Street. He wore only a pair of Muay Thai boxing shorts and a crust of sleepy dust. His thick white hair was tousled and his eyes puffy. He hadn't planned on being awake before eight and it was only a quarter past six. Daeng had gone down to set up for the morning noodle rush and had responded to the loud knocking at the shutters. She had checked the man's credentials before rousing her hungover husband. Even though Siri was only 153 centimetres in his sandals he still managed to rise half a head above the intruder in the slate grey safari suit.

'Who are you?' Siri asked.

'Is this your place of abode?'

'Has anybody told you that answering questions with questions inevitably leads to your vanishing up your own—?'

'Siri!' Madame Daeng caught him just in time. It was unwise to rile a bureaucrat, even a very small one. Both men looked up when she pulled back the double shutters to give the Mekhong River a better view of the inside of her shop. The early sunlight glittered on the water like a shoal of day stars. A solitary fisherman rowed his boat against the current and seemed to be travelling backwards – perhaps more than seemed.

'As I told your …as I told the comrade,' the man said, 'I am Koomki from the Department of Housing Allocation.'

Siri's stomach clenched. Somewhere deep down he'd been expecting this visit. He backed up two steps and sat down on the bare wood. Daeng had begun to prepare the ingredients for the day's *feu* noodle soup at the rear of the shop.

'Dr Siri,' Koomki continued, 'we have an inconsistency in our files.'

'And what would that be?' Siri asked as if he didn't know.

'You, Comrade.'

'Madame Daeng,' Siri called to his wife, 'did you hear that? I'm an inconsistency.'

'That's why I married you, sweetness.'

The man from housing blushed.

'I think you'll realize soon enough that this is hardly a joking matter,' Koomki said. 'Is this your place of abode or not?'

Siri resented Koomki's tone. 'No.'

'You're standing here naked but for a pair of shorts and this lady is clearly your wife—'

'Oh, no, I'm not,' Daeng interrupted.

'Not his wife?'

'Not a lady.'

The man was plainly out of his depth with this couple. He held up his clipboard to his damp bulgy eyes and read from it. 'Dr Siri, you are registered as the householder of allocated government accommodation unit 22B742 at That Luang.'

'Then that's obviously where I live,' Siri assured him.

'Well, it's clear to our department that although there are a number of people living in that bungalow, you are not among them.'

'And what's your definition of living?' Siri asked.

'I…er…'

'I assume you have one?'

'It's…it's the place where you sleep.'

'Really? So insomniacs would never qualify for government housing?'

'What?'

'You have to admit our government's causing us a lot of sleepless nights. In fact, I'd wager most people aren't sleeping at all. I do have a bed on which to lay my head at my house but when I find myself wanting at two a.m., I climb on my motorcycle and come here to find a little rest.'

'Or to the house of one of his mistresses,' Madame Daeng added.

'Quite.' Siri nodded.

Koomki turned to Daeng, who was smiling broadly beside the hearth. The steam from her broth curled around her face and filled the occupants of the room with a wanton desire to eat. The stomach of the man from Housing growled.

'Comrade,' he said to Madame Daeng, 'I warn you that lying to a government cadre is a very serious offence.'

'Honestly, I barely see him,' she said with an earnest look in her eyes. 'As you'll know from your files there's only me registered here. Of course, I do have other paramours popping in from time to time.'

Siri smiled and scratched the tingle where his left earlobe used to be.

Koomki seemed to realize that he was having the mickey taken out of him. As he didn't have humour to fall back on, he resorted to regulations.

'Comrades, according to the rules, you are not allowed to sublet government housing. Thanks to the benevolence of the republic, you are given permission to remain in your house rent free. As soon as you desert it, you forfeit the right to reside there. You certainly may not rent it out.'

Siri nodded. 'Well, then there's no problem, is there?'

'Why not?'

'Because, a, as we've established, I do live there, and b, none of the people in my house pay rent. They're my friends.'

'Your friends?' The man laughed for the first time. 'Then you're a very popular man, Dr Siri.'

'Thank you.'

'Yesterday I counted nineteen people coming to and going from the That Luang residence. Eight of them have registered your house as their official domicile. There was also a monk who we have no record of at all. What's a monk doing at your house, Comrade?'

'He's my spiritual adviser. You know, like when the prime minister's wife sneaks off to the temple to ask about fortuitous dates for staging national events?'

'Then I suggest he's advising you subliminally because he would appear to be deaf and dumb. He seemed unable or unwilling to tell me to which temple he is attached. And we all know that monks are not permitted to stay in private housing. Which brings me to the question of prostitution.'

Siri raised his bushy white eyebrows and turned to his wife. 'Do we know any questions of prostitution, my dear?'

'The question "How much?" springs to mind,' she replied.

The Housing man was getting more and more flustered and the scent of Daeng's noodles was very seductive.

'The question refers to two young women residing at your house who have criminal records for engaging in prostitution.'

'Tsk, tsk, and they're plying their trade from my house?'

'Not exactly.'

'That's similar to "no", isn't it?'

'We are still investigating that charge. It's one of the reasons I've been sent here to fetch you. We have a hearing scheduled for you at seven thirty.'

'Am I under arrest?' Siri stood and held out his wrists.

'Well, no. I'm not a—'

'Because if I'm not under arrest and if you don't have at least four burly thugs waiting outside to haul me away, it looks like you're going to have to conduct your little trial without me.'

'That isn't an option, Comrade.' The man's voice was beginning to crack. He fumbled through the sheets on his board. 'I have a summons here signed by the director of Housing.'

'Oh, then that's different.' Siri nodded. 'Could I get a better look at that?'

Koomki held it out and, in one smooth sweeping movement, unexpected in a man of his age, Siri grasped the sheet in his hand and was halfway across the shop. Daeng took a step back. Siri folded the paper neatly before placing it on the earthenware hearth in which burned a merry fire. It crumpled to black within seconds. Where the mouth of the man from Housing had previously been, there was now a large gaping hole.

'And, if you'll excuse me,' Siri said, wiping his hands, 'I intend to have a little breakfast before heading off to work.'

The man seemed unable to move. 'That was government property,' he managed finally.

Siri went over to Koomki, put his arm around him, and led him to the front of the shop.

'You blatantly destroyed government property,' the man stammered in case Siri hadn't heard the first time.

'Then it's an eye for an eye. You see, I am the national coroner, which makes me government property too. I am owned exclusively by the Justice Department. Yet you come here and attempt to destroy my reputation. A little slip of paper is cheap by comparison, don't you think?'

Siri had Koomki on the uneven pavement now, but before sending him on his way, Siri leaned close to the man's wet eyes and said, 'So please tell your colleagues that if they have any charges to bring against me, they should have me picked up by the police. They may then pursue my case through the courts. Otherwise, leave me alone. I'm not going to get into a panic about a couple of minor officials in an office playing pocket politburo. And if you even consider confiscating my house I'll have you up in front of the Party union representative before you can get to verse two of "The Red Flag". I've been a fully paid-up member for longer than our own prime minister. Don't forget that.'

He launched Koomki on his way and stood back. It was always good to have a little sport before breakfast. Siri laughed and took in a breath of early Vientiane. It had become a peaceful place. The only ugly sounds floated across the river: motorcycles and tape recorders, loud-speaker trucks urging people to buy plastic buckets and sweet potatoes. Somewhere, a man was shouting at his wife, sharing their family scandal with his Lao brothers and sisters. Thais weren't a race you'd ever accuse of peace and quiet. Their televisions and radios had two adjustments on the dial: off and loud.

Madame Daeng wheeled her cart out to the pavement and joined Siri in his revelry. She put her arm around his waist.

'Poor man,' she said.

'Him or me?'

'Comrade Koomki. I don't suppose I need to tell you what you just did probably wasn't a good idea.'

'Good idea? He comes here, spying, at six o'clock on a Saturday morning to see if I'm wearing pyjamas ...?'

'I know.'

'What's the country coming to? Is this what we labored in the jungles for thirty years to produce?'

'I know.'

'Bloody little bureaucrat with his clipboard and lists. If he were 50 centimetres taller I might have given him a right hook.' He showed her his right hook, and she felt his muscle. 'Even the old one-two.'

'My hero.'

They gazed at the retrograde fisherman until he turned to look at them and waved. They waved back.

'But it probably wasn't a good idea,' Siri agreed, recalling all his other dust-ups with government officials.

'Probably not. Did you know you had ladies of ill repute at your house?'

'He has to be talking about Mrs Fah's nieces.'

'She didn't mention their old career?'

'All she said was they were back from the islands. She could have meant a resort vacation for all I knew.'

'More likely the internment camps on the reservoir. But if they were released it means they've served their time. And if they were really on Don Nang with hardened criminals it wouldn't have been a very pleasant experience. The last thing they want is nosy cadres breathing down their necks.'

'It's the last thing any of us wants. According to Fah, they both lost husbands to the war and children to disease. They're long overdue a gust of good fortune.'

'Well, they did find a kindly old gentleman to take them in off the streets. And what about your monk?'

'Comrade Noo? He did well to keep his mouth shut. If they'd found out he was Thai they'd have whisked him off to Immigration, never to be seen again.'

'Your house is getting out of control.'

'So it would appear. Since Nurse Dtui and I moved out to our respective love nests it's been hard to keep a check on who's moving in or out. I suppose I should stop by there tomorrow and do a head count.'

'I'll come with you. It's always a laugh to spend time at your house. It makes me feel…I don't know, saner.'

Phan often considered the possibility that he might have the 'everything' that other men craved: a regular job that allowed him to travel, several government letters of identification, and looks that naive country girls found interesting. And of course he had a truck. A man with a truck was somebody in Laos. With its solid double-plated frame and its growling Chinese engine, it broadcast his power. Of course he didn't own it but nobody needed to know that. Being allowed to drive a department vehicle was almost as good. He liked the way they watched him pass, the dull nowhere girls sitting on their front porches, hoping for life to come by and call for them to climb aboard. If he chanced to stop they'd almost turn pirouettes and crash face-first onto the dirt.

That power had taken control of him. It wasn't simply that he could bed them; that was easy. Mothers sometimes brought their daughters to him and asked whether he'd like to take them for a trial run. No, it was the knowledge that he could woo a respectable girl – untouched, unsullied, saved for something special – that he could talk his way into the family home, make a seemingly genuine display of his affection, and have them all believe he was a legitimate catch.

His record had been five days: the platonic seduction, dinner with the parents, a display of credentials and bank statement, trip to the registry office in the nearest town – all before the week was over. It still amazed him how quickly he had taken possession of her. The document said she was his. All he needed was to take her maidenhead, and then her life. Was there anywhere else in the world where you could claim ownership of another human being in such a short period of time? He didn't know of it. Perhaps there was a place in Africa or South America where parents were so desperate to see their loved ones secure that they'd overlook little discrepancies, take shortcuts with paperwork.

These were desperate times. 'She had her opportunity,' they would have said. 'This nice fellow came from the city and he fell in love with her. But he was only in town for a month before his project ended. We couldn't let a chance like that go by, could we now?' All they wanted for their daughter was a good, financially secure suitor with polite manners, reasonable looks, connections with the Party…oh, and a truck would be nice.

All he required was beauty, virginity…and a long, squeezable neck.

He walked from the headman's house, where he'd secured a mattress for the night. The sun was setting behind the grey-mauve mountains and the insects were at evensong, filling the valley with a monotone soprano. A crest of pines surrounded the village of bamboo-and-elephant-grass shanties with odd corrugated roofs. Most huts had twig fences around them and flowery borders of bougainvilleas and steamy blue convolvuli. It gave the place that nice feeling that always made Phan uncomfortable.

On his work roster this little place was classified as a town. But he'd travelled and he knew what a town should look like. Being located on a provincial main road didn't change a thing as far as he was concerned. A village was a village. Even some of the provincial capitals were no more than villages: broad, spread-out ramshackle villages with concrete blocks here and there. Villages filled with ignorant, unpleasant people who would never appreciate the finer things in life.

He nodded at householders, deliberately stopping to chat and state his business. In a hamlet this size, that news would find its way around before the evening meal. After twenty minutes of casual, hands-in-pockets strolling, he'd already come to the edge of the village. There was nothing but a dirt trail leading off into the woods up ahead. He sat beside a urine green pond where a lanky crane stood on one leg, staring back at him. A toad stirred in the grass at his feet. He eased his foot under its belly and volleyed it out into the water.

As all patient hunters learn, sitting quietly for long enough will invariably draw prey. Phan hadn't been at his post for more than ten minutes before he heard the voices of young children approaching along the dirt track. Through the reeds he could make out a dozen or so shirts of various degrees of whiteness. The children disappeared

*into the long shadow of the mountain, then re-emerged,
laughing and frolicking into the last of the sunlight. And
with them was the perfect woman. She held books: probably a young teacher returning from school with her flock.
She was slim but had full breasts. Her buttocks were
shapely enough to cause her phasin skirt to bunch a little
below the belt. There was nothing worse than a woman
with no arse. But her face, oh, her face was perfection, no
sun damage or moles or acne scars or hairy sideburns. She
would do very nicely. So soon after his last honeymoon but
still he had no intention of letting up. He was insatiable.*

*One of the children saw him sitting by himself by the
pond and nudged her playmate. Soon, all eyes were on him,
the young teacher's included. Strangers were a rarity, and
well-groomed, presentable strangers might have dropped to
earth from another planet. The children stopped and stared
at him and were admonished by their teacher.*

'Some manners, children. This isn't the zoo,' she said.

*She nodded an apology to the stranger and shepherded
everyone along. She would look back, he knew. How she
did so would tell him whether she was married or single. A
married woman would be flush with the confidence that
comes from having snared a husband and consumed him.
Once penetrated, a woman became a slut, soiled, easy pick-
ings. A wife's whoring nature would inspire her to turn
back with a brazen, inviting smile.*

*He waited. At the very last minute she turned. It was a
brief, almost accidental look. Her face flushed crimson with
embarrassment when she saw him looking back at her. She
quickened her pace and was eaten up by the vegetation that
bordered the track. But it was enough. She was his.*

Insatiable and irresistible.

*

When Dr Siri arrived at Mahosot Hospital at 8:15 there was a dog asleep in his parking spot. It had to be his spot, today of all days. There was just the one place shaded by a bashful-desire tree for the hottest part of the day and he'd put his territorial marker on it in the shape of an unarmed claymore mine with his initials on it. There were twenty other empty spaces to sleep but the dog appeared to have the same criteria as the doctor. Siri beeped his horn. Nothing. He edged forward. No movement. He was considering whether to just drive on over the animal when the dog looked up. His eyes were hepatitis yellow with no visible irises.

'Saloop?'

When he was still alive, Saloop had been Siri's dog. Or perhaps it would be fairer to say that Siri had been Saloop's man. The dog had adopted Siri, saved his life once, and become a fixture in the yard of the bungalow at That Luang. Then one day he'd been murdered by the neighbour in cold blood – brained with a garden shovel.

The doctor was surprised but not shocked to see him. He'd seen worse. He had an uncomfortable relationship with the spirit world. Through no fault of his own, Siri hosted the soul of Yeh Ming, a thousand-year-old Hmong shaman. It appeared the spirit had come to rest in him following negotiations with Siri's father. He'd been too little to remember anything about it. His father had not bothered to stick around in Siri's childhood memories. For as long as he could remember, Siri had been visited in his dreams by the ghosts of departed patients. Over the past two years, those spirits had begun to slip out of his unconscious and haunt him in his waking hours. He didn't allow them to frighten him.

Siri was certain that if he were more intelligent or a better detective, he'd be able to interpret what he was being shown. He often arrived at the eureka moment long after the fact, when the mysteries had been solved by more conventional, mundane methods. His forehead was permanently bruised and disfigured from his constant slapping at it when he realized what the spirits had been trying to tell him. Perhaps it was due to his inadequacies as a host that he had only confided his infirmity to three people: his lab nurse, Dtui; his best friend, Civilai; and his wife, Madame Daeng. They'd taken it quite well, considering. Inspector Phosy of the Central Intelligence Unit had arrived by means of a policeman's instinct at the conclusion that Siri wasn't all there. But he was not averse to a good ghost story either.

Siri had learned to observe rationally. There were times when he braved nightmares like a confident swimmer, knowing he'd end up on the bank unscathed. There were malignant ghosts like the *Phibob* of the forest who hounded Yeh Ming's spirit. They constantly hummed around him like vindictive wasps, waiting for a moment of weakness when they could sting. Had it not been for a sacred amulet at his neck, Siri would certainly not have made it to his second marriage. But the vast majority of spirits were harmless.

Siri sat on the saddle of his Triumph and shook his head as Saloop rose creakily on his dead legs. The scientist in Siri wondered what had happened to his inner cynic. He'd mocked his way through a temple education, raised a philosophical finger to the Virgin Mary while studying in Paris, and made fun of the shamans and fortune-tellers upon his return to Asia. Perhaps this was their revenge: bringing him eyeball to eyeball with a dead dog inquiring after his health.

'How are you, boy?' he asked.

Saloop had, not surprisingly, lost his big-smiling, waggy-tailed savoir faire since he'd passed away. He scratched halfheartedly and drooled green bile. He stepped across the loose bricks and into the vegetable garden, where he started to dig. Siri decided that a filmmaker might have had trouble representing the scene. Saloop was undoubtedly digging deep into the earth but the actual dirt wasn't moving. There was no hole, yet the dog was in it. He emerged with a bone in his mouth and took one step towards Siri.

A bicycle bell sounded behind the doctor and he turned to see Dr Mut, the urologist, attempting to reach his parking spot. When Siri turned back, the dog, the bone, and the non-hole were gone.

By the time Siri entered the morgue, Nurse Dtui and Mr Geung, the lab assistant, were already at work. Siri heard their voices in the cutting room so he threw his shoulder bag on his desk and went to join them. They were standing on either side of a body. He knew it must have arrived that morning while he was convening with the dog. He'd been there till eight the previous evening, and as it was an offence to die outside office hours in Vientiane, this body wouldn't have been allowed in the morgue until eight that morning. The tobacco leaves in which it had been wrapped were on the floor beneath the table.

'Hello, my staff,' Siri said with a smile.

'G...goo...good morning, Comrade Doctor,' said Geung. No matter how many times he'd attempted it,

Geung had never once managed to get out the greeting in one breath. Down's syndrome was a bugger.

'Mr Geung, what have you done with your hair?' Siri asked. 'You look like a—'

'Like Elvis?' Dtui interrupted. Already a well-rounded girl, she was now twice her normal size, swollen with her first child. She was a country lass, born in the troubled north-east, and she'd never crossed an ocean. But she had spent a good many years with her nose buried in Thai pop magazines so she knew the world – or at least the important parts of it. Siri was a movie buff so he knew of Elvis from *Jailhouse Rock* and *G.I. Blues*.

'I was about to say a mountain goat,' he confessed. 'What have you done to him?'

'It's a fra...a fra...What is it, Dtui?' Geung asked.

'A fringe, babe,' she reminded him. 'It's our new look. I was getting sick of staring at his greasy centre parting, so we've had a bit of a makeover. I came in early and gave him a shampoo and a snip. I think he looks very handsome.'

'I...I'm gorgeous,' Geung told Siri.

'Irresistible. Let's just hope no female goats pass by the morgue,' said Siri. 'Right, who do we have here?' He took a step back and noted for the first time just how beautiful the naked corpse was. Although tastes differed, few would doubt that she had the proportions most girls dreamed of. She was around seventeen with perfect bone structure and very little excess fat. But there was something inexplicable about the condition of the body.

'Name unknown,' Dtui told him.

'Who brought her in?' he asked.

'A headman and local Central Committee man from Vang Vieng. They said the body was found yesterday morning. They seemed in a hurry to get her here. Drove overnight.'

'What were the circumstances?'

'They wouldn't tell me. They looked a bit shell-shocked when I asked. The cadre gave me a sealed envelope for you. It's on your desk. Obviously something a lady shouldn't know.'

'I'll get ready and take a look at the note. Where are her clothes?'

'This is the way she arrived. They wrapped her in tobacco leaves for the journey to keep the smell down.'

The warning signals sounded for Siri immediately. A naked girl found dead suggested a rape. That would be reason enough for men from the country not to discuss it with a young nurse. But after reading the note he understood there was another disturbing element to the death. A local hunter camped out in the woods had heard the sound of a truck late at night. At first light he'd gone to investigate and found the victim. She was tied to a tree with ribbon. She'd been seated with her arms and legs around the trunk. There was far more to this than merely an assault. When Siri returned to the cutting room, Dtui and Geung were wearing their aprons and masks. The temperamental air conditioner on the far wall grumbled. Siri handed Dtui the note. There were no secrets in the Mahosot morgue. He could see she was disturbed by what she read.

'I don't think I'm looking forward to this,' she confessed.

But for her unplanned pregnancy by Inspector Phosy, Nurse Dtui would have been in the Eastern Bloc by now, studying to take over Siri's job. So, as was his habit, Siri called on her to make the initial appraisal of the body.

'Would that it were mine,' she began.

Geung threw her oft-quoted words back to her. 'Men like f-f-fat women,' he said.

'Can we get on with it?' Siri said impatiently, but he knew her remark had been made to disguise her discomfort.

'Sorry, Doc.'

Siri pulled up a stool and sat with his arms folded. 'All right. What do you see?' he asked.

'She must have been found pretty soon after she was killed judging by the lack of insect or animal damage to the corpse.' Dtui stepped up to the table and touched the victim's neck. 'The cause of death was strangulation.'

'How can you tell?' Siri asked.

'Bruising of the strap muscles.' She prodded at the neck. 'Probable fracture of the hyoid.'

'I agree,' Siri nodded. 'The perpetrator?'

'Man. Big hands. The thumbprint's twice the size of mine.'

'Any defensive wounds?'

'Not really. But look, she doesn't have much in the way of fingernails. They're trimmed down to nothing. If she tried to pull him off she wouldn't have left any scratches on her own neck. Don't see any other bruising apart from the big hand print on her neck.'

'I agree,' said Mr Geung, sweeping the hair out of his eyes.

Siri smiled. 'Thank you, Dr Geung.' Geung's laughter helped to lighten the darkening mood in the room.

Dtui pulled back the girl's thick hair and inspected her scalp. 'No head wounds, small mole just below her hairline above the ear.' She worked her way down the body. 'One of her fingers is broken,' Dtui continued, 'but there's no bruising so it looks like it happened post-mortem. She might have been damaged in transit.' She leaned over the dark untrimmed mound of hair at the girl's pubis and put her hands together in apology before probing. 'No outward signs of bleeding or bruising at the vagina, thank heaven.'

She walked to the bottom of the table and looked at the girl's feet. 'This is the thing that gets me,' she said. 'Look at her pale skin. It's beautiful. No sun damage, no blemishes. It's so white, nearly opaque; it's almost as if she had a vitamin deficiency. She's like an advertisement for Camay soap. But then we come down to these creatures.'

The girl's feet and ankles were dark and rough. It was as if she were wearing grubby brown socks. The skin was sun rusted but her toenails were bleached almost pink and the soles of her feet were puckered and soft as tofu. Siri left his perch to take a look.

'You're right,' he said. 'That is most odd.'

'Any idea what could have caused it?' Dtui asked.

'Not a clue. See anything else?'

'Well' – Dtui returned to the girl's hands – 'it isn't as spectacular as the feet but look at this.'

She lifted one of the girl's arms. The back of the hand was as pristine as the rest of her, but the palm was a mass of calluses and blisters. The skin was as tough as pomelo rind.

'That's odd too,' Siri agreed. 'So far, this young lady is a compendium of contradictions. Do you see anything out of place when you compare the body with the cadre's report?'

Dtui looked at the paper again but nothing leaped out at her.

'No, I don't,' she confessed.

'The ribbon?' Siri prompted.

'No, I ... wait!' She lifted the hand one more time and was

obviously annoyed with herself having missed it. 'No welts on her wrists,' she said.

'And that tells us ...?'

'That she was tied up when she was unconscious, or after she'd lost the will to fight.'

'Or?'

'Or he tied her up after he'd killed her.'

'I think it's time to see whether she has any deeper secrets to tell us.'

The autopsy proceeded as usual although Siri was loath to defile such a beautiful young lady with his scalpel. She had been in very good heath. Siri envisioned a diet with little sugar or starch and a healthy supply of fruit. Photos of her lungs and liver might have graced a Department of Health THIS COULD BE YOU poster.

Up to this point it had been a strangulation case, no less horrific for its simplicity but not a difficult diagnosis. Yet murders by strangulation were almost unheard of in Laos. The ability to kill a person with bare hands was rare. Many believed if a person was holding a body when the life drained from it, that person was likely to provide a conduit for the spirit of the corpse and be haunted for eternity. For that reason, few Lao were prepared to handle the dead. Siri and his team were extraordinary in many respects. To physically squeeze the life out of another human being, the killer would have to be a peculiar type of monster. Yet even this far into the autopsy, Siri had still to learn just how evil the girl's murderer was.

They had suspected sexual assault of some kind but the absence of blood around the mons had made a closer inspection a lesser priority. They didn't have the facility to test for semen other than the senses of the eye and nose but

Siri was obliged to take samples. It was obvious as soon as he began the examination of her vagina that the opening and surrounding flesh must have been thoroughly cleaned. He looked up at Dtui, who involuntarily took a step backward. There was evidence of severe trauma deep in the vaginal passage, evidence that the membrane of the hymen had been newly ruptured, and then—

Siri heard a gasp emerge from his own lips. He looked up to see Dtui cover her mouth and run from the room. Mr Geung had held his ground but his eyes were full of tears. Both he and Siri stood looking in disbelief. Buried deep inside the girl was a black stone pestle. It must have been inserted while she was still alive. The silence in the morgue was broken by Geung, who was sobbing uncontrollably. 'This is v…v…very bad.'

'Yes, Geung. It is very bad indeed.'

Siri's own emotions did not show in his light green eyes or in his voice. But inside himself he felt a terrible rage that wrung his stomach muscles. He immediately promised himself that he would not leave the earth until the perpetrator of this heinous crime had been dealt with in equal measure. This death was not the result of an inevitable act of war; it was not the destruction of an enemy. It was the cruel and sadistic defilement of a beautiful young woman for reasons that a soldier or a nurse or a reluctant coroner could never begin to understand.

When Dtui returned to the table her angry eyes were bloodshot and her cheeks damp. She had nothing to say. She put on an unsoiled mask and stepped up to the table. Siri had removed the pestle and placed it on a stainless steel tray.

'We'll need to take a look at the stomach contents,' Siri told her. 'The girl must have been drugged in some way.

There were no contusions or abrasions on the thighs or labia so I don't think she put up a fight. She was either unconscious or paralyzed and unable to resist. Given the nature of the crime, I'd—'

Dtui threw the scalpel to the floor.

'How can you be so calm?' she shouted at the top of her voice.

Geung jumped with shock. Dtui rushed to Siri and pushed at his chest. 'Feel something, why don't you? Stop looking at her as . . .' A sob caught in her throat. 'As if she's meat.'

Tears overwhelmed her. Siri put his hand out to her but Geung stepped in between them and reached for his friend. She slapped at him but he fought his way inside her flailing arms, put his strong arms around her, and hugged her to him until she no longer had the will to fight. Together they rode out her sobs.

2

BO BEN NYANG

Despite the heat, Saturday lunch was alfresco on a log beside the languid Mekhong. Comrade Civilai had brought baguettes he'd baked himself. Since his retirement, Civilai had spent much of his free time in the kitchen. As an expolitburo member he'd been allowed to keep his ranch-style home in the old American compound at kilometre 6 and the gas oven it contained. Civilai had taken to baking like a pig takes to slops. His expanding waist size was testament to his experimentation in the kitchen. Whereas the populace often arrived at an empty market of a morning, there was no shortage of ingredients available for the senior Party members. Even Civilai's large bald head seemed to be putting on weight. He was the first to admit that his baguettes were modest compared to those of old Auntie Lah behind the mosque but he was getting there, and Siri was his official taster.

'How is it?' Civilai asked, watching his best friend chew on the crusty shell.

'It tastes less like tree bark than usual,' Siri admitted.

Siri had considered cancelling his luncheon date. That morning's autopsy still haunted him. His anger hadn't subsided but he'd long since learned to keep his feelings to himself unless sharing them would help with a case in some way. He could fool most people most of the time, but he knew bluffing astute Civilai would be another matter. And perhaps it would be useful to get his friend's thoughts on what had transpired in Vang Vieng the previous day.

'Come on, little brother,' Civilai pleaded. 'I've used her exact recipe. I bribed her with a half bottle of rum to get it.'

'And it's a commendable effort. But you need more than a recipe. You need all those elements that can't be accounted for: the patina of the kiln, the sweat of the workers, the experience. A real baguette is a time capsule of every little stage that's gone into the making of it.'

'So you don't like it?'

'I didn't say that. It's pleasant.'

'You're a tough audience, Siri. I should know better than to ask on one of your bad days.'

'What makes you think I'm having a bad day?'

'Your face is as long as that thing.'

He raised his chin towards the Mekhong. The river was almost humble in March, like a large dirty puddle doing its best to fill its banks. Once again, the dry-season gardeners had planted their vegetables along its shores and marked off their allotments with string and slips of paper with their names or marks on them. That was the limit of the security system. They figured that if someone was so hungry they were forced to steal a head of lettuce, then they deserved to have it.

'Got anything to drink in that bag?' Siri asked.

'From your tone, I'm assuming you wouldn't settle for chrysanthemum juice?'

'Something with a bite.'

Civilai fumbled deep in his old green kit bag and emerged with a flask. He unscrewed the cap, took a whiff, and handed it to Siri.

'It'll probably go down better if you don't ask me what it is,' he said.

Siri took a swig and felt a handful of burning tacks embed themselves in his liver.

'Ouch! Holy Father of the Lord Buddha,' he said.

'Potent, isn't it?'

'We used something like this to strip paint off tanks.'

'Give it back then.'

'Not on your life.' Siri took another swig.

They sat for a while, willing the flies to leave them alone, admiring the industry of a river rat ferrying mushrooms to and from her hole.

'How's Dtui?' Civilai asked, allowing Siri his own sweet time to tell what was troubling him.

'A month short of giving birth to what looks like a small bulldozer,' Siri said.

'And the marriage?'

'They seem content.'

'I meant yours.'

'Me?' At last a happy thought. 'I'm a very lucky man, old brother. I'd forgotten what a pleasure it was to watch a woman breathe in her sleep...see her chest rise and fall.'

'Steady, you'll be writing poetry next.' Siri was silent. 'You haven't?'

'Only a short one.'

'You're like me, Siri. Can't get through life without a woman. Too bad you'll have to settle for just the one.'

'One what?'

'Wife. Our friends up at the roundabout are introducing a law against polygamy. I know the average lowland Lao in his right mind can't handle more than one wife, so it would appear to be one more kick in the testicles for the hill tribes.'

'How do you find out all these things?'

'They keep me in the loop. A driver comes by once a week with politburo news, a copy of *Lao Huksat* newsletter, and a calendar of meetings I don't bother to go to. Want to know the highlights of the week?'

'Go on, make me laugh.'

'My favourite is the fact that they've decided all spirit houses have to be registered.'

'By the occupants?'

Civilai laughed. 'Oh, and there's a new ban on contraceptive devices, not that anyone could afford one anyway. It appears they're offering rice tax deductions to families with more than three children. Got to shore up the dwindling proletariat.'

'They offering to feed them too?'

'Not as far as I know. Then there's the usual list of Western paranoia measures: a moratorium on blue jeans to go with the one on long hair. And they'll be sending inspectors around to coffee shops to make sure the lighting isn't too dim.'

'So you can see the stains on the tablecloths?'

'Dim lighting apparently leads to lasciviousness and lewdness.'

'Which in turn leads to pregnancy and a higher population. I wish they'd make their minds up.'

'It would all be hilarious if it weren't true.'

'How's our old friend collectivism?'

'It's all in the advanced planning stage.'

'They're really going ahead with it? They're madder than I thought.'

'Collectivism: the gathering of farmers who have nothing to meet once a week to distribute it.'

'That just about sums it up. The communists in Russia introduced it to help the peasants rise up against the oppressive landlords. We haven't got any oppressive landlords.'

'They'll probably hire one or two before they start the programme.'

'I'm sure I'd be on their list.'

'How so?'

'I'm about to go to jail for absentee landlordism and pimping. A fifty-centimetre-tall official from Housing came by this morning and told me I have to give up my house.'

'And all the freaks it contains?'

'They think I don't live there.'

'You don't.'

'I know.'

The two old men smiled and shared a banana.

'Hot, isn't it?' Civilai said at last.

'Bloody hot.'

'This place seems to switch from the cool season to the bloody hot season without passing through a tepid or a lukewarm season on the way. You'd expect to find Crazy Rajid stark naked in the river on days like these.'

'Hmm, now you mention it, I haven't seen him walking aimlessly around town for a while.'

'Me neither.'

'I hope he's all right.' Siri's brow furrowed.

'I'm not sure how you'd go about checking up on an insane homeless Indian. He might have just curled up and died and nobody would be any the wiser.'

'I think I'll ask around. But for a few wonky genes here, and an overdose of vodka there, it could be you or me walking endless circles around Nam Poo Fountain in our underwear.'

'Speak for yourself. You know what Nietzsche says about madness?'

'No.'

'Me neither.'

Siri laughed. 'Ah, Civilai, you're a waste of perfectly good skin and body parts.'

He took another swig of the vindictive spirits. He detected a hint of turnip but he really didn't want to ask what it was made of. It hurt his insides and he decided it was exactly what he needed. He decided also that it was time to tell Civilai about his morning.

All Siri wanted to do after lunch was go home and sleep, but he'd arranged to meet Inspector Phosy at the morgue. Saturday was officially a half day; so when he returned, Dtui and Mr Geung had already left. He unlocked the door and went directly to the cutting room. He unfastened the freezer and pulled out the drawer. His beautiful Madonna was wrapped in a blue plastic sheet that he rolled down as far as her neck. He took a step back and looked at her pale mask of a face. She had been so lovely. What had led to this? Why could he not rub some consecrated sticks together and summon her spirit? Why was his supernatural power so ineffective when he could most make use of it? One or two answers from the beyond and he'd have the bastard who did this. He hated his own psychic impotence every bit as much as he hated the maniac who had erased this beauty's life and stolen her dignity.

'She must have been very pretty.'

Siri hadn't heard Phosy arrive. The inspector – upright, middle-aged, and muscular – looked none the worse for his seven months of marriage to Nurse Dtui. He ate like a horse, but it melted off. He had raven black hair that Dtui assured everyone didn't come from a bottle, and a keen, curious face.

'Did Dtui tell you everything?' Siri asked, forgetting his greeting manners.

'Yes, she was home for lunch. She wanted me to tell you she was sorry for—'

'I understand. Do you have any idea who'll be handling this case? I want to be involved.'

'You already are,' Phosy told him. 'It's me.'

'I thought you only handled political issues these days.'

'It was Comrade Surachai's idea. He's the committee member who rode in with her this morning. He knew about me from Kham, my old boss. Surachai has some clout with my chief. The folks up at Vang Vieng are frightened there might be a killer on the loose. So let's get to it.'

Siri was delighted. He'd worked with Phosy on a number of cases; he thought they made a splendid team. Siri had been ramrodded into the coroner's job, but it did give him the opportunity to vent his detective proclivities. As a penniless young medical-school student in Paris he had been deprived of the type of raunchy entertainment other men his age sought. Instead, he'd found solace in the two old-franc cinema halls and in libraries where Maurice LeBlanc, Gaston Leroux, and Stanislas-André Steeman took him on noir journeys through the nettle-strewn undergrowth of the criminal world. His hero, Inspector Maigret, had convinced him that there could be no better career than that of solving crimes and putting blackguards behind bars.

There hadn't been much detecting to be done in the jungles of Vietnam and northern Laos in his army days; so his dream, like most of the dreams men harbour, had turned to snuff and been huffed away by history. Until now.

'Where do we start?' Phosy asked, a question every closet member of the sûreté de police yearns to hear. Although brilliant in his own way, Phosy never pretended to be anything he wasn't. He knew his limitations.

'You already have a picture of the girl?' Siri asked, although he knew Phosy's subordinate, Sergeant Sihot, had arrived that morning to meet the body and taken a Polaroid instant photograph. The camera was one of the police department's latest crime-fighting tools.

'Sihot went back with the cadre to Vang Vieng. He'll show the picture around and try to get an identification.'

'Good.' Siri nodded. 'Then I suggest we look at the pestle.'

Rinsed clean now and tagged, the object sat innocently on a shelf above the dissection table.

'It's not your common or garden variety,' Phosy noticed, weighing the heavy, blunt tool in his hand. 'Unusual size; somewhere between a cooking implement and a medicine crusher.'

'Black stone. Looks expensive,' Siri agreed.

'I'll have someone show it around, too, and see what we can come up with. Does the body tell us anything?'

Siri walked to the corpse and pulled back the plastic wrapping. He held up the callused fingers and indicated the sunburned ankles. He and Phosy ping-ponged ideas back and forth for almost an hour but still they were unable to come up with anything plausible. The state of the corpse left them both baffled.

Dtui usually put her foot firmly down on any plans her husband might have to work on the weekend, but this case had become personal to her. She'd told him to do everything he could to avenge the girl's death. He would leave that afternoon for Vang Vieng to join Sergeant Sihot. Siri vowed to invest more thought into the condition of his Madonna while the policemen were away.

To the great displeasure of many, Madame Daeng's noodle shop was not open on Sunday. This was Siri's day off and she insisted on spending every one of its twenty-four hours with her husband. He had no objection whatsoever. They both loved to walk but Daeng's arthritis limited their treks. Invariably, they would head off on Siri's motorcycle to beauty spots that in another era would have been crowded with happy people. These days they often enjoyed their picnics alone.

But Siri had designated this Sunday a Vientiane day. The capital was somewhat ghostly when they set out at nine. Stores were shuttered, many for so long the locks had rusted to the hasps. Houses were in permanent disrepair. The dusts of March had settled on the city like a grey-brown layer of snow. Roads, even those with bitumen surfaces, looked like dirt tracks. There were no obvious colours anywhere, only shades. Even the gaudiest billboards had been reduced to a fuzzy pastel. The most common sounds they heard as they cruised the streets were the sweeping of front steps and the dry-clearing of throats.

Theirs was not an aimless tour of the city. Siri and Daeng passed all the spots at which Crazy Rajid had been a feature: the Nam Poo Fountain, the Black Stupa, the three old French villas on Samsenthai, and the bank of the river. As far as they knew, that was the young man's territory. Siri stopped at every open door he passed and chatted with neighbours. Yes, they knew Crazy Rajid, although not by name. Siri began to wonder whether he and Civilai might have christened the poor man themselves. Some had given the vagrant food; most had offered him water at one time or another. Some had tried to engage him in conversation, but it appeared that nobody other than Siri, Civilai, and Inspector Phosy had ever heard him speak, and even to them he had uttered only a word or two.

Everyone considered him a feature of their landscape and all agreed, 'Now you come to mention it, I haven't seen him for a while.' The last time anyone recalled a sighting had been the previous Thursday. That meant the local crazy man had been absent for ten days. Details were sketchy at best. Nobody makes a note of seeing a street person. But the account of one witness was accurate enough to give Siri cause for concern.

Ba See sold old stamps and coins from a tiny shopfront near the corner of Samsenthai Road and Pangkham. It was unlikely she made a living from it but she enjoyed sitting on her threadbare wicker armchair and watching the street.

'Every Friday,' she said. 'Regular as clockwork for the past two years he'd turn up at five thirty p.m. on the dot. Don't know how he managed it. Never saw him wear a watch, or much else for that matter. He'd go over to the first of them colonials across the street.' She pointed to three ancient French buildings behind a low white wall. At one time they'd been white, but time and weather had turned them as ugly as a smoker's teeth.

'He'd go over and bang on the door,' she continued. 'No point in it at all. There are six families living in there, government workers from the provinces, and they've all got their own rooms. The front door's never locked. But he didn't ever go in. He just stood there knocking. People came down to see what he wanted but he never wanted anything. Only wanted to bang by the looks of it. Every damned week. Then, last Friday, he didn't show up. I was waiting for my regular five thirty bang but he didn't come. It surprised me. Even some of the women in the house came down and looked out the door like they were expecting him. Day before yesterday, he didn't come again. Must be something wrong.'

Siri and Daeng went to the old building and asked the few people who were home. They supported Ba See's story. Nobody had any idea why he knocked on the door every week, and nobody had seen him for the last two Fridays. Siri leaned his head against Daeng's shoulder blade. They were sitting on his bike. No greater love has any man than to let his wife have a turn at driving his beloved motorcycle.

'So what do we do next?' Daeng asked.

'If we had TV we could put an artist's impression of him on the evening news.'

'Failing that?'

'Failing that I think we've come to the end of our leads for the day. Let's mark it down as ongoing and move on to the next impossible situation.'

'Your house?'

'Are you up for it?'

'If you are.'

They pulled up in front of Siri's old bungalow and conducted a quick surveillance of the property. There were some six children frozen like statues in the front yard. Daeng turned to Siri, who could only shrug. On the roof was what looked like a handleless red-and-white-polka-dot umbrella forming a dome in the centre of the tiles. A makeshift clothesline had been strung up between a tree and a very ornate spirit house, one that hadn't been there on Siri's last visit. An assortment of brightly coloured ladies' undergarments hung from the rope like distress flags on a ship. Thai religious music filled the street in front of the house, and one of the front windows bore brown tape in the shape of a cross.

'I don't know,' Daeng said. 'Fighting the French in the jungles is one thing . . .'

'Be brave, ma Pasionaria. A warning, though: I may have to feign anger. I'd appreciate it if you didn't burst out laughing.'

'I'll do my best.'

Siri's habit of collecting strays had begun when his original lodging was blown up and he was relocated to the suburbs. It hadn't seemed logical for a single man to live alone in such a mansion. Several down-and-outs had passed through over the previous year. Some had stayed. On the current roster, as far as he knew, were: Mr Inthanet, the puppet master from Luang Prabang; Mrs Fah, whose husband had been haunted to death, and her two children, Mee and Nounou; the two hopefully inactive prostitutes, Tong and Gongjai; Comrade Noo, the renegade monk fleeing the Thai junta; and a blind Hmong beggar, Pao, and his granddaughter, Lia, who had been swept from the road in front of Daeng's shop before the police could tidy them away. Then there were the baby twins, temporarily named Athit and Jun, awaiting collection, and that was a story in itself.

Siri and Daeng walked toward the front door and paused to look at the frozen children.

'I think they're dead,' said Daeng.

'Stuffed probably,' Siri added.

'You could do anything to them and they wouldn't feel it.'

'You mean if I stick my finger up one of their nostrils ...?'

Nounou, beneath the young *lumyai* tree, burst into laughter, and the others came to life giggling and pointing at their playmate.

'You lost,' they shouted.

'That's not fair,' Nounou pouted. 'Grandfather's not in the game. He's not allowed.'

Siri laughed, put his hands together in a polite *nop* of apology, and escorted Daeng inside. The source of the music was a large cassette recorder in the front room. It was so loud the machine was dancing back and forth on the concrete floor. Siri bent down and turned it off. Halfway down the hall, the handle of the roof umbrella hung down from a hole in the ceiling with a bucket attached to it. Through the open bedroom door to their left, they saw Pao and his granddaughter lying on a mattress. The old man's eyes stared wide at Siri even though the sound of snoring suggested he was in a deep sleep. Lia smiled and waved.

It wasn't until they hit the backyard that they found other signs of life. Comrade Noo was lying in Siri's old hammock like a Roman emperor. Ten people, some of whom Siri recognized as neighbours, others as the official residents of the house, were seated cross-legged at his feet in some kind of trance. Siri had no qualms about disturbing them.

'Tell me you aren't conducting a Buddhist ceremony in the back garden of my house,' he barked.

The acolytes came out of their reverie as one and greeted Siri with *nop*s and 'Good healths'. Comrade Noo lifted his head and smiled broadly at his benefactor.

'It's merely a meditation session,' said the Thai. 'A cleansing. Some of the neighbours asked if they could join us. They miss their religion. I hope you don't mind.'

By 1978 the opium of the people had been powdered down to fine mist. Fewer than three thousand monks remained in the entire country, and they were growing their own alms and making a living teaching. An illegal Thai monk performing a service in the garden of a government worker might just be construed as treason. It would very likely warrant a prolonged stay for all of them in the re-education camps in the north. Siri hadn't arrived a moment too soon.

'Mind?' he shouted. 'Mind? I want everyone not registered in this house out of here this minute. And take your petrified children with you. Now!'

This proclamation didn't exactly lead to a frenzy. Given all they'd suffered in their lives, the Lao no longer panicked, nor did they move very fast. There was an orderly departure during which they exchanged friendly conversation, made obeisance to the monk, and strolled past Siri, who stood with his fists on his waist.

'Hello, brother Siri,' said Inthanet. 'We don't get to see you nearly enough these days.'

'Is that so?' Siri replied. 'Well, the way things are going, you'll be able to come to visit me in prison for the next few years.'

'Why?' asked Mrs Fah with an expression of surprise on her face. 'What have you done?'

'It's not what I've done,' he replied. 'It's you lot. This house is under surveillance, and you've broken every ordinance there is.'

Inthanet smiled and came out with the inevitable, 'Bo ben nyang!'

If the founding fathers of the great European languages

had been at all aware of the efficacy of the Lao expression *bo ben nyang,* they would certainly have invented their own versions of it. It magically expressed, That's all right, it's not important, I don't care, you're welcome, no problem, plus several more obscure nuances, but with a Lao slant that suggested there was no matter of such great importance in the world that one needed to get one's knickers in a twist. The slender panic grass would continue to grow, and the orb of the sun would not cease its lethargic lob from horizon to horizon. It was a heal-all balm of a phrase, but there were times when it could be utterly infuriating.

'That's easy for you to say, old man,' said Siri through clenched teeth. 'I don't see your name on the lease. No,' he addressed everyone. 'Changes have to be made here, starting today.'

'Perhaps you'd like an orange cordial to help you cool down, uncle,' said lady of the night Gongjai.

'I don't want to be cool,' Siri replied. 'I want my head as hot as I can make it so you understand I'm not just speaking for my own benefit.'

'So you don't want a drink?' Gongjai tried again.

'I didn't say that. I just don't want you thinking it's going to make me any calmer.'

'Right, I'll go and mix it.' She smiled. 'And you, Madame Daeng?'

'Please.'

'Or you could have some rice whisky,' said Inthanet. 'It's not yet cooled off from the still but it—'

'Don't tell me you're brewing your own hooch here too,' Siri interrupted.

Inthanet laughed. 'Of course not, brother. Old Khout from the ice works brings it in payment for teacher Noo's serm—for his meditation services.'

The monk lifted his eyes towards heaven and smiled, showing his few remaining betel-ravaged teeth.

Once everyone except Comrade Noo had a drink in front of them, Siri, seated beside his wife on his old wooden cot, called the house meeting to order.

'Right,' he began. 'Madame Daeng will be taking the minutes and will post them on the bathroom door when we're finished.'

Daeng held up her pen to show them it wasn't an idle threat.

'Rule one,' Siri continued, 'no vulgar underwear visible at the front of the house.'

Gongjai and Tong were about to protest, not at the rule, but at the description of their underwear. Their aunt settled them down and reminded them whose house they were staying in.

'Rule two, down comes the spirit house.' There was a momentary mumble from Inthanet. 'I have it on good authority that officials will soon be going from building to building registering spirit houses and we don't want any more government people nosing around here than we already have. If there are resident spirits, apologize to them, and move it round the back where no one can see it.

'Rule three, no more religious services in, behind, or in the close vicinity of this house.'

'I was merely—' Comrade Noo began.

'You're hiding out, you damned fool,' Siri interrupted. The girls looked shocked. 'You aren't even supposed to be in the country. Even our own monks don't feel safe performing services. I didn't invite you to stay here so you could turn the place into the great Vientiane alternative temple. From today, you're an *inactive* monk. You want to preach, you go back to Thailand.'

'But—'

'There's no but. You quit or you're out. Rule four, where are the twins?'

'In the refrigerator,' Inthanet said calmly.

'What?' Siri felt Daeng stiffen beside him.

'It's an old one I found at the dump.' The puppet man put them at ease.

Mrs Fah added, 'We laid it on its side and converted it into a double crib. Very comfortable.'

'They're asleep,' said Tong.

'Good, right.' Siri nodded to Daeng. 'In that case, I need one of you to volunteer to register them at Births, Deaths, and Marriages as your own. We can't have unregistered children here. It would be on a temporary basis, until they're collected by their real relatives. I'd ask Madame Daeng here to do it but I think that might stretch credibility.'

'We can do it,' said Gongjai, 'me and Tong. We've been taking care of them since they got here.'

Madame Daeng spoke up. 'I don't know, girls. There'll be some ugly questions about who the fathers are.'

Tong laughed. 'Auntie, don't you think we've heard all the ugly questions there are? They drained what little dignity we had left a long time ago. One more day of insults isn't going to leave any more bruises.'

'If you're sure?' Daeng said. They nodded. 'Thank you.'

Siri wasn't cut out to be a landlord. He'd started sweating long before the sun edged over the roof. It was getting hot out in the yard, but he didn't want to interrupt himself by taking a recess. Mrs Fah brought a small fan out onto the veranda at the end of a long extension cord and set it on swing. It didn't make any difference at all to the temperature.

'Finally,' Siri said, 'rule five, Inthanet?'

'Yes, *mon général*?'

'Should I assume the front window is your doing?'

'Yes, Comrade,' he smiled. 'Indirectly.'

'And should I gather that it's a result of a brick flying over the next-door fence?'

'A 1972 Asian Games commemorative mug,' he corrected.

'That's rather dangerous, don't you think?'

'She did wait till the children were out of the house.'

'That's a small mercy. But, my friend, it really is time for this feud to cease. There was a period when you and Miss Vong were very fond of each other. Talk of marriage, I seem to recall. We can't have any of the neighbours out for revenge. Do you know what I mean? I want you to apologize to her.'

'For what?' Inthanet asked indignantly. 'Being married to someone else?'

'For not telling her you were before you started to woo her.'

'It slipped my mind.'

'The fact that you have four children and nine grandchildren slipped your mind?'

'No, just the married part. My wife left me a long time ago. Long before the kids were out of the house. I'd erased her from my mind.'

'Right, then that's the angle we'll go with – amnesia. It isn't going to be easy, I grant you, but I want peace in this neighbourhood. Got it?'

Inthanet nodded.

'Good, then I think that's it.'

'The umbrella,' Daeng reminded him.

'Oh, yes. Perhaps someone can tell me why there's an umbrella poking through the roof.'

Lia, the blind Hmong's granddaughter, sheepishly put up her hand.

'Sir?'

'Yes, love?'

'I'm do it. I'm make hole in roof.'

'Why?'

'Grandfather tell it danger make fire in house if no hole in roof to make smoke go away. I use broomstick. Stand on chair.'

'Well, you're a very strong girl,' Siri said. 'That was a very tough roof.'

'Take one hour.'

'But does your grandfather realize he shouldn't light fires in the house?'

'Hmong house have hole in roof.'

'I know. But this house has a gas range and an open window. Can you explain that to him?'

'I tell.'

'Thank you.'

'I put the umbrella up there in case the rains come early this year,' Inthanet explained. 'Used the bucket to stop it blowing away.'

'Right.' Siri understood. 'But if I bring some new tiles, do you think you could get up there and fix the hole?'

'No problem.'

'Thank you.'

'*Bo ben nyang!*' said the old puppet master.

With a group sigh of relief, the meeting ended; it seemed to

Siri that all the issues had been resolved quite amicably. The women had retired to the kitchen, where smoke from the range escaped through an open window. The smell of cooking filled the house. Siri and Inthanet were seated on the front porch, working on a second bottle of rice whisky. Crazy Rajid was still on Siri's mind but, like him and Daeng, all the people at the house were immigrants from the provinces. The only Vientiane resident was Miss Vong next door and she was off on a one-week training programme in the north. Then something occurred to him. He called Lia over.

'I sorry, sir,' she said.

'It's OK, love. It's not about the roof.' He took her hand and smiled. 'When you and your grandfather were begging around the city, do you remember seeing a half-naked man?'

'India man,' she said straight away.

'Yes, that's it. His name's Rajid, or maybe it isn't. He's a little bit ...' He circled a finger around the side of his head.

'I know he.'

'Good, well, he's missing. We can't find him. Nobody's seen him for ten days.'

'I hope he no sick.'

'So do I, Lia. Do you know about any places he might like to go to hide? Have you seen him anywhere apart from downtown?'

'No, sir.'

'That's OK. We'll keep looking.'

'Maybe he father know.'

'You mean, *your* father?'

'No, sir. He father. India father.'

'Rajid has a father? How could you possibly know that?'

'One day he take us go eat. Meet father.'

'Where?'

'India restaurant near market. He father cooking. Big fat man.'

The dinner was simple but Phan had learned to stomach the inadequate swill they served out here in the boondocks. He inquired about the recipe and charmed the girl's mother by going so far as to write it down in his notebook to give to friends in Vientiane. He told her his hobby was collecting authentic ethnic recipes, and hers was one of the best. He was a consummate and convincing flatterer. He savoured the bitter stench as if it were nectar from the gods and let his eyes wander only briefly to the still-blushing face of Wei.

Not bad this – only his second day and he was already in the circle: cross-legged on the bamboo matting, telling funny stories to the younger ones, sharing mechanical insights with the older brother. Not over the top. Modest. Not the entertainer who causes people to doubt his sincerity but the quiet, almost shy man who only speaks when spoken to. Perhaps he asks a question about the area: the wildlife, the irrigation system. The perfect guest.

Wei sat on the far side of the circle ignored by this interesting stranger all but for his eyes. Yet she knew, as they all did, that she was the reason for his being there.

On Saturday night he had presented his credentials to the headman and, according to protocol, dined with the old man and his wife. He might have mentioned the young teacher he'd seen at the pond, might have blushed a little, but he hadn't pursued the matter. Once mentioned, the subject was dropped. Of course the old wife had asked him about his marital status.

'I haven't found the right woman,' he'd told her.

(Another blush.) He mentioned that he had only just arrived at the financial plateau upon which one could build a family life. (One more blush.) 'I'm looking for a smart girl who loves children.'

He'd noticed the old couple exchange glances at that point and knew the trap was set.

On Sunday morning he'd cleaned his truck and spent the next seven hours or so in the space beneath the headman's hut beside the loom. He had his back to the street and was writing at a makeshift table, poring over sheets of very complicated-looking documents. Serious. Dedicated. It was hot so he wore only shorts and an undershirt that showed his well-defined shoulders. Every footstep overhead on the old bamboo sent down a shower of dust but he ignored the inconvenience. They brought him water and lunch and he ate while working. He could tell that people were passing on the street, talking about him, stopping to admire his dedication. Nothing could disturb him until, at three o'clock, he was done. He leaned back on his stool and stretched.

He put on a pair of sand shoes and walked through the village in search of the inevitable game of takraw. *After asking directions, he found it behind the school – teenagers and married men in a knockout competition, standard rules. A three-man team owned the court until it was beaten. He didn't push himself on to a team, just sat and admired the skills of the players and chatted. When he was given his chance to play he didn't outdo the locals even though it wouldn't have been hard. He did just enough to fit in.*

Children came and laughed and poked fun. Teenaged girls came by, pretending not to be interested in the game, secretly whispering together about his fine muscles and his interesting face. And Wei came. She came with a queer friend. Phan couldn't abide queers. What was she thinking? Didn't she have any pride? Perhaps she was just kind. He put it out of his mind, became wrapped up in the tournament: slapped backs, told jokes, lost when he had to, put on a show, and took off his shirt.

He wouldn't have been disappointed if he'd had to wait three or four days for the invitation. That was normal. He knew he had her. But at the headman's house that evening as he was showering off sweat and dust in the backyard, the old lady called to him, 'Better put on your best shirt, young Comrade Phan. You've got a date for dinner tonight.'

Wei's father wasn't a wealthy man, but he had buffalo and the knack of breeding them. It gave him a steady income and allowed him to keep his promise to his wife that their children would study up to the level of their abilities. This was a minority Tai Dum village, and opportunities were not readily available to hill dwellers. Wei had done well at the local primary school, and they'd sent her off to stay with an aunt in town to become a teacher. At the age of fifteen she'd received her pedagogical certificate from the provincial governor and come home to the two-room school she'd left three years earlier. Now, at seventeen, she had lived her little dream and was beginning to wonder whether she'd used up all her luck. Then he'd arrived.

She looked at him over the rim of her glass and wished to the gods that she could keep from blushing. The last thing she wanted him to think was that she was merely a girl.

46

3

THE OVERSIZED MONDAY

Days had always had a standard length and breadth until
that Monday. It began at six a.m. for Siri. He was awakened
by Daeng stroking his temple. The sun had not yet risen so
he saw her outline by the light of the Thai streetlights across
the river. Silhouettes had always been a weakness of his.

'I might need a few minutes,' he said.

'It's not *that*.'

'Why else would you be caressing me gently?'

'Because I'm not the type of girl to slap you and scream and
say, "There are strange men gathered opposite our shop."'

'And are there?'

'Three of them.'

'Anyone we know?'

'The little one, Koomki. The others are bigger. I think
they're planning an attack.'

Siri laughed. 'What should we do?'

'Well, imagine that I'm a young married woman and my
husband's just come home unexpectedly.'

'You want me to climb into a closet?'

'No, I think you should go out the back door, being very
careful not to disturb the fowl, and hop over the fence into
the garden behind ours.'

Siri laughed again and listened to the silence.

'You're serious.'

'Yes.'

'You want me to flee from the Department of Housing.'

'Just until we can sort everything out, get the twins registered and the bungalow fixed up.'

'Where does my dignity fit into all this?'

'I was thinking this might preserve some of it. Unless you want to be dragged to a hearing.'

'You're right. Where should I hide out?'

'Go to the morgue. You'll be safe there. It's a shame you've alienated the people who could help you. A word from Judge Haeng and all this would go away. Won't you consider talking to him?'

'I'd sooner eat my own foot.'

'I thought you might say that. But don't rule it out. Think about it, for me.'

He looked at her erotic outline against the window and decided there was very little he wouldn't do for her.

There wasn't a great deal to do in a morgue at six thirty in the morning. Siri sat at his desk and tidied the files and pens that lived there. He decided to focus his mind on the conundrum of why a beautiful young woman had such gnarled feet and calluses on her hands. He returned to the freezer and slid out the tray, then talked through what he was seeing as if he were Dtui itemizing and explaining.

'No sun damage,' he said. 'So...never outside or only when covered in some way. Covered from head to foot, or to ankle. Why would anyone go to so much trouble to stay out of the sun? And then, having gone to the trouble, leave their feet exposed? Madness.' And these weren't feet baked from the sun and hardened by walking. They were soft. The only feet he could think of with a similar consistency were . . .

There was a sound from the office. Too early for Dtui, and he would have heard her footfalls, but Mr Geung might have sneaked in to sweep and dust. That was his early-morning hobby. He took pride in the cleanliness of the morgue. Who could say what time he normally left his cramped dormitory for the comfort of a place he loved?

'Morning!' Siri called. But there was no answer.

He walked through the shadowy vestibule and into the curtained office. There was nobody there. His missing earlobe tingled. The amulet at his neck felt warm against his skin. He knew there was a presence here. His first hope was that the corpse in the cutting room was about to confide in him at last. He headed back there. Halfway across the vestibule, a chill ran up his spine. A cold damp feeling caressed his skin, and he stopped midstride. There was a smell like wet earth in the air, a scent that seemed to take hold and squeeze him tightly. He knew at once it had nothing to do with the dead girl.

He heard a rustle behind him in the empty office and turned his head in time to see a shadow cross beyond the door. He stepped back into the doorway, and there on the floor at the centre of the round rug lay Saloop, drooling. It was a difficult moment. Siri had an affection for his dog, and his instinct was to lean down and pat him, tickle his ears. The animal used to like that. Surely a spirit dog would appreciate a little attention. But Saloop hadn't come for petting. He stood and barked, although the sound was delayed for two seconds due to the difference in dimensions. He turned in circles as if he wanted his old master to follow him, even though there was nowhere to go.

Siri stepped past the door and saw immediately what Saloop was making all the fuss about. The doctor had considered himself unshockable. He'd seen the spirits of dead soldiers in legions. The ghost of a woman he believed was his own mother followed him around like an albatross. He'd held consultations with a monk at Hay Sok Temple who was clearly not of this world, but the figure sitting at his desk was enough to put the willies up even the most hardened shaman.

She was unpleasantly overweight, ugly as a lopsided toad, and unmistakably naked. Her skin, if it could be called skin, was a squirming mass of live worms. They crawled in and out of her eye sockets and her mouth and nose. Siri edged farther into the room and could see that what he had thought at first was a beer belly was probably an eight-month term of pregnancy. Her stomach glistened with sweat. He was nauseated by the sight of her but knew he had to observe. He knew the image wouldn't last long. He waited for a word, a sign, but he could only smell the moist earth and feel the shudder of his amulet.

'Please,' he said. 'I'm not very good at this. Couldn't you …?'

But, as he'd feared, his words seemed to blow away the ugly woman and the dog like smoke. And all that remained was a feeling of doom.

When Dtui and Geung arrived together at eight, they found Dr Siri sitting at his desk staring at his knuckles.

'Goo …good morning, Comrade Doctor,' said Geung.

'Anybody else and I'd say you looked like you'd seen a ghost,' said Dtui. 'But in your case …'

'Just a little tired is all.' Siri smiled. 'I'm only being haunted by the Department of Housing. I could use a nap. They won't leave me alone.'

'I heard about that,' she said.

Geung hurried off to clean up the spotless morgue. Dtui sat on the spare chair in front of Siri's desk.

'The other day ...' she began.

'It's all right. I understand completely.'

'I mean, I know you care just as much as anyone.'

'Don't worry.'

'Thanks. Doc, I've been putting a lot of sleepless night-time thought into our girl in there.'

'Me too.'

'The feet?'

'Paddy fields?'

'Two great minds. It's the only thing that makes any sense, although it doesn't make sense at all. She had to have been shrouded from head to calf to work in the fields. Most farm women wrap themselves up when they can to prevent sun damage, but it's hot out there. They put on one layer of clothing at the most. It's not enough to stop them from tanning. Most of them are already dark skinned from when they're little. By the looks of her, this girl hadn't ever seen the sun. Do you think she might have had an allergy to sunlight?'

'Without sun she'd have to supplement the lack of vitamin D somehow. Her skin's very pale, but there's no evidence of an allergy in her pigmentation. I can read up on it, see if I've missed a condition. Failing that, it appears she just wanted to stay out of the sun. The only part she wouldn't have been able to cover was her feet. I suppose rubber boots might have worked.'

'I'd bet she tried that for a while until she realized how many diseases you can pick up in sweaty boots in this climate. I tried it myself for a while when I was little and ended up with every skin disease you can imagine.'

'It is odd, though. If it isn't an allergy, there has to be some other reason we haven't thought of. I'll work on it. Have you heard from Phosy?'

'I got a message from him last night. Said he'd give you a ring later this morning. Didn't sound like he'd found much out.'

'All right, let me just get this autopsy report finished for Director Suk.'

'Are you sure you're all right?'

'Yes, why?'

'You really do look like you've seen a ghost.'

Siri smiled, but he was starting to believe that what he'd seen wasn't merely a ghost. It was an omen.

Phosy rang at ten thirty. The clerk from the administration building trotted downstairs, across the forecourt, and into the morgue to let Dr Siri know he had a phone call. By the time Siri had walked briskly back to the clerk's office (his trotting days were behind him) the connection had been severed. It was half a cup of tea later before Phosy managed to get through again. Siri was beside the phone.

'Siri speaking. Any luck?'

'I went to the crime scene and looked around,' Phosy told him. 'The only thing I found there was a circle of candles: the red ones with short wicks you get at temples.'

'How large was the circle?'

'Diameter of about four metres.'

'That's interesting.'

'We've shown the photo all over the district. You'd think someone would recall a pretty girl like that. But no joy.'

'Phosy, have you been to the farms?'

'Some, but mostly around town. Why?'

Siri explained their shrouded-rice-worker theory. Phosy seemed sceptical.

'It would have been unbearable,' he said. 'How could anyone work the fields wrapped up ...and why?'

'If it did really happen,' Siri said, 'there'd have to be a good reason for it. You might want to ask if anyone's seen a girl like that working the fields.'

'All right. Anything from the stomach contents?'

'I'm just about to take them over to teacher Oum at the lycée. She was away at a seminar all weekend. It's the first chance I've had. I hear they've released the chemicals from customs.'

'The ones the Soviets donated?'

'The Vladivostok Schools Cooperative.'

'You mean they've been at the docks for a year?'

'It's an improvement. My new French forensic pathology textbooks have been stuck there since early '76. By the time they're cleared you'll be able to use them on me.'

Siri put the double plastic bag of stomach contents into a cloth shoulder bag and set off on his motorcycle. Teacher Oum's chemistry class was the closest thing Siri could get to a lab. In his breast pocket he had his Chiang Mai University toxicological colour key pamphlet. It contained a rather limited range of tests that, with a bit of luck, might give clues as to any poison or drug remaining in the system. More often than not, they didn't work. He wasn't feeling particularly lucky today. In fact, the more he considered the spectres of that morning, the more he felt as if his luck was about to run out.

He wanted to go for a ride in the countryside to improve his mood, but the contents of the bag needed to be refrigerated as soon as possible. He turned right in front of the old French governor general's mansion that held court at the start of Lan Xang Avenue. Its grounds had been ignored since the arrival of the Pathet Lao, and all the exotic plants and expensive flowers and shrubs had gone to seed. It was a petty revenge for sixty years of colonialism. Even towards lunchtime there was scant traffic on the main avenue. With its own Lao Arc de Triomphe, Lan Xang had delusions of being the Champs-Élysées. At its widest it could accommodate ten and a half cars or fifty-seven bicycles but today it welcomed only Dr Siri and a small pack of dogs, all dusty.

He passed two government buildings, Finance and Foreign Affairs, which, until a week ago, had been mere departments. Overnight they had become ministries. He remembered a meeting in the caves of Vieng Xai where the old cadres had voted unanimously that when they came to power, they wouldn't encumber their work with the linguistic ornaments of the decadent West. They didn't need ministers or ministries because that would distance them from the common people. No, for them titles like 'Comrade Bounlert in charge of agriculture' would be sufficient. But the temptation to be Somebody had obviously proven too great and the Department of Information had announced that all departments, including itself, would thereafter be called ministries, 'merely to avoid confusion among foreign diplomats'.

At last he rode beneath the arch of the old French lycée. So as not to disturb classes, or, as teacher Oum would have it, wake up the pupils, he switched off his motor and scooted along the driveway to the building that housed the chemistry department. He'd been in graveyards less silent. Education, it appeared, had given way to copying large tracts of text from a blackboard. It saved the vocal cords of the teachers and the brain matter of the children.

He waited in Oum's tiny office until the bell sounded for lunch. Siri had been forced to repeat his high school education in Paris and the sounding of a bell there had been the signal for euphoric screams of freedom and laughter and gaiety. Here at the lycée it was more of an alarm clock that sent sleepy children to their meal. Teacher Oum burst from her classroom like a claustrophobic chick from an egg. She was thirtyish and roundish with an infectious smile. She ran into her office in a panic.

'Oh, Siri,' she said. 'I need a cigarette.'

'You don't smoke.'

'I started last Wednesday. I'm addicted already.'

'But why?'

'I needed something after three hours of the new curriculum. I couldn't scream or run head first into a wall. Cigarettes were the next best thing. Like my new decorations?'

Siri looked around the walls at the neat shelves that held brand-new bottles of chemicals all labelled with little black skulls and crossbones and Russian lettering. Oum struck a match and sucked at the flame through a Red A cigarette.

'Are you sure you should be lighting fires with all this around you?' Siri asked, not in jest.

She coughed her response. 'With a bit of luck, the whole' – cough – 'the whole place will go up.' Cough. 'What can I do for you?'

Siri went to the small refrigerator.

'I've brought you stomach contents,' he said, removing the bag.

'How sweet. Gary used to bring me chocolates.'

Gary was the Australian who had deflowered young Oum during her study period in Sydney. Apart from chocolates, he'd left another gift. She'd named the child Nali. He was seven now, and his red hair made him hard to disguise.

'How's Nali?' Siri asked.

'His Aussie genes are starting to show through. He punched a four-year-old girl last week.'

'Perhaps it's rebellion against the smoking.'

'He'll have to get used to it. I'm planning to have a lot more vices before he grows up.'

'Good for you.'

Oum was spooning stomach contents into six Petri dishes. 'What are we looking for?'

'I'm guessing traces of a sedative, a very strong one.' He went back to the fridge and took out another small vial. 'I brought this too. I wasn't sure we'd be able to do anything with it. I didn't see anything in the book.'

'What are you hoping to find?' she asked.

'Traces of semen.'

'Ah, so this was a rape?'

'I just need to know whether he . . .'

'I get it. It's too bad we're so limited in what we can do here. You need a real lab, Dr Siri.'

'I'll tell the president.'

'Let him know you've got a ready-made assistant to work in it too. I tell you what. This is a long shot, Siri, but there may be a way. I read about it when I was in Sydney. You need an ultraviolet light. It shows up the phosphates.'

'And you just happen to have an ultraviolet lamp lying around?'

'I hope that wasn't sarcasm, Doctor, because yes, we do. It's over in the gym. They used it at the school discotheque in the good old days. I have no idea whether it'll work but it's worth a try.'

'Indeed it is.'

'I'll get on to it after school this evening. Let's look at these fellows first.'

While they worked their way down the list from the handbook, Siri decided to describe the case. Given Dtui's reaction, he was reluctant to spoil Oum's day, but he knew in the small world they shared, she'd hear about the strangling sooner or later. He left the part about the pestle to the very end. Oum dropped the pipette into a glass bowl with a crash and pushed herself back on the chair.

'I'm sorry,' he told her. 'There was no delicate way—'

'No, Siri. This story. I've heard the selfsame thing.'

'What do you mean?'

'The beautiful girl strangled, tied to a tree …the pestle.'

'How could you have heard it so soon? It only happened on Friday.'

'No, Siri. It happened a long time ago.'

'Where did you get it from?'

'Here, at the school. It's one of those legends the kids pass around to scare the daylights out of each other. I put a girl in detention when I heard her telling it. I thought it was sick for children to be coming up with stories like that.'

'Well, believe me, Oum, this wasn't a story. When did you hear it?'

'A year ago? Maybe two.'

The anger rose in Siri's throat. 'He's done this before, the bastard. Do you remember the student?'

'Kumdee Vilavong. She's also big on dirty jokes and scandal. I put her in detention all the time. I'm quite fond of her.'

Siri stood. 'Can we go and talk to her?'

'What? Now?'

'Yes, right now.'

4

HINDIPENDENCE

The lunchtime rush at the Happy Dine Indian restaurant was over and the proprietor was sitting with his waitress in the open frontage looking at the street. At eleven, they'd sprinkled the pavement out front with a watering can. For about thirty minutes it kept the dust from flying into the tin lunch trays. They'd repeated the dousing at twelve and one. It was 1:15 and no evidence of their efforts remained. The hot pavement had devoured the water as soon as it made contact. That might explain, in some small way, why the lunchtime rush had numbered five people, one of whom had brought his own drink. Everybody agreed the Happy Dine had gone downhill since the old regime.

A motorcycle went past, braked, and turned back. It kicked up a dust storm. The waitress pulled up her T-shirt to cover her nose and exposed her belly. The proprietor looked down forlornly at his once white shirt. Dr Siri emerged from the cloud and cast a faint shadow across both of them. He quickly explained that he'd already eaten lunch, thus curtailing their excitement before it got out of hand.

'I'm here to see your chef,' he said.

'We have nobody here of that name,' said the proprietor. He was one of the southern Indians who had weathered the takeover of '75. His accent was so thick, it would have stuck to the wall if you'd thrown it. Siri wasn't absolutely sure it was Lao he was hearing.

'The father of the crazy man who walks around the streets?' Siri tried again.

'My chef is not available for other positions. He is bonded,' said the proprietor.

Siri stared at him.

'He's out the back, uncle,' said the waitress. The young man glared at her, but she ignored him.

Out the back actually meant 'out the back'.

The kitchen was at the rear of the restaurant in the yard roofed over by a large green tarpaulin with grease stains. Attached to a cross beam were two remarkable fans. Someone had come up with the bright idea of removing the covers and attaching long streamers to the blades. The intention had obviously been to keep insects away from the food and keep the cook cool at the same time. But the weight of the streamers had slowed the rotors to such a pace that the device merely stirred the hot air and the flies together like ingredients in a large stew. A fat man in a navy blue undershirt and long black trousers was on the far side of the small yard washing dishes in a bucket.

'Excuse me,' Siri said.

The man looked over his shoulder with a shocked expression. His was a bulbous chocolaty face with a nose that looked like it might pop. He dropped the dishes into the unsoapy water and hurried over to Siri, wiping his hands on his belly. He crouched as he walked in order to keep his head below the visitor's. He smiled broadly and rocked his head and performed a very wobbly version of the Lao, hands-together *nop*. Siri was afraid the man might drop to his knees.

'Yes, sir? Yes, sir?' he said, apparently delighted to see

Siri. This out-of-shape Indian was in his fifties, and Siri doubted the man had known a year of those fifty when he wasn't being bossed or bullied. He had the air of a man whose idea of Nirvana was a place where the canes were shorter and the whips merely made of horsehair.

'Do you speak Lao?' Siri asked.

The man nodded several times. 'Yes, sir. How can I help you?'

'You could stop bobbing up and down for a start. I'm getting motion sickness.'

'Very well. Yes, sir.'

Siri pulled over two bathroom stools and signalled for the man to sit on one. But as soon as Siri sat on the other, the Indian dropped to the floor like a sack of soft noodles. It appeared to be familiar territory for him so the doctor conceded.

'What's your name?' Siri asked.

'Yes, sir. I am Bhiku David Tickoo.'

'May I call you Bhiku?'

'Sir, I would be an honoree.'

'Very well, I'm here about Rajid.' Bhiku smiled silently. 'You don't know who that is, do you?'

'No, sir.'

'Thought not. It's the name we've given to the young man who walks half naked around the streets.'

'Ah, sir. Then that would be my son, Jogendranath, as named after the great reformist.'

'Really, well that's quite a mouthful. Could I just call him Rajid for now?'

'As you wish, sir.'

Without warning, Bhiku climbed uneasily to his feet and hurried into the shop. Siri wondered whether he'd offended him by renaming his son, but he returned in seconds with a glass of misty water. He lowered himself to the ground once more before handing it to Siri.

'Forgive me, sir. Where were my manners?'

Siri knew better than to drink unidentified water so he merely touched his lips to the surface.

'Thank you, Bhiku. I was wondering whether you might know where Rajid is right now. Nobody's seen him for ten days.'

'I know this, sir. I too am very concerned.'

'Does your son ever tell you about places he likes to go? Places where he hides out?'

'Sir, it is sad that I am to say this, but my poor son has not uttered a word since our family tragedy.'

Siri personally knew that not to be true but he didn't see this as an appropriate moment to say so.

'If it's not too difficult for you,' Siri said, 'I'd like to hear that story.'

'Oh, sir. It is such a small tale for such a great man to waste his time with.'

Siri laughed. 'Dear Bhiku, I really am not a great man.'

'Forgive me for begging to differ, sir, but you are Dr Siri Paiboun. You were pointed out to me at the hospital. You are the greatest man in the entire hemisphere.'

Siri wanted to laugh again but it felt oddly irreverent to do so. He absentmindedly took a sip of his water. 'You shouldn't believe everything my wife tells you,' he joked to shake off the embarrassment.

'I have seen it with my own eyes. My son adores you.'

'He does?'

'Yes, sir. He has informed me of your nature and your ability.'

'You said he can't speak.'

'And that is true, sir. But he writes.'

'Cr— Rajid writes?'

'Indeed, sir. He writes beautifully. I taught all of my children as my father had taught me. Although my son's body and mind have been taken by the *Asuras,* his true self is still with us in his script.'

'Could I see it?'

'I am delighted to show you, sir. Unfortunately, you cannot read his words for yourself as they are in Hindi, and he writes in old verse. But there are several stanzas dedicated to you, Doctor.'

Siri was astounded. Crazy Rajid, aka Jogendranath, had always been a character on the fringes of Siri and Civilai's lunches, swinging in trees, bathing naked in the Mekhong, occasionally masturbating. The thought that he might, like a coma patient, have been aware of everything that was being said, while unable to express himself, made Siri feel a sudden pang of guilt. The two old men could be unkind at times.

'What did he write?' Siri asked.

'Yes, sir. He mentions your kindness, and the kindness of your friends. You brought him clothes, fed him, included him in your celebrations. I know that others treated him well – it is the Lao way to be kind to those less fortunate – but I feel that you did not look down on him.'

Siri was touched.

'I'd like to hear about your tragedy,' Siri said.

'If you insist, sir. In a nutshell, we – my wife and two daughters and two sons – were travelling to Burma by boat. For a better life, it was. I had been offered work in a factory there. Alas, the boat was not as strong as our resolve. There was a storm. Only myself and Jogendranath survived. We were adrift for four days. By the time we were rescued, my son had lost hold of his sanity.'

'So, you and he ...?'

'Some work in Burma, sir, until the junta put a crackdown on us illegals. Then to Thailand and casual work. Then a kind Punjabi invited us here. I had cooked for him in Rangoon. He was coming to open this restaurant in Vientiane. He sadly is demised now. It is his son who runs it today.'

His life story had been told in five minutes, and there was sorrow in his large puffy eyes.

'And Rajid?'

'He has periods when he remembers me. At other times I am absent from his mind, sir. We have not spoken since the final day on the boat.'

Siri knew the Indian could speak. He'd heard him. He wondered what blockage there was between son and father. What was Rajid thinking that made him ignore the man who had carried the boy's infirmity like a boulder on his back across a continent? Siri looked at big, soft, smiling Bhiku and wondered what wicked fate had dragged his life into the bogs.

'Bhiku,' he said. 'You strike me as an intelligent man. You read Hindi, and you speak my language quite beautifully ...'

'You are too kind, sir. I also have smatterings of Thai and Burmese ...not to mention English.'

'That's what I thought. So why – and there's no offence intended here – why are you grovelling about in this depressing restaurant earning ...what do they pay you?'

'Food and board, sir.'

'Then that's even worse. Why are you here earning nothing at all when you could hold down a decent job?'

Bhiku smiled. 'It is my fate, sir.'

'What does that mean?'

'My wife and I . . . and my children, we were born untouchables. Our caste dictates that we were destined to suffer – and life has certainly proven that to be true, sir.'

'Oh, Mr Tickoo.' Siri shook his head and sighed. Not for the first time, a very strong urge came over him. If this wasn't a needy case he didn't know what was. Before he was taken by the wormy woman, Siri was determined to rescue Rajid's father from servitude and set him free. He just had no idea how to go about it.

'All right.' Siri came back to the here and now. 'Let's talk about where your son might be.'

'Yes, sir. I have no awareness of this. I too am most worried. I have spent all my free time scouring the streets and the river. I even reported it to the police but they laughed at me.'

'That doesn't surprise me. When was the last time you saw him?'

'Twelve days ago.'

'Well, I met someone who saw him ten days ago, on the Thursday.'

'I expected to see him on the Friday. He always used to go to the old French mansion on Fridays and stop off here first with a verse.'

'Any idea why he went there?'

'Oh yes, sir. My old employer bought that house from its French owner. He lived there during the heydays of Vientiane. So much life and vitality in the city then. Those were the days when the Americans still painted the town green. The restaurant was terribly popular. We had a singer, and we made as much on drink as we did on food. I had three co-workers. We only closed on Friday. And every Friday evening, our employer would invite the workers to eat at his house. It was a tradition. For Jogendranath it was the only time he sat down with what could be called a family and ate a civilized meal.

'It didn't occur to me at the time, but I imagine it brought back memories of our own family. When our old owner passed away and his boy took over, the tradition was stopped. But my son continued to go to the house. There was no explaining to him. That's when I realized how important the Friday meals must have been. He knocks on the door every week at 5:30.'

'But for the past two weeks he hasn't knocked,' Siri said. 'Do you think something might have happened to him?'

'He is my son. I have worried about him every day of his life. I used to go to him and try to convince him to come home, but I have to admit that I lost him some time ago. Now he is a child of the streets and all the dangers it contains.'

'But his writing?'

'Sometimes he drops it off here. At others he leaves it at the door of the old house. I believe that is the location of the first riddle.'

'Riddle?'

'Yes, sir. He is very classical, my son. I believe that but for the tragedy, he would have been a scholar in the classics. A university lecturer. Of course our caste would have prevented this but I believe in my heart he had the ability. In his odes he writes that he is a prince. In order to find his palace of the One Hundred and Eleven Eyes, the common man must solve three riddles. The first riddle talks of the lace beneath the old French lady's skirt. I wonder if he sees the colonial building as an old French lady.'

'Do you have all three riddles?'

'Solving the first will lead to the second, and so on.'

'Have you looked under the old lady's skirt?'

'Sadly, sir, I don't have my son's head for literature, or yours for science. I am a humble cook.'

'Right. We can discuss that later. Do you have the full riddle somewhere?'

'It is upstairs.'

'Do you have time to translate it for me?'

'It would be my pleasure, sir.'

5

DOOMED

When Siri got back to the morgue there were three messages waiting for him. Unfortunately, their waiting area was between the ears of Mr Geung. Nurse Dtui was off at a nursing lecture at the new Ministry of Health so the messages had been given orally to the morgue assistant. It took a while to extract them. The easiest to understand was that a small man and two taller men had been by asking where Dr Siri was. The doctor knew exactly who they were and was pleased he'd been out of the office when they came. But he knew he had to go on the attack against the thugs from Housing. The second message was that Inspector Phosy would call, although the time had become lost in the muddle of juggling three pieces of information at the same time. The third message was impossible to decipher.

'A...she w...wasn't her. But the other h...her was was on...on dragging.'

Siri knew his friend had reached his 'full' mark and didn't press him. He left Geung in the cutting room and went into his office to see if Dtui had left a note. Halfway across his room he stopped. There were a dozen worms squirming on his desk and they didn't hurry away when they saw him. The same ominous feeling came over him, the vague scent of damp earth, the sense of time running out. He heard a step behind him.

'Dr Siri?'

If his skin hadn't been on so tight he would have jumped out of it. He turned to see the hospital clerk in the doorway.

'Yes?'

'Doctor? Are you all right?'

'Yes.'

'You have another phone call.'

This time, Phosy was still on the line when the coroner reached the administration office. Siri wondered exactly how much red tape would have to be unwrapped to get a phone extension over at the morgue. He didn't need all this exercise. His lungs had been giving him trouble of late. He wheezed once or twice into the mouthpiece.

'Siri?'

'Phosy?'

'Any news?'

'Lots. Just let me…catch my breath. You go first.'

'Nothing at all from the photo. I did meet a weaver who recognized the ribbon. She gave me the name of a shop in Vientiane that sells it. It isn't available up here apparently. That might lead to something. And I've been sharing your theory about the shrouded rice worker. I got some interesting reactions to that. I told people to spread it around and one farmer got back to me. He told me the driver of the truck that picks up his excess rice for the government tax mentioned something similar once.'

'How similar?'

'Well, you know what stories are like up here. It was about a woman he'd seen working the fields who wasn't really a woman.'

'And she was a ...?'

'The locals told the driver she used to be a woman – and this is from him, not me – but she drank from a cursed pool, and it turned her invisible. So they wrapped her up from head to foot so she wouldn't frighten outsiders.'

'And he believed them?'

'He's a truck driver.'

'Did your farmer recall where this invisible woman was seen ...or not seen?'

'He couldn't remember. But we're looking for the driver. We've got his name. It shouldn't take long. Are you ready to speak yet?'

'I am, and it's important. Let's hope we don't get cut off. I went to the lycée and met teacher Oum. I mentioned the condition of our corpse, and she'd heard the same story from one of her students over a year ago.'

'The same story?'

'The beautiful girl, the strangulation, the tree, the pestle.'

'Shit.'

'Exactly. I went to meet the girl. She told me the story again exactly as she'd heard it: a mirror of our case. I followed the trail. We found the girl who'd told our girl and the boy who'd told her, and on and on. At last we arrived at a rather shy, quiet lass who'd started the whole ball rolling. She was from Luang Nam Tha in the north. The lycée's still pretty exclusive, but she'd been awarded a Cuban scholarship from Comrade Castro. She was reluctant to tell us where she'd heard the story, but teacher Oum bullied her into giving up her source. It appears she'd heard it from her sister, and her sister's a nurse.'

'In Luang Nam Tha?'

'Yes, which attaches a grain of truth to the rumour.'

'You have the sister's name?'

'And address. Am I not the complete detective?'

'You're Inspector Migraine incarnate.'

'It's Maigret, Phosy. But thank you. Should I leave that avenue of investigation to you?'

'Of course. Siri, I can't believe this animal has committed the same atrocity more than once.'

'Fortunately we live in a place where things like this are so scandalous people continue to talk about them.'

It was the first chance to meet and speak in relative privacy. Phan had done his duty the previous evening. He'd charmed the immediate and extended family. The grandmother, eleven sheets to the wind, had declared him 'a very jolly boy who would be a great asset to the family'. The father had translated proudly for Phan. The others had shushed her and told her there was no such plan in the works but Phan knew they were all thinking the same thing. His foot was in the door. His was a skill many men yearned to possess and he had it in droves. He was now ready for the prelude to the kill.

'You shouldn't be here,' she said.

Phan had driven the truck up a particularly troublesome hill to arrive at Wei's school from the far side. The track from the village was too narrow to navigate so a huge detour had been necessary to arrive there in the vehicle. But the old Chinese truck was a vital player in this drama. Phan arrived just as the bell sounded for the end of the day's lessons. The children gathered around the truck like ants on a wounded caterpillar. He did tricks for them: produced boiled sweets from their ears, made gooseberries vanish. He was the Messiah. Wei had walked out to meet him.

'I know. I apologize,' he said. 'I finished work early. I didn't have anything to do. I remembered your mother saying you'd hurt your toe. She said it was painful for you to walk.'

'It's only half a kilometre along the track.'

'Even so, I thought you might like a ride.'

The other teacher had come out to watch the show with a big smile on her face.

'It…it isn't appropriate,' she said. Wei's cheeks were as stained as rose apples.

'I mean you and the children, of course.'

'By road, you have to go all the way around the mountain.'

'I have to anyway. Look . . .' He leaned closer so the children couldn't hear. She smelled grease on him and some kind of disinfectant soap. 'I didn't want to embarrass you, really. I just…I just thought I could help. If you prefer, I'll leave you to walk.'

She looked at the children gathered expectantly around the truck, then back at him. So tall, so polite…so interesting.

'All right, for the children's sake,' she said at last. 'They don't get many opportunities to ride in a truck. It will be nice for them.'

They screamed all the way back to the village. Wei sat in the passenger seat with a smile on her face that wouldn't go away. Their countryside, the scenery she knew too well, was suddenly unrecognizable. From the window of his truck it had become…magical. A feeling had come over her she couldn't understand. Part of it was physical, as if she needed to wee but knew she wouldn't be able to. Her insides danced. It was all part of the spell. She had suddenly been whisked up in a hurricane that blew through her world.

The children from outside the village were dropped off individually at their huts. They strode proudly from the truck as if a private limousine had delivered them. Phan saluted like a chauffeur when they thanked him. They would remember the experience for years. He dropped the children who lived in the village at the hand-pump diesel stand in the dead centre of town. The provincial roadway that passed through the village was barely two dirt lanes wide. Buses and military vehicles carried their own spare petrol so the diesel stand was largely for decoration. When Phan had filled up there twice he doubled the owner's monthly revenue.

Wei was about to follow the children but Phan touched her arm. 'Wei, could I talk to you?'

'It isn't—'

'Appropriate, I know.' He smiled. 'We're in the middle of town. There are eyes everywhere. We have a hundred chaperones. How dangerous can it be?'

'I didn't say ...' She was tongue-tied. She spoke all day for a living but here she was ... couldn't put a sentence together.

Phan leaned against his door, as far from her as he could be. He clutched the wheel like a shield and stared at the road ahead. 'I had ... I had no idea, no plan,' he began. 'I came only to work. I've been to a hundred, two hundred towns like this. I've done my surveys, made my calculations, and left. I've enjoyed meeting the people, sharing jokes and experiences. But I've never ...'

Wei was looking out of her own window so he couldn't see the crimson her face had become. 'I don't think you should say any more.' She pushed open her door a centimetre or two.

'No, I have to say this or I would never forgive myself. I have never felt this way before. I have to leave soon and we will probably never see each other again. And, if we don't, I want to leave you with this…this overwhelming emotion I've had since I first saw you by the pond. It's not…I wish I were more…wish I were better with words. Because when I saw you something flooded into me and I don't know how to describe what it was. You've changed me.'

Never, never had she heard such words. In all her seventeen years she'd never heard a man truly express himself. This was Laos. Men held in their feelings. You could be around them all their lives and not know they had one emotion between them. So this was overwhelming. It was as if his large hand had reached inside her rib cage and squeezed her heart. She couldn't breathe. She threw open the door of the truck and walked unsteadily away.

Phan watched her go, reached across, and closed her door. The woman who pumped the diesel was leaning on the counter in the tiny bamboo service hut. She smiled. He smiled back and shrugged. She held up her thumb.

This was too, too easy.

It was only four thirty of the same, incredibly long, Monday. Siri was sitting on a wooden bench at the new Ministry of Justice. He'd heard of their dilemma. Prior to the ministerization, Judge Haeng had been an appropriate department head in the eyes of the administration. He was a judge, albeit a fast-track, Soviet-trained judge, and he was from a wealthy family. So, as a department head, he fitted the bill. But as a minister, even though it was fundamentally the same job, he was found lacking. Being a minister had certain inherent expectations. How, for example, could anybody barely turned forty be a minister? A minister had to look experienced, with the lines of wisdom etched onto his countenance. Haeng had acne. What diplomat would want to shake hands with a spotty minister?

So a room on the top floor of the Ministry of Justice was being refurbished for the arrival of the new minister. Siri watched agile old men climbing the bamboo scaffold like spiders on a web. They chipped away the clay hornets' nests and replaced broken louvres. Nobody yet knew who the new minister would be, so, temporarily, Judge Haeng remained in charge. It had been a very painful slap in the face for him and his mood reflected it. This was certainly a bad time to be asking him for favours.

'He'll see you now, Doctor,' said Manivone. She was the receptionist, the head of the typing pool, and the real brains behind the Ministry of Justice. Siri was sure that without her, Judge Haeng would be driving a motorcycle taxi.

'What hat should I wear?' Siri asked.

'My first choice would be something hard and shock proof,' she said, walking beside him along the open-air corridor. 'But as it's almost going-home time, I'd go with cap in hand. The Vietnamese adviser's in there so the judge has to keep hold of his temper and act humble. If you come across as pathetic he might take pity on you.'

'I don't do pathetic very well.'

'I know. But don't rile him. You know what he's like when you rile him. Play it by ear.' Siri knocked and turned the doorknob. '...or earlobe,' she added and laughed behind her hand.

Siri was smiling when he entered the room. Haeng continued to do whatever it was he was doing at his desk

74

and ignored the intrusion. Comrade Phat, a Vietnamese with few teeth but no shortage of charisma, looked up from his corner table and greeted Siri in Vietnamese. Siri replied in kind and Phat laughed. This was probably a bad start if Siri wanted to win over the judge. Judge Haeng's Vietnamese wasn't good enough to catch the joke. He would naturally assume the worst.

Siri sat on the rickety chair in front of Haeng's desk and awaited his audience. The judge seemed to be composing a memorandum. He wrote like a child with his tongue poking slightly through his lips. Siri had always seen him as a boy although Haeng was clearly middle-aged. He didn't have any respect for the young fellow.

'Siri?' said Haeng, as if he'd just noticed him. 'What is it?'

Obviously the judge was in a bad mood; Siri was in need of a clever tactic or two to win him over. He tried the most obvious first.

'I just came by because I was astounded when I heard. After all you've done for the Justice Department, your impeccable record. How could you have been passed over?'

Siri had lied to Manivone. Pathetic wasn't at all beyond him. But Daeng was right. The only way to get Housing off his back was to have Haeng on his side. Few men would have seen Siri's blatant pandering as anything other than what it was. But Haeng obviously wanted to hear it.

'Why, thank you, Siri,' he said. 'It's always heartening to hear a hurrah from the soldiers in the ranks.'

'And you are an inspiration to the men, Judge.' Siri was temporarily interrupted by the clearing of a Vietnamese throat. 'I often find myself repeating your Party mottoes.' He didn't bother to add, 'At drinking sessions for a good laugh.'

'Well, I'm touched, Doctor.'

'Oh, yes. And one of my favourites, and I hope I've got this right, goes, "If a mother cries in Pakse we feel sorrow in Xam Neua. If a daughter is born in Bokeo, we burp her in Khamuan. It is the duty of a good socialist to consider every Lao a member of his family." That still brings a tear to my eye, that one.'

'I think you have the essence of it, Siri. Well done.'

'That motto changed my philosophy, Judge.'

'It did?'

'After you uttered those words I went out and invited my new family into my home: the poor, the blind, the previously immoral, the widowed, and the dishonest.'

'Siri, you aren't referring to your present house, are you?'

'Why, yes.'

'I've been there, remember?'

'Wasn't it marvellous to see your dream turn into reality? I tell everybody, even the Department of Housing, that my living arrangements were inspired by Judge Haeng.'

'You do?'

'Certainly.'

'Well, I suggest you un-tell them.'

'What?'

'You are a senior Party member and the national coroner. You have to command respect. Yet your house is a zoo, Siri. I thought your marriage might settle you down, force you to kick that band of scavengers out onto the street and make you live like a respectable senior citizen. It's a government residence, not a guesthouse.'

'Oh, I get it. A Party motto is perfectly sound advice until it's put into practice. Say it after me by all means, but don't actually do it. We don't really want everyone in Khamuan wiping the snotty little Bokeo tyke's arse.'

'Siri, you always resort to vulgarity when you lose an argument.'

'How would you know? You're never around when I lose an argument.'

Judge Haeng stood and shuffled papers on his desk. He was in a black huff.

'Dr Siri, these are working hours. I have neither the time nor the inclination to discuss your personal life. If you have technical or medical information for me I am happy to listen. Otherwise, please don't disturb me. And now I have a meeting.'

Siri was fuming inside, which caused the smile on his face to pucker his cheeks.

'Oh, I completely forgot,' he said calmly. 'I do have some medical and scientific information to pass on to you.'

'Well, let's have it. I'm in a hurry.'

Siri coughed and recited, 'A fart is fifty-nine per cent nitrogen, twenty-one per cent hydrogen…'

Haeng pushed back his chair, grabbed his papers, and strode to the door.

'…and nineteen per cent carbon…'

The door slammed.

'…dioxide.'

Siri pursed his lips and stared at the brown marks on the backs of his hands. He fancied he saw familiar country outlines from the atlas there.

'What's the other one per cent?' asked Phat.

'Depends what you had for dinner,' Siri told him.

There was a beat before both men burst into laughter.

'Dr Siri,' said Phat, drying his eyes on a torn-off rectangle of tissue paper. 'How have you survived in the system this long?'

'Actually, Comrade, they did away with me several years back. I've returned to haunt them.'

'So it would seem, Siri. So it would seem. Trouble with Housing?'

'They aren't happy with the class of people I have living with me.'

'Are they paying rent?'

'Not a brass *kip*.'

'I'll see what I can do.'

'Thank you.'

The door opened. Judge Haeng returned to his desk with a pronounced limp, and collected his forgotten walking stick. He ignored the two disrespectful old men and shuffled out. The laughter resumed.

The morgue seemed to have frozen in time since Siri had left on his mission to the Ministry of Justice. Nothing had moved, not even Geung, who still stood with a toilet plunger hoisted above his head trying to coax a ceiling lizard to drop into it.

'Are you training it?' Siri asked.

'I...I want to take it ou...outside. It shits on th... the...the gurney. I don't want to kill it. It's Buddha's crea...creature.'

'Keep your voice down, Geung. The Ministry of Not Mentioning Religion might hear you.' Geung was bemused. 'Look, I'll give you a little hint. Spray it with water. I don't know how I know, but when you do that they can't hold on for some reason. Try it. But when you get it outside give it a stern talking-to so it doesn't come running back in. All right?'

Geung's laugh clanged around the room. 'Ha, who...who's mad enough to talk to a...a lizard?'

Siri laughed and patted his friend on the back. 'Sorry, my little comrade. Sometimes I forget who it is I'm addressing.'

'Oh...oh!' Geung hopped on one leg. 'I remember.'

'What?'

'The last message. Teacher Ou...Teacher Ou...Oum.'

'Wants me to get in touch?'

'Something...drug.'

'All right. Thank you. Good job. If I'm not back by six, you can lock up.'

Geung saluted and turned again to the job at hand.

'It's definitely Meprobamate,' said Oum, her voice sounding like ice rattling in an empty glass over the telephone line. 'It reacted with furfural.'

'I thought it might be something like that,' Siri replied. 'How heavy was the dose?'

'The reaction was really strong. I'd say it was quite concentrated.'

'Enough to cause loss of consciousness?'

'Not impossible.'

'Let's hope so. I'd hate for her to have been aware of what was going on. In a way I'm glad it was Meprobamate. The symptoms of an overdose are more like a coma – drowsiness, loss of muscle control, unresponsiveness. There are other drugs that paralyze the nervous system. You can see what's going on but can't lift a finger to stop it. I'd prefer that she was unconscious or at least numb.'

'Oh, and the contents of the stomach,' Oum remembered. 'Did you go through them before you brought them over here?'

'I did take a look. Didn't recognize anything.'

'The little green fellows?'

'Berries of some kind? Seeds?'

'I wouldn't bet my life on it, but they looked a lot like capers to me.'

'And they are?'

'They're used for seasoning. I had them once or twice in Australia. You get them in Italian food. Not the kind of thing you can find locally.'

'So they would be imported and expensive.'

'If I'm right.'

'Not the type of thing a farm girl would include in her diet.'

'Not at all.'

'I'll pass that little clue on to Phosy. Any luck with the ultraviolet light?'

'I just got back from the gym. It isn't the type of place I hang out normally, but I did your test. I don't think we should read too much into this. The machine only has two settings, and neither might be the right one to reveal phosphates, but nothing made an appearance on the sample you gave me.'

'So either the perpetrator didn't ejaculate . . .'

'Or the school has a crap piece of black light equipment. Can you come over and pick up all your evidence? My fridge is full.'

Siri did as he was told. On his way back along That Luang Road with both his shoulder bag and his mind full he switched off the engine, cruised, and contemplated on the long downward incline. If the lycée legend was true, if there really had been a similar murder, then how could they be sure there weren't others? This wasn't Europe. There was no network to cross-reference commonalities between crimes. In Laos, local police forces described their cases in two ledgers and when these were full, one would be placed on the shelf in the police station, and eventually the other would be sent to Vientiane and filed at police headquarters under the province from which it had come. If two similar crimes occurred in two different provinces, there would be no way of telling.

His thoughts were disturbed by the aftermath of a small accident at the Victory Monument roundabout just in front of the bland court building. A black government limousine pulling out of the driveway had been hit by a motorcycle sidecar piled high with cartons of eggs on their way to an embassy reception. The front bonnet of the car was a giant omelette. Two young police officers were holding back onlookers brandishing spoons and plates. The chances of two motorized vehicles colliding in Vientiane were less than that of a bird of paradise defecating on your best hat. Poosu, the Hmong god of small accidents, must have been bored that evening.

The limousine was empty and there was no motorcyclist apparent at the scene, so the police had obviously taken the suspects in for questioning. The Lao language had no shortage of bawdy egg jokes, so Siri was certain this story would be twice around the city before he got back home. His momentum had brought him this far, and he was about to switch on his engine when, among the legs of the crowd, he spied Saloop, his ex-dog. It was dark, and the onlookers were lit only by a single lamp at the front of the courthouse, but there was no mistaking the shape and piercing eyes of Saloop. He sat with his back to the accident staring directly at Siri. His head followed the doctor as he glided slowly past, and that same, hopeless, sands-of-time feeling came over Siri. It couldn't be ignored. Somebody was going to die, and Saloop was there to make the announcement.

Although it was after six the morgue door was open. Siri assumed Geung was still attempting to coax his lizard outside. But when he walked in he found Inspector Phosy sitting at his desk.

'Dr Siri, you look like you've seen a ghost,' he said.

Siri was getting sick of hearing this description.

'It's road dust,' he said. 'It'll wash off. How did you get back so soon? I just talked to you on the phone.'

'The cadre representing Vang Vieng had a helicopter pick him up so he could make the cabinet meeting tomorrow. They're starting work on the three-year development programme. I hitched a ride.'

Siri sat at Dtui's desk and wiped his face with a cotton skullcap.

'Any news?' he asked.

'Nothing in Vang Vieng. I thought I could do more good here. I left Sergeant Sihot up there showing the photo around.'

'And the truck driver?'

'That's why I'm here. He's based at the new Cooperative Development Works. He's due in from Pak Lai tomorrow. I'll catch him when he arrives.'

'And the nurse in Luang Nam Tha?'

'I'm taking the regular flight up there tomorrow afternoon, the Lord willing. I'll talk to her and see if that leads anywhere.'

'You can't phone her?'

'Doctor Siri, you surprise me. What happened to the man

who just eighteen months ago didn't know which end of a telephone to talk into?'

'The Senior Citizens' Union encourages us to embrace new technology.'

'Then they should encourage Luang Nam Tha to get a few telephone lines put in. It's like contacting Great-Uncle Lou at a séance, and that's an insult to séances. Not even the governor's got a phone yet. He has to drive down to the Chinese road project and use theirs.'

'You realize Dtui will blame me for your going away again.'

'Why should she?'

'She blames me for everything. Everybody does.'

'Doctor, you seem a little down.'

'Oh, it's nothing. Just an old man contemplating the impermanence of life.'

'Has something happened?'

'Seventy-three years have happened.'

'Have you had a medical examination I don't know about?'

'No. It's . . . ah, *bo ben nyang*.'

Siri arrived at the shop at the end of the noodle rush hour. Daeng was dishing out supper as fast as the pot could boil. If the Thai secret service had trained their binoculars on her shop that evening, they would never have believed Laos was undergoing an economic crisis. They'd have considered the second devaluation of the *kip* to have been a ruse and rumours of financial ruin to be a dastardly communist plot. But they wouldn't have known the real reason everybody flocked to Daeng's shop. A bowl of the most delicious noodles north of the Singapore equator cost the equivalent of five pence and few could refuse such a temptation. There was nobody like her in the capital. Even travellers from outside the district had begun to turn up as word spread. Delicious food, low prices, minimal chances of contracting hepatitis.

Siri sneaked in over the fence and through the back door. He whistled to Daeng, who turned around from her kettle.

'Psst. Is the coast clear?' he asked.

'Darling, you're alive,' she shouted. A dozen diners looked up and Siri retreated behind the door frame. 'I was sure Housing had assassinated you.'

Siri hurried to the staircase and held up two fingers, which signified Daeng's special Number Two, seasoned with tree frogs and jelly mushrooms. Then he vanished upstairs.

By eight thirty the tables were wiped and the shutters pulled. Nobody stayed out late any more unless they were Eastern European experts or connected to somebody important. Daeng went up to see how her husband was doing. He was scooped over his desk. She kissed the lighter of his ears.

'People our age don't do that,' he said.

'Then they're mad.' She kissed him again. 'What are you doing?'

'I'm reading a Hindi riddle.'

'And we mere humans struggle with the *Lao Huksat* newsletter.'

'It's been translated.'

She pulled over a rattan stool and sat beside him, her hand on his thigh. He told her about his meeting with Crazy Rajid's father and the incredible fact that the silent and troubled Rajid could write beautiful poetry. Daeng said it reminded her of a rubber plantation, such a clutter of trees that seemed to have no order at all until you looked at them from the right angle. Then they were all lined up and parallel.

'So, what do we have from our demented poet?' she asked.

Siri held up the paper and recited like an ancient scholar,

> Beneath the old French lady's skirt
> Black lace and too much pink
> The cold daughter of the daughter
> Hides in a dark corner.

'It probably rhymed in Hindi,' Daeng decided.

'And made sense,' Siri added.

'But it is potentially cracking good fun. Like a treasure hunt clue. Let's go for it.'

'Bhiku seems to think the old French lady is one of the colonial buildings on Samsenthai.'

'He does? So let's go there.'

'Don't you want to relax after a busy day?'

'What I want after a busy day of noodling is to use my sadly inactive brain. Grab a torch. I'll get changed into my mystery-solving outfit.'

They decided to walk the short distance to the three colonial buildings on the main street. Daeng firmly believed that arthritis could be cured by ignoring it completely, that it would give up and go away. So far the ploy hadn't worked. Odd lamps burned in closed shops along their way. The streetlights attached to public buildings were poorly placed and seemed to leak light rather than express it. They cast deceptive shadows on the footpaths that might have been ruts or two-metre-deep holes. Luckily, Siri and Daeng had their torches with them.

When they arrived at the first of the three old ladies, it was evident that the new generation of government officials retired early. Only four of the fifteen or so windows shone dully with electric light. Like most of the houses of the moneyed families of the old regime, this ancient lady had been hurriedly converted to accommodate several families. They all shared one bathroom and lived their lives crammed in one room. Senior Party members sometimes had two. Siri had lived in such a house when he first came to Vientiane. There was no supervisor to make complaints to. If something broke down, as things often did, the residents would get together, pool their resources, and fix it. That, as they said, was what communism was all about.

There was nobody to ask permission from, so Siri and Daeng decided to nose around. Colonial homes in the tropics generally were built without basements because in the monsoon season they tended to fill with water that ruined everything in them. They decided to skirt the building from the outside, shining their torches. They arrived back at the front door with nettles attached to their trousers but no hint of lace undergarments.

'I suppose we should go inside,' Siri suggested.

'After me,' said Daeng, scooting up the step.

The front door was solid teak, obviously very old. When they pushed, there was a defiant creak from the hinges. Three rooms led off the long passageway that stretched before them. The hallway itself was covered in once stylish – now sadly worn – linoleum. A staircase on their left rose darkly to the second floor. Two rooms on the right were residences. Hasps had been attached to the outsides of their doors and one had a name on a small rectangle of card taped beside it. It was too dark to read it. The only light in the hallway came from the third room, a bathroom on the left beyond the stairs.

Attracted like moths to the light, Siri and Daeng went in. It was spotlessly clean. Different coloured plastic bowls and scoops seemed to demarcate each family's spot.

'See a trapdoor anywhere?' Daeng asked. She exhibited none of the characteristics of an interloper sneaking around someone else's house. She had been a spy for the Lao underground so a stranger's bathroom presented no threat to her.

She sat on one of the tiny plastic stools. 'Come on, Siri, use your imagination. He came here every Friday as a child. He would have had a chance to explore. All the adults are sitting at the table drinking wine, having a good time. Young Rajid wanders through the house by himself. Think like Rajid.'

'Perhaps I should take off my clothes and play with myself.'

'That's the spirit.'

Siri stopped pacing. 'No, that's it. Think like Rajid. He may be a scholar deep down, but on the surface he's a randy beast. What if we're thinking too deeply?'

'The old French lady's really an old lady? One of the neighbours?'

'And the lace . . .'

'Is her underwear. And there's too much pink under there. Brilliant! All right. How does he get to see her undies?'

'Well, assuming she didn't strip off at the dinner table I'd say we're in the most likely place.'

'Nowhere to hide in here, really, and the window's too high.'

Siri sat on the Western toilet and looked around.

'There,' he said, pointing at the baseboard in which there was a small rectangular grate no bigger than a business envelope.

'He must have been a lot smaller when he was young.' Daeng laughed, getting on her knees to take a look.

'The stairs,' Siri said. 'This grate is directly under the staircase.' He was hurrying towards the door when he bumped into a muscular man in a towel. 'Good health,' he said.

'Good health,' said the man, obviously surprised to have collided with a strange old gentleman in his own bathroom. He looked at the old lady on her hands and knees on the bare concrete.

'We're just about to move in,' said Siri, 'so we've come to ...to ...'

'To measure for curtains,' Daeng helped him out. She climbed to her feet and followed Siri into the hall, taking more time than necessary to study the man's torso. He blushed and hurried to close the door.

'Curtains?' muttered Siri as they walked to the stairs.

'Yes.'

'In the bathroom?'

'Why not? You would have said something like toilet inspector.'

'What's wrong with that?'

They stood at the foot of the stairs, wondering how anyone could get inside the staircase. A Peeping Tom would have to be directly beneath it. Siri tapped at the front of the wooden steps with his toe. The first and second emitted resounding thuds. The third plonked and seemed to give way a little. Although the panel had been stained the same colour as the others, it was obviously a plywood substitute for the original. Siri knelt on the first stair and carefully pushed one side of the loose panel. It was held in place only by its snug fit between the steps. It gave way easily and he was able to wrest it free without its falling into the gap beneath.

'See anything?' Daeng asked, hunkering down beside him. They heard the scampering of cockroaches, perhaps the patter of a mouse.

'The gap's too narrow to crawl through,' Siri decided.

'Well, thank goodness for that.'

'But I can see a skinny little Indian getting in here easily enough.'

'What's that over there?'

They both leaned into the gap. The bathroom light shone yellow through the grill three metres ahead of them. To the left of the grill there was a shadow. It was about thirty centimetres tall and had all the makings of a hairy creature lurking, ready to pounce.

'Shine your light on it.'

'I left mine in the bathroom.'

'Me too.'

'Did it just move?' Siri asked. 'Perhaps not. If I had a stick I could give it a poke.'

'Don't go away.'

Daeng went back to the bathroom and walked in on the man as he was tossing water over himself with a ladle. He opened one eye and looked at her through the shampoo.

'Excuse me,' she said, grabbing a mop and their torches.

'No problem,' he replied.

She paused briefly in the doorway to glance back, then took the mop to Siri. It was just long enough to reach the hairy object in the corner. It didn't leap to life when Siri prodded it. The torches revealed its identity. With a little manual dexterity, Siri was able to coax the object towards them. Daeng reached down and grabbed it by the hair. It was a porcelain doll: *the cold daughter of the daughter.* Her clothes were tattered and insect ravaged but her hair and face looked as gay as on the day she first arrived in the tropics with her French owner.

'You don't suppose if we pull its string it might tell us the next riddle?' Daeng asked.

'This young lady pre-dates talking dolls by about fifty years, I'd say, but look.' Siri had lifted the frayed dress to reveal a conservative pair of knickers and, in the waistband, a tightly rolled slip of paper. 'Ah, Rajid, sleazy as ever.'

6

IN THE BELLY OF THE BRAINLESS ONE

It had been four days since Phan had begun courting Wei, the schoolteacher. Everything had gone very smoothly. He and her brother were best friends, her parents called him 'son', and Granny would have had him in her attic bunk in the blink of an eye. Wei wasn't as eager as some. She had to save face at the school, he imagined. But she was certainly in love with him. He hadn't exactly asked her to marry him, not in so many words. But there was an unspoken inevitability. It was his last night in the village. His work in the region was done for this trip. He'd weaved his magic so deftly he imagined more than a few villagers would shed tears to see him go.

There were only two more steps: tonight's tearful goodbye and one, perhaps two, love letters. That should do it. But first there had to be the question. It was a final test. If she got the answer wrong she couldn't have him, not ever. It would mean the end of all this hokum. Ironically, the wrong answer might actually save her worthless life. By now he'd developed an instinct about it but he needed to hear it from the girl's mouth and read the truth in her eyes.

He was sitting by the same urine-coloured pond, ignoring the mosquitoes that sucked at his blood. The sun had set, and he was weaving a grass goldfish by the light of a small *kerosene lamp. He heard the crunch of two sets of footsteps on the gravel. It was a very good sign. She wasn't alone.*

She saw him there in the warm orange glow of the lamp and felt Nook squeeze her hand. It was a scene from the *Ramayana* she'd seen in an illustration. Rama, with his princely aura, sitting by the lake of Manas. She'd found no fault in him, not one in four days. He was a sincere, hard-working government cadre, warm and funny and strong, and…not handsome exactly, but noble looking. A face that would age well. She'd become somebody different since he'd arrived: somebody better. Her village and her life were so much more important when she saw them through his eyes. And she …? She had become…no, that was it. She had become.

He watched her say goodbye to her queer friend and walk towards him. But the queer didn't turn around and go back. He was her chaperone. Excellent that she had one but why choose that aberration? Why would a man, born with all the right attributes, aspire to be female? It was sickening. Phan felt the nausea rise in his throat. But he had to ignore it. He had to ignore the freak and concentrate on the task at hand.

He rose when she approached and gestured toward a large rock. He'd placed his folded windbreaker on top of it for her comfort.

'Hello, Phan.' She looked at the completed grass sculpture in his hand. 'Can I see it?'

'It's for you,' he said.

'It's beautiful.'

She blushed when he handed it to her.

'It's only a fish,' he smiled.

'I know. Fish are my favourites.'

'You're very easy to be around, Wei.'

'I hope so.'

'You know I'm leaving very early in the morning?'

'Yes, we'll be sorry to see you go.' She cursed herself. She wasn't saying any of the things she meant.

'I can't tell you how much I'll miss this town, and especially you,' he said.

She blushed again and looked out at the water.

He continued. 'Wei, I have a question I need to ask you. It's something I've never asked anyone before. It's very personal, probably the most personal question a man can ask a woman.'

She felt a mixture of joy and trepidation but no words came to her.

Phan kept going. 'I've been agonizing about it all day. But it's vital that I know. You see? My family…my upbringing was very proper. I was instilled with ideals that seem to have lost value in this day and age. If I ask I know you'll think me rude and old-fashioned. And still I don't know how to put my question. Wei, everybody possesses a gift. They are born with that gift and decide when they should share it, although some people don't realize its value and…no, I'm not doing very well. Wei, you might find this hard to believe but I have never been with a woman, sexually.'

She let out all the air she'd been holding back in one loud gasp. Her face turned the colour of an overripe chilli.

'I kept my gift until I found somebody worthy to give it to. I need to know…' he continued.

'Phan, it's all right,' she said, but she was far too stunned to look him in the eye. She spoke to the surface of the pond. 'I understand, and I don't think you're rude or

old-fashioned at all. You don't need to be embarrassed. I
think it's lovely. I haven't either…I mean, with a man…or
anyone.'

*He liked the fact that she was tongue-tied, and he
laughed with her. He reached for her hands. They were
damp and trembling, most unpleasant. It was just as well he
hadn't touched her fingers earlier or he might not be here in
this situation now. But it was too late to turn back.*

'Then I can't think of any reason why I shouldn't go to
speak with your parents.'

*She pulled her hands away, not because she wanted to
but because it was proper to do so. She stood and turned
her back to him. Her hands went to her face.*

'It's not that bad, is it?' he asked.

She spoke through her finger mask. 'No, it's…I'm
pleased.'

*Good, a woman of few words. Nothing worse than one
who wouldn't shut up – gushing, annoying. When at last
she was able to pull herself together and turn back to him,
he showed her the ring. It was a single gold band.*

'Where did you…?'

'It was my mother's,' *he told her.* 'I always carry it with me
in her memory. It's an old tradition our family picked up
from the French. I know I can't give it to you till I talk with
your father, but I was curious to see whether it fitted.' *He
took hold of her slimy hand again and slid the ring onto what
in the West they called the engagement finger. It paused
briefly at the joint then eased down towards the knuckle. He
always got it right. He had a dozen rings of varying sizes in
the truck and could judge with impressive accuracy which
would fit.* 'I'm afraid it's rather plain. It's just a symbol of my
sincerity. I promise I'll do better with the wedding ring.'

'Oh, no, Phan. It's perfect.'
'No, Wei. It's you who's perfect. Trust me.'

They'd passed the midpoint of the week in Vientiane and there still was no new evidence in the strangled woman case. The ribbon that had been used was sold in two or three shops in the city but the shopkeepers couldn't recall selling it to any suspicious characters. The pestle was made in Thailand and was expensive. Only one shop sold them, a store that specialized in exotic imported fare. The woman who owned the establishment hadn't sold more than one to any of her customers. The strangler would have had to travel to Thailand to buy them there before travel restrictions had been imposed.

Inspector Phosy's meeting with the truck driver had proven fruitless. The man claimed that his sighting of the shrouded farmer and the invisible woman story were made up. Either that or he'd heard them from another driver. He couldn't remember who because, assuming that really was how he'd come by the story, he must have been drunk at the time. Phosy had given the man his telephone number at police headquarters and told him that if the fuzziness ever cleared, Phosy would give him half a bottle of Thai rum in thanks.

Later that same day, Phosy was bumped from the Luang Nam Tha flight in favour of some visiting VIPs from North Korea and several Party officials. He didn't have any strings to pull higher than that. On Wednesday the flight didn't take off as the visibility at their destination was poor due to crop burn offs. So it was Thursday, and he was killing time at the morgue before heading off to Wattay Airport for his third attempt. They were all in the cutting room – Siri, Dtui, and Mr Geung. Phosy was leaning against the freezer door.

'B...be careful, Comrade Ph...Phosy,' Geung said. 'You might f...f...freeze your eggs.' Geung laughed uproariously and the others chuckled along with him. The egg joke frenzy had gripped a Vientiane that was obviously in need of cheering up. When word got out that the prime minister himself had been in the limousine involved in the great scramble it had become something of a national campaign. *Molum* singers, the common man's humorists, had already performed several live versions of the saga. It had even found its way into Geung's simple humour reservoir.

'Steady, Geung.' Dtui smiled. 'We don't want little Malee hearing dirty jokes at her age.'

Geung bent forward and touched Dtui's enormous belly. 'Sorry, Malee,' he said.

'How much longer do you plan to keep the girl on ice?' asked Phosy, tapping on the freezer door.

'Really, I don't like to keep anyone in there for too long,' Siri confessed. 'If we don't find a family for her soon we'll have to take her to the temple and give her an anonymous send-off. They don't like that.'

They all knew what he meant.

'Anything on Crazy Rajid?' Phosy asked.

'No sign of him,' said Siri. 'It's been two weeks already since anyone last saw him.'

'Of course he might have just wandered off,' Phosy reminded them. 'That's what street people do. He could be anywhere.'

'I don't know.' Dtui shook her head. 'He wandered pretty close to home as a rule. I mean to his dad's home.'

'Who'd have thought Crazy Rajid had a father?' said Phosy. 'And could write. Wonders will never cease. Any luck with the second riddle?'

'Not exactly,' said Siri. 'I think the combination of its being written by a madman and translated from Hindi makes it doubly difficult.'

'But he isn't a madman, is he, Dr Siri?' Dtui asked. 'I mean, he wasn't born crazy. It was a trauma in his child-hood that made him like this.'

'You're right,' Siri agreed. 'And he may very well have a treatable condition for all we know. But we don't have the expertise or the resources here to do anything for him. We can barely treat basic medical conditions.'

Phosy took the note from Siri. 'It's obvious there's a sane person in there somewhere or he wouldn't be able to write things like this.' He unrolled the paper and read aloud,

In the belly of the brainless one,
Made in Thailand.
Watched by four thousand eyes.

'Well, I wouldn't go so far as to call it sane,' said Dtui.

'It's a riddle, Nurse,' Siri reminded her. 'It's supposed to be confusing.'

'Then it succeeds,' she decided.

'Made in Thailand. Made in Thailand.' Phosy seemed to hope that repeating it might make it clearer. 'Should we be thinking dirty?'

'I think Madame Daeng and I have been through all the dirty possibilities,' said Siri with a slight blush.

'Is . . . is four thousand m . . . more than a m . . . million?' Geung asked.

'No, mate,' Dtui told him, 'it's not that many. But it's a hell of a lot of eyes.'

'We thought "brainless one" might refer to the grand

assembly building,' Siri confessed. 'But we would never know which seat to look under.'

'The national stadium?' Phosy offered.

'Come off it.' Dtui laughed. 'When was the last time they got more than fifty people watching anything there?'

'True.'

'Because if...if...if it's a million...' Geung persisted.

'It could be the spot where the Thai military intelligence put their telescope to watch what we're doing over here,' Dtui suggested.

'Not sure Crazy Rajid can swim that far,' Siri smiled.

'...then th...there's at least a m...million eyes at...at...at Wat Si Saket.'

'Then there's...What was that, Geung?' Dtui asked.

'Wat Si Saket,' repeated Geung.

'The little Buddhas.' Phosy nodded his head. 'There are certainly a lot of them.'

'It isn't out of the question,' Dtui agreed.

'But what's the "made in Thailand" connection?' Phosy asked.

Siri clicked his fingers so loudly the others were afraid he'd broken a bone.

'Of course,' he said and added another handprint to his forehead. 'Shame on me. They taught us all this stuff at the temple in Savanaketh. Why is it I can remember verbatim French radio jingles for chocolate biscuits and not the history of my own country?'

'Probably because—' Dtui started.

'It was a rhetorical question, Dtui.'

'Sorry.'

'Wat Si Saket,' Siri began, 'is the oldest surviving temple in Vientiane, and that's probably because, when the Thais flooded in to rape and sack and pillage in eighteen some-thing or other, they didn't want to destroy anything that reminded them of home. The temple was one of Prince Chao Anou's creations. He was educated in Bangkok and was probably more Thai than Lao. The Thais set him up as a puppet king here, and he built old Si Saket in the Thai style. Made in Thailand. *Voilà*.'

He walked to Geung and planted a large kiss on his fore-head. Geung wiped the kiss away violently but grinned with pleasure.

'I don't know why we just don't hand all our mysteries directly to you, Geung,' Phosy said with very little sarcasm in his voice.

'Any thoughts on the lady in the freezer, Inspector Geung?' Dtui asked.

'Sh…she's very pretty,' Geung decided.

'So who's the brainless one?' Phosy asked. He shouldered his bag for the trip to the airport.

'It could refer to us,' Siri conceded. 'But I think I shall take Madame Daeng for a cultural soiree at the temple this evening.'

'Well, I'm husbandless tonight, so I'm coming too,' said Dtui.

'I'm husbless t…too, so so am I,' said Geung.

'That's settled then.' Siri laughed. 'It looks like Si Saket Temple will be doubling its annual quota of visitors in one evening.'

Siri had been speaking only partly in jest. The residents of Vientiane had become very self-conscious about being seen in temples. People had begun to worship discreetly. Their faith had not been dented by the constant notices and the loudspeaker broadcasts decrying the curse of religion, but they found it prudent not to advertise their beliefs. The government interpreted the empty temple grounds as evidence that socialism was a more powerful dogma than Buddhism.

This perhaps explains why, on that warm evening in March, the visitors arriving at Si Saket had to find the keeper of the keys in the nearby compound and convince him it was vitally important to the security of the nation that they gain access to the inner sanctum of the temple immediately. As there were no lights, they were forced to buy sanctified orange candles from the abbot and place them at intervals around the rectangular cloister. This created a splendid, albeit rather creepy, atmosphere. The walls on all four sides contained small alcoves from floor to beam, and each nook had its own Buddha image in bronze or silver or stone: three-dimensional dharmic wallpaper.

'How many eyes would you say?' Siri asked Daeng.

'At least four thousand. Do you suppose he counted them?'

'Nothing about Rajid would surprise me. It does make me think we're in the right place. All we need now is to decide which is the brainless one.'

'We could ask them all twenty general-knowledge questions.'

'By my calculations that would take longer than I have left on this earth,' he said. He smiled uneasily and Daeng glared at him. 'What? Why are you giving me that look?'

'Has something happened to you this week that I should know about?'

'What do you mean?'

'I mean has the spectre of death landed in your morgue and handed you an invitation?'

Daeng's comment was intended as a joke but, like a hammer thrown from the far side of the room, it had somehow managed to hit the nail on the head. Siri felt a now familiar clenching at his heart. Every day the harbingers had visited him. Worms travelled the extremities of his desk, and the scent of damp earth filled his lungs. Saloop was everywhere – beside the road, beneath the table in the cutting room, outside the shop in the undergrowth opposite. Tonight, as they walked to the temple, the dog's yellow eyes had glared from every alleyway and nook. Death was closing in on Dr Siri, but it was news he'd decided to keep to himself. There was no point in depressing anyone else.

'I don't know what you mean,' he lied.

'Oh, Siri, you've managed to swing every other conversation we've had this week around to death.'

'I have not.'

'You have. You've mentioned graves at least twenty times.'

'Let me hear the tapes.'

'Take my word for it.'

'Daeng, I'm a coroner. It comes with the territory. If you wanted sweet talk you should have married someone at the boiled candy works. Death is my stock-in-trade.'

'Then why do I get this niggling feeling it's getting personal?'

'Because you're not as young as you used to be. Elderly people start to have delusions.'

'Is that so?'

She might have wrestled him to the ground at that point and twisted his arm behind his back had it not been for a shout from Dtui at the far end of the cloister.

'Doc, Auntie Daeng, I think we've found brainless.'

They joined Dtui and Geung in front of a small gallery of much larger Buddhas, some up to one metre tall. They stood or sat as if in a line-up of suspects: similar but different. And the fellow who stood out from the crowd had a head that ended above the ears. He was made of hollow cast iron and had obviously experienced a traumatic event that had removed the top of his head and half his back. His vintage and historical significance allowed him a place in otherwise complete company.

'Looks like a candidate,' said Daeng. 'Anyone feel like sticking their hand in there?'

Geung raised his arm.

'Yes, Mr Geung?'

'I will.'

'Go ahead.'

Geung put his hands together and muttered a quick prayer of apology before very excitedly reaching down into the bowels of the Buddha. He rummaged around for a few seconds before re-emerging with a small roll of paper. He handed it to Siri, who unrolled it to reveal a page of unfathomable Hindi letters.

'Mr Tickoo,' Siri shouted, 'Bhiku.'

'Wake up, Mr Tickoo!' Daeng yelled even louder, her voice echoing around the silent neighbourhood. They stood in front of the shutters of the Happy Dine Indian restaurant, looking up at the gaping open window on the second floor. Geung's dormitory at Mahosot and Dtui's police hostel room weren't far from the temple, so they'd agreed to walk each other home, leaving Siri and Daeng to pursue what was hopefully the last instalment of the riddle. They all hoped this final clue would lead them to Prince Crazy

Rajid's palace. Mr Tickoo's face arrived at the window with a smile that lit up the sidewalk around them.

'It is even more fiendish,' said Rajid's father. Mr Tickoo was sitting inside the restaurant with Siri and Daeng. The fluorescent tube above them was buzzing and cutting out every now and then like at an amateur discotheque. It was annoying but the note kept them spellbound. They watched the Indian consider and contemplate and finally compose. They sipped their tea impatiently, waiting for the last word of the last line. When it arrived and Bhiku looked up with a satisfied smile, they pirouetted the notepad around to see its Lao translation.

> *One million pachyderms*
> *And one spirited bear*
> *Look sadly at the all-night sun.*

Siri looked up from the paper as if he'd won the national lottery.

'Why so smug?' Daeng asked.

'I've got it,' he replied.

'Already?'

'More by luck than intelligence, my love.'

'Well, that's no fun at all. Don't tell me the answer. Let me get it for myself. Pachyderms ... the old word for ...'

'Elephants,' Siri put in.

'I said don't tell me. I knew that. So obviously a million old elephants equals Lan Xang. Name of the ancient kingdom of Laos.'

'And?'

'Several businesses.'

'The largest being?'

'The Lan Xang Hotel?'

'Spot on.'

Mr Tickoo clapped his hands. 'My word,' he said. 'It's like watching the gods laying out their plan for the universe. Such brilliance.'

Daeng and Siri looked at each other.

'Don't let yourself be diverted by conceit,' Siri said.

Daeng continued, 'I know I'm close here. A bear. The logo on a bottle or a can? No? A bearskin rug? A certain configuration of stars? Spirit…a drunken bear? A dead bear? A dead bear at the Lan Xang Hotel…the empty cages.'

'You are remarkable.' Siri smiled and squeezed her hand. The riddle had only been simple for him because it paralleled a case he'd handled the previous year. The Lan Xang Hotel had previously imprisoned live animals for the edification of the general public. One black bear had been the star attraction until it was freed. Siri could imagine Rajid wandering into the Lan Xang grounds and watching the poor old girl behind her bars. Somewhere there lay the secret to the location of Rajid's palace.

'What time is it?' Siri asked.

'Who cares?' answered Daeng.

The grounds of the Lan Xang were spacious for a Lao hotel. There was some thick tropical vegetation, native flowers that had been dug up and replanted in unnatural rows, and a swimming pool that was starting to look more like a lotus pond. It had so many leaves floating on it a skinny teenager could have walked across its surface without getting wet.

Siri and Daeng had strolled through reception arm in arm as if they owned the place. They dismissed the night clerk with a 'Don't even think about asking us a question' look and ambled towards the door that gave access to the grounds. To any observer they were merely guests who intended to take a short promenade before retiring to their suite. Once they were outside they were alone. Squashed up against one wall there were four cages that had housed a variety of wild inmates in their time. Currently they served as an aviary. There was a crane in one, a dowdy hornbill in the next, a couple of dubious characters that looked like chickens in heavy make-up in the third, and a male peacock with barely enough space to spread his impressive tail in the last.

'Where was the bear?' Daeng asked.

'That one.'

Siri pointed to the sad hornbill.

'She looks depressed,' Daeng decided. 'Why can't they let her just wander around the grounds?'

'That's the problem with birds. They have this nasty habit of flying.'

'She's lovely. I doubt there are many of these left in the wild.'

'It's her own fault. Look at all that meat. She'd make three square meals. She's in the cage for her own protection.'

Siri had spent much of his life in the jungle and had eaten every endangered species there was. In those days a man didn't give a hoot about the survival of an avian family lineage. It was them or us. If a hornbill with a machete had run across Siri in the bush and hacked him to death, he would have succumbed in good grace: a victim of the survival of the fittest rule. He believed that if God made you colourful, overweight, and delicious and didn't give you any survival skills, you deserved to get eaten.

Daeng obviously didn't see it that way. Siri knew straight away what his unblushing bride had in mind. There were large padlocks on the cages, but he knew his lady had ways and means.

'Can we solve the last riddle before you liberate her?' he pleaded.

'What does he say about the sun?'

'The all-night sun.'

They looked up simultaneously at the single electric bulb that dangled in front of the cages. There were other bulbs that hung here and there from the same untidy cable. One hung by the pool, another by the garbage bins. The extension to the cages was nailed to a tree.

'Our night sun's up that tree, Siri.'

'I can see that.'

'Well, you surely don't expect me to climb up there in my condition?'

Siri had climbed enough trees in his life, but none since he had turned seventy. He held up his fist.

'Surely not,' said Daeng, but she knew this was the only solution. She raised her own fist to the same height as his and stared into his eyes. Their version of rock-paper-scissors was elephant (fist), mouse (palm), and ant (little finger). The elephant crushed the mouse, the mouse squashed the ant, and the ant crawled up the elephant's trunk and paralyzed his brain.

They shook their fists twice and disclosed their opening gambits for the first round: Siri-elephant, Daeng-mouse. The second shake was Daeng-ant, Siri-elephant. All even. Everything came down to the last shake. They glared into one another's eyes and let loose their final creatures.

Siri-mouse ... Daeng-ant.

'Shit,' said Daeng.

Luckily she was wearing fisherman's trousers and not a skirt. There was no need to disrobe. She walked once around the tree and homed in on her branch of choice. Faster than Siri's eye could follow she was up on the first hub and above the dangling bulb.

'You're only part human,' he called up to her.

She edged along the branch. 'I don't see anything that looks like a note,' she said. 'We might have outsmarted ourselves again.'

'Can you get closer to the bulb? They'd have to replace them regularly so take a look at the socket.'

Daeng hung like a sloth. She reached down and, sure enough, wrapped around the socket and held in place with a rubber band was a slip of paper: the last clue. A map.

'Are we or are we not a team?' she asked.

It wasn't easy to disagree with a sixty-six-year-old lady hanging upside down from a tree.

'We are indeed,' he said.

7

AN INVISIBLE RICE FARMER

Phan had the letter written already. His handwriting was impeccable: not one questionable vowel or missing tone marker. The paper was headed Department of Water Management, and the contact details had a false telephone number and post office box number. All he needed to add was the date and the name of the recipient.

Dearest – *How did she spell her name? Oh, yes* – Wei,

I am back in Vientiane, although my heart is still in your village with you and all the wonderful people I met on my trip. I cannot concentrate on my work because you are in my mind all the time. My life has suddenly changed because of you.

I received wonderful news today. I have to return to your area on – *he checked the schedule on the wall* – March 26 to do a follow-up to my project there. I will only be there for a day or two. When I heard this news I felt so happy because it means I can see you again. I have been afraid we wouldn't get together for three or four months. Sadly, this will be my last trip of the year. It pains me that our marriage will be such a long way off.

That is why I want to make this presumptuous suggestion. The thought of being apart from you for so long makes me feel ill; so, if you are willing, I have a solution. My darling, what if we were to marry during this coming visit? I know it's short notice, and you might have trouble making arrangements, but I would be so happy if you could return to Vientiane with me as my wife. I have a nice home here, and I believe we would have a chance to go to Eastern Europe soon for my work. I would be so honoured if you could be there at my side.

I would understand completely if this is not convenient for you, but I hope with all my heart that you agree. I apologize if this letter is too formal and not chatty. I have never had the opportunity to write a letter of love before, so I'm not certain how to go about it.

I miss you so much that my eyes are wet with tears as I write this. I pray that you are thinking of me and that we can be together soon and for ever.

With all my heart,
Phan

He shook his head and let out a little puff of air. He wrote the name of his betrothed and her address on the envelope and ran the gummed edge across the damp sponge that sat permanently on the desk before sealing it. There was a long-distance bus scheduled to leave the next morning for Natan. He'd give the driver a few kip to drop it off on his way through her so-called town.

He had to play the game carefully. There were so many things that could go wrong. The last one – the ridiculous white girl with her imperfect hands and ugly feet – white cotton socks on the wedding night. He put that down as a fault in his vetting process. But she was beautiful, there was no question about that at all. Every man in the district wanted her. And who won her? Phan, the man.

That's why he was so proud of his kills. Five already in a little over two years, and that wasn't including the whore. He never included the whore. She was ancient history. This was his new life with its new meaning. Five was a good catch. And this Wei, she didn't have the looks of the last girl but she had bearing and education. Those two attributes didn't exactly add up to class but she was a step up. He was honing his skills, attracting a better-quality victim. Naïveté in the inferior female gender knew no barriers. They were all pretty damned gullible.

Between Madame Daeng's hours at the shop and Dr Siri's commitments at the morgue, there were only a few times when the couple could get together for adventures. These amounted to before six in the morning, when Daeng started to get her noodle broth brewing; after eight p.m., when the evening rush subsided; or Sundays. As they hadn't returned from the Lan Xang Hotel until after eleven the previous night, not even the excitement of having a hand-drawn map was enough to deprive them of a few hours of sleep. They'd opted to leave their search for Crazy Rajid's palace until the following night. Siri's morning was occupied with sweeping imaginary worms off his desk and forming a philosophy of life in time for his death, and with having the strangled lady investigation dropped squarely on his lap.

When two clearly drunk but ominously heavy men wandered into the morgue at nine, yelling and screaming with the scent of stale rice liquor on their breath, Siri was inclined to send them packing.

'This is a hospital,' he said. 'At least have the decency to sober up before you come staggering around here.'

He didn't have anything against drunks per se – goodness knows he'd been one often enough – but there was a time and a place. Nine in the morning in a morgue was neither.

'You a doctor?' asked the less sotted of the two. 'We're looking for a doctor.'

'I'm a coroner,' Siri told him. 'Come back when you're dead.'

'What's his name?' one man asked his colleague.

'Who?'

'The doctor they told us. Come and see Dr – shit, what was his name?'

By now, Geung and Dtui were at the office door squaring up to the intruders, ready to throw them out.

'Dr Sorry,' slurred the other drunk.

'Siri,' said the first, 'Siri Pai…something.'

'I think you two should go away and come back when you regain possession of your minds,' Siri told them. He stepped over a sleeping dog that nobody else saw and came around to their side of the desk.

'But the police sent us,' said the first man.

'They sent you here? Why?'

'We was looking for the inspector.'

He held out a slip of paper with Phosy's name and number written on it but dropped it and watched it float under the desk. His colleague fell to his knees to give chase.

'Don't bother,' Siri said. 'I saw it.' But the second man was already on the trail of the elusive slip of paper. He tried to rise when he heard Siri's voice but, forgetting he was under a desk, banged his head on its underside and crashed back to the floor. This caused both men to laugh hysterically.

'Dtui, get my gun,' said Siri. Siri didn't have a gun but Dtui ran off to get it anyway.

'No,' shouted the first drunk. He threw his hands in the air. 'Don't shoot. The cop said if I could remember who told me about the invibisible rice worker he'd give me a half ...I mean a full bottle of Thai rum.'

It suddenly dawned on Siri what this was all about.

'I take it you mean "invisible"?'

'That's what I said.'

'The woman who works the fields covered from head to foot?'

'Yeah!'

'Who told you?'

'He did.'

He pointed to the legs of the second drunk, who had apparently passed out under the table.

'Mr Geung, could you please extract this gentleman from under my desk?'

Geung was stronger than he looked and had the large man out and in a sitting position in a matter of seconds.

'Thank you,' said Siri. He leaned over the groggy driver and glared at him. 'Hey, you!'

'Me?'

'Yes. You saw the woman?'

'I did?'

'The one they convinced you was invisible.'

The man's eyes stared ahead as if recalling a nightmare. 'Oh, she was. She was.'

'Where was she?'

'Just a shape ... nothing ... inside the ...'

'Where – was – she?

'In the field.'

'All right. My fault. Bad question. Where was the field?'

'Where?'

'The district.'

'Ban Xon.'

Ban Xon was only seventy kilometres from Vientiane and most of the road there was straight. Siri would have preferred to travel with somebody else, if possible in a car or truck. Civilai had a car, but he drove so slowly the twins would be reaching puberty by the time they got back. Neighbour, Miss Vong, had a truck, but she still wasn't speaking to Mr Inthanet so there was no hope of getting help there. Judge Haeng could probably sign him out a Justice Ministry car, but Siri would sooner slide naked down a splintery plank than beg the boy for anything else.

So Siri was on his Triumph, the hot air blow-drying the features off his face. Dtui had wanted to ride pillion, but there was too much of her now, and Siri feared the potholes and bumps might prematurely bring on labour. So he was alone: Easy Rider. He and Civilai had watched the film in Hanoi, dubbed in French. Siri wanted to look up and smile at the sky like Peter Fonda, but he knew he'd be on his back counting stars if he didn't study the road all the way. Motorcyclists in Laos didn't get to appreciate a lot of scenery. He didn't take any stretches fast enough to feel his hair flapping against the side of his head but he was able to smell the scent of the share-a-fistful blossoms that edged the highway. At that speed there wasn't a worm on earth that could keep up with him. For a man standing at the exit of existence, it was exactly what he needed.

He arrived in Ban Xon mid-afternoon looking like he'd been dipped in powdered cinnamon. He removed his goggles and stared at himself in the mirror. He was a perfect photographic negative of the Lone Ranger. He needed a wash very badly. He went into the nearest coffee stall, ordered water and coffee, and selected a packet of Vietnamese munchies that hung from a string at the front of the shop. He dusted himself down and washed from the communal clay water pot. When he was presentable he sat down to drink his coffee. Inevitably, it tasted of road dust.

The shop owner was a heavily built and – after a little coaxing – jolly woman in her fifties. She was the same well built, jolly woman who ran the coffee shops and noodle stalls the length and breadth of the country. He'd seen her everywhere: the same smile, hair in an untidy bun, the same bawdy humour. The same washed-out pastel blouse and threadbare purple *phasin*.

Siri was the only customer and the woman must have been starved for company because she sat with him as soon as she'd served the glass of coffee. Once all the preliminaries – work, travelling from, age (you look much younger), marital status, children, etc. – were out of the way, she got around to 'What brings you to Ban Xon?'

'I'm here to see the invisible woman,' he said and smiled.

'You know, Granddad?' She leaned on the table and it creaked. 'It beats me how that silly rumour got so much mileage. I have people stop here all the time asking if it's true.'

'And it's not?'

'You're a doctor, Granddad. How likely is it?'

'I see things all the time I can't explain.'

'Well this is just...just silly. There was a perfectly good reason why the girl was wrapped up like that.'

Siri's heart did a little dance. 'So there *was* a girl?'

'Oh, yes. And you could see her. Very pretty. She came to dances and village events. All after dark, of course.'

'Why, of course?'

'She had a condition. Some medical thing to do with the sun. Everyone knew about it. People round here like to tease strangers who pass through. I suppose that's how the invisible woman story started.'

'Why do you talk about her in past tense?'

'Oh, she's gone, Granddad. Stroke of luck, if you ask me. Married a very eligible young man and left.'

'When was this?'

'Over a week ago now. I was at the wedding party. It was a good do.'

'So you saw the groom?'

'Interesting-looking chap. Nice personality. Very happy man, I'd say. I wouldn't have minded a fling with him myself. He's something important with the roads department if I remember rightly.'

The rice farm was four kilometres out of town along a dirt track that was all deep ruts. By the time he reached his destination, Siri had attained the dexterity of a gramophone needle. It didn't take a great detective to see how poor the family was. The house was loosely woven elephant-grass panels on a bamboo-and-wood frame. The roof was thatched. There was a bamboo conduit that snaked down from the hills, bringing water from a spring to a large oil drum. Three chickens scratched around in the dirt, and an anorexic dog, one that Siri didn't recognize, slept under a bush of thistles. Siri called out. There was nobody home.

In March there was no water in the paddies; so the farmer's work was to repair damaged levees and clear land for new fields. Siri passed the little altar that held offerings to the spirits of the land. With the kind cooperation of Lady Kosob, the rice goddess, there would be early rains, and they would not fall in torrents that destroyed the earth embankments that separated the rice troughs. It was clear the offerings had been too paltry to raise this family from poverty. There were only two small paddies attached to the farm but they appeared to be deserted. After a long, circuitous walk, Siri finally found a sunburned man and two teenaged boys sheltering in a flimsy grass-roofed lean-to. There wasn't an ounce of fat between the three of them. The youths seemed drugged with ennui.

'Good health,' Siri said with a big smile on his face. They returned his greeting, apparently unfazed to find a stranger in their midst. 'I'm looking for Comrades Boonhee and Mongaew.'

'Well you've found Boonhee,' said the man, returning Siri's smile. 'What can I do for you, brother?'

Siri sat beneath a short chicken-guts tree and fanned himself with the manila envelope he carried.

'I'm too old for this,' he said. 'All this travelling will have me in my grave.'

'Long time before that happens I'd bet,' said Boonhee. He brought over a plastic ice bucket with a screw top. Inside was a small tin cup floating in water. Siri forwent his aversion to unidentified liquids and helped himself to a cupful. The water was hot but deliciously sweet, probably due to a high concentration of streptococcus.

'I'm Siri Paiboun from Mahosot Hospital in Vientiane,' he said.

'I reckon I've been there once,' said Boonhee. 'You lost?'

'No, I'm in the right place. I wanted to talk to you about your daughter.'

'Ngam?' The man seemed pleased. 'You've met her, have you? How's she doing?'

'Comrade Boonhee, has she been in touch with you since she left?'

The farmer laughed. 'Look around you, brother. It's not the easiest place to contact.'

'I can see.'

'So, what did she say? Are they off to overseas yet?'

'Is that what she told you? That they'd be leaving the country?'

'It's what the young man told us: Phan. Said he was getting posted to…I don't know, some country over in Europe somewhere. Her mother'd remember the name of it.'

'When was the last time you saw Ngam?'

'The party. The night of the ceremony. It was the seventh.'

'Comrade Boonhee,' Siri sighed, 'does Ngam have a small mole, here?' He touched his temple above his ear.

'A small one, nothing a bit of make-up wouldn't— wait, what are you doing here talking about our Ngam's mole?'

Siri sighed again and removed the photograph from the

envelope. 'Mr Boonhee, can you come and sit over here with me, please.'

'I can stand well enough.'

Siri held up the photograph to the farmer who, despite his courageous words, was rocking unsteadily.

'What? Where'd you get that? That ...that's not a normal picture. Why's her eyes closed?'

Siri often wondered how wealthy he would be if he'd received a franc for every time he'd said, 'I'm sorry.'

'What you sorry about? What is this?'

'Ngam's dead, Comrade.'

The two lethargic boys stood and ambled over to look at the photo. Boonhee couldn't find words.

'I'm from the morgue,' Siri said. 'I've been waiting for her family to get in touch. She needs a ceremony.'

Boonhee's face twisted into a confused, working-out-a-puzzle type of expression. He looked up at Siri as if the answer might be somewhere on the doctor's face.

'Her mother's going to be ...I don't know. What happened?'

'She was murdered, strangled to death.'

There was the longest pause before Boonhee asked, 'Do you know who did it?'

'No.'

Another gap.

'Does Phan know?'

'I don't know.'

'Someone should tell him.'

Siri left the obvious conclusion to find its own way into the farmer's mind.

'Do you know how we can get in touch with him?' the doctor asked.

'He's with roads.'

'The Highways Department?'

'Something like that. The people that build the roads.'

'So you don't have an address, papers, any way to contact him?'

'Ngam had all that. She took it all with her.' Siri could see that the man was forcing himself to stay on his feet so as not to lose face in front of the boys.

'Do you remember his family name?' Siri kept pushing.

'Ngam would know all that.'

'You didn't sign the marriage documents?'

'We don't write nor read. Not me or her mother.'

'Where is your wife? Perhaps she'd remember something about him.'

'She's over at Nit's place helping out.'

'Comrade, I'm sorry to keep asking questions. I know this has to be hard for you.'

'You can ask.'

Unless it surpassed all physical means, grief wasn't something you shared with strangers in Laos.

'Do you have any pictures of the wedding?'

'Why do you want them?'

'Well, if we don't have an address for Phan it might be the only way to find him.'

'Nit had a camera. The film was in it for a year or more. When he went into town to get it printed there wasn't nothing but white.'

'I see. Is there any way we can get your wife back here to talk to? I think she should hear this.'

'You're right.' Boonhee nodded at one of the silent youths and the boy set off across the fields at the speed of light. It had seemed hardly possible he could move so fast.

Boonhee's wife was frozen into a fit by the news. Her husband had told her himself and shown her the photograph. She'd fainted. When she came around it astounded Siri just how many tears her dehydrated little body could produce. Still she couldn't speak. Boonhee and Siri led her into the shanty and watched her lie on the thin mattress. Her body was curled in a knot of misery. Boonhee left her and walked with Siri to his bike.

'What else do you need?' he asked the doctor.

'Why was she covered? I mean when she worked in the fields.'

'Ngam? She was allergic to sunlight.'

'No she wasn't.'

'Eh?' Boonhee stared at Siri.

'I'm a doctor.'

8

PALACE OF THE ONE HUNDRED
AND ELEVEN EYES

As he rode back towards Vientiane, Siri considered every astonishing fact he'd learned. He couldn't bring himself to believe it. Ngam had been a pretty baby. The parents had been astounded they could ever have produced such a prize. They changed her name to Ngam, which meant beautiful, to reflect her looks. They knew she'd grow up to be as pretty as a picture. But Mongaew, her mother, understood that to be truly beautiful in Asia, a girl had to be white. In all the advertisements, in the magazines, in the travelling film shows before the takeover, all the classic beauties had skin as white as china.

When she herself was little, Mongaew had fantasized about her own life. If only she were white, she might grow up to be Miss Sangkhan at the provincial festival parade. She'd get to carry the four-faced head of Phanya Kabilaphon on the decorated chariot. It was all an unreachable dream. She was neither white nor particularly attractive. But now she had been blessed with a miracle: a girl child who might truly grow up to win the competition. If only – if only they could keep her skin from the sun. So Mongaew and Boonhee invented an illness for her, an allergy that prevented her from exposing her skin to sunlight. She'd seen a specialist in

Thailand, she'd told the neighbours. The girl might die if she were to go outside in the daytime.

Ngam, of course, had believed her parents and done as she was told. She played at home with her brothers and covered herself from head to foot when it came to harvest time. A kindly teacher from the local school felt sorry for the girl and volunteered to come by in the evenings to give her vitamins and a modest education. When Ngam reached sixteen her mother used the money she'd put aside to record her daughter's beauty at a professional photographer's in Phonhong. She sent the resulting snaps to the organizers of the festival. One committee member came to the farm to see the girl, to verify that the beauty they'd seen in the photograph was not a trick of the light. She had been astounded that such a vision could rise up from these humble origins. She assured the parents that their daughter was guaranteed a spot in the next year's competition, and – off the record – that Ngam was so lovely the organizer couldn't see anyone beating her.

Mongaew was elated. She knew exactly what this meant. Every year, the winner of the Miss Sangkhan beauty pageant was handed a substantial sum of prize money. She would receive countless offers to advertise beans and cement and farm implements and soft drinks, all for a fee. But, most important, what wealthy man would not want to marry the most beautiful girl in the province? What a prize she would be. Money would flow onto Mongaew's head like honey from heaven. All the planning, the inconvenience, would have been worth it. All their financial problems would be over. Mongaew had gambled with her girl's life and won.

The following year, amid the political upheaval, and with the Royalists scurrying across the Mekhong, the Miss

Sangkhan beauty pageant had been cancelled. 'Next year,' she was told. 'Next year everything will return to normal, and your daughter will take the Miss Sangkhan crown.' But in some stuffy socialist meeting, a decision was made that beauty competitions were one more vestige of the decadent society the Party was trying to sweep out. The shows insulted women. They were cattle markets. They were demeaning. And so, all beauty pageants were banned immediately.

Ngam had reached her peak at sixteen. Few winners of the Miss Sangkhan crown had been older than seventeen. She was aging rapidly, and there was no indication that the Pathet Lao would change its mind. The world of Mongaew and her family had come crashing down. But there was hope that their daughter's beauty might still rescue them from poverty. In desperation, Mongaew started taking her girl to night-time wedding receptions in the district. Some evenings they'd walk for two hours to the house of the happy couple. Mongaew had decided that if Ngam was not to be the star she deserved to be, at least she would be married to a local man with influence. Perhaps the son of a cadre.

And one night, her revised prayer was answered. The man from Vientiane was so dashing. He was supervising a road project, staying with the headman, well mannered with a wonderful sense of humour. He was groomed and polite, and he had a truck, of all things. Mongaew fell in love with him at first sight. And, it was evident to everybody in attendance that night that the visitor had an eye for Ngam. Things seemed to happen so fast from there on. It was like a fairy tale played at three times its normal speed: an engagement, love letters from the capital, a brief return visit, a reception and, in the blink of an eye, their daughter was gone. All Mongaew had to do now was sit and wait for the cheques to arrive. But all she got was a coroner from Mahosot and news that her precious daughter was dead.

As Siri rode along the dirt highway, he couldn't get the thought of the charming stranger out of his head. Phan, the nickname of a hundred thousand: Sisouphan, Thongphan, Bouaphan, Houmphan, all whittled down to Phan. No address, no family name, no photographs. He came. He saw. He destroyed. Already Siri had the antagonist taped to the dartboard of his mind. At last, somebody to blame. Someone to hate. A small lead in the case. A family to claim a lost body. A very successful day, but not a happy one.

'You're late,' Daeng told the cinnamon-coated man who'd arrived at her shop after dark. There was a bright flash from the vegetation across the street. They both looked up in time to see a man with an old-fashioned camera turn and run down the riverbank.

'I think someone just took a candid photograph of us,' said Daeng.

'*Pasason Lao* newspaper doing a photographic feature on celebrity couples in Vientiane, I wouldn't wonder.' Siri smiled.

'You're sure it wasn't the Department of Housing?'

'No, they're such nice people. Why would they go to so much trouble?' They walked hand in hand into the closed shop. 'What time is it?'

'Nine.'

'Too late for a palace hunt?'

'It's up to you. You look exhausted.'

'You can't see how I look. I have a two-centimetre-thick layer of grime on me. A quick bath and I'll be fine. I could use some excitement.'

'Have you eaten?'

'I wouldn't say no to a number two. I hope you sold enough noodles this week to pay for the cost of today's petrol.'

'Can't you claim it on your expense account?'

'I'm a coroner playing policeman. Who's going to pay for that? Phosy was uncontactable in the north, so I took it upon myself. Nobody rewards individual initiative in this regime.'

'Don't worry, my love. I'll support your intrigues even if I have to resort to selling my body.' She kissed his dusty cheek. 'As long as you tell me exactly what happened today, in gory detail.'

'Accompany me to the bath, Madame Daeng, and I'll disclose everything.'

The map was beautifully illustrated like a wayward doodle, but its intricacy made it hard to follow. The river was easy enough to identify as it was a long chain of tiny smiling fishes. The outline of Nam Poo Fountain was the eastern-most point. The Kokpho turn-off, which ultimately led to the airport, was marked with an aeroplane. Daeng drove them about four hundred metres beyond the intersection and parked. There were still patches of forest on this stretch of the river, and it felt so remote it seemed impossible that there was a city just half a kilometre away.

'All right,' Siri said, holding his torch up to the map. 'There's something that looks like a snake drinking from the river.'

'Hmm. You'd expect snakes to change location from time to time, unless it's a dead one.'

'Or unless it's a pipe. Perhaps it's not drinking at all.'

'An overflow?'

'It could be.'

Siri waded through the tall lemongrass to the river's edge and waved his light up and downstream. There was no obvious plumbing. He was about to return to the road when he felt some kind of mound beneath his feet. It was more solid than the crunchy clay all around. He traced its path with his foot until he arrived at the mouth of a pipe.

'Any luck?' Daeng called out.

'More like divine inspiration. I was right on top of it. I'm at the serpent's jaws.'

'Is it wide enough to crawl through?'

'Perhaps for an Indian fakir. Not for two old souls like us.'

He returned to the bike and looked at the map once more.

'Then it's easy,' said Daeng. 'We follow the pipe at surface level.'

They shone their lights across the road in the direction from which the pipe originated. There was nothing but bush. It was a long vacant lot between two empty houses. It seemed to be crammed with all the remaining monsoon forest in the country.

'How do we get through that?' Siri asked.

'Determination,' Daeng replied and produced a frightening machete from her shoulder bag. She crossed the road and shone her beam along the green barricade. Siri joined her. 'Right, down there,' she said.

She had picked out a low, dark tunnel of leaves that looked like a small animal track.

'That would involve crawling,' Siri pointed out.

Daeng was already on her hands and knees hacking at the leaves.

'I'll go first and let you look at my bottom,' she said.

'Aha, lead on, my Amazon.'

The slow, bestial crawling lasted no longer than five minutes before they arrived at a clearing. This was no accident of nature. The clearing was a perfect square, twelve by twelve metres, probably levelled for a building project then abandoned. At its centre, just as the map promised, was Crazy Rajid's palace. In the illustration it had all the splendour of the Taj Mahal with domes and minarets and a platoon of guards. In the real world it was a structure made entirely of old television sets. They were piled six high in one continuous square with no apparent entry point. They appeared to be cemented together with river mud. The turrets were formed of radiograms spaced along the parapet. Siri and Daeng stood behind their torches in awe of its weirdness.

'Now how do you suppose he did that?' Daeng asked.

Siri shook his head and laughed. 'Offhand I see three possibilities. One, the TVs were already abandoned here and he just rearranged them into a palace. Two, they were dumped in the river by the consumerist Thais and washed up by the overflow. Or, three, he just rescued dead and dying TV sets from around the town and carried them here. Whichever it is, it's good to see he hasn't been wasting his time for the past ten years.'

They walked around the outside of the structure to see if there was a way in. There was not.

'You don't suppose he's inside there, do you?' Daeng asked.

'Rajid, are you in there?' Siri called.

There was no answer.

'How do we get in?' he asked.

'Must be a magic word. What was the old Roman spell?'

'Abracadabra.'

'Abracadabra,' Daeng repeated.

Nothing happened.

'Well, as we've solved the riddles and come all this way,' Siri decided, putting down his pack and walking to the television wall, 'I think we only have one way to claim our prize.' He reached up to the top of the wall and pulled at the volume control of one of the smaller sets. As one might expect, river mud does not make a particularly effective cement. The mortar crumbled and the set fell at Siri's feet. 'Aha,' he sang. 'We have breached their defences. The palace will soon be ours.'

Daeng joined him in his pillage and within seconds they had a fairly large gap through which to step. At the centre of the compound lay the open grate of a large drain. This was obviously Rajid's entry and exit point. Apart from some fifty forks jabbed into the earth all around, the only furnishing was a cardboard box. Siri picked his way between the forks and opened the flaps.

'Anything interesting?' Daeng asked.

'Bones,' Siri told her.

'My word. Whose?' She was on her knees again inspecting the cutlery.

'They're old. I mean very old. And there's broken pottery in here and what looks like hair.'

'Oh dear.'

'What is it?'

'The forks. They're gravestones.'

'Eh?'

'Frogs, by the look of it although I'm not planning to go through the lot to see if they're all the same.'

'I remember he has a fondness for amphibians.'

'Does any of this help us to know where he's gone?'

'Not at all.'

'But you have to admit he is a wonderfully peculiar little chap.' She used the fork to replace the dirt on the frog she'd just unearthed and said a short prayer for its soul.

9

THE LAO PATRIOTIC WOMEN'S ASSOCIATION

Siri sat on the wicker chair in front of Madame Daeng's shop, going through the contents of the box one more time. In total, there were ten mostly broken bones, five shards of pottery, and a small tangled mass of hair. Daeng was inside preparing the breakfast so their conversation was shouted.

'I can't imagine where he got all this stuff,' Siri yelled.

'What?' She couldn't hear him above the sound of the charcoal cracking in the flames.

'I say, some of these shards seem really old.'

'How does the bone look in the cold light of day?'

'None of them is complete but I'd say this one is part of a humerus.'

'How can you be sure it's not a goat's hind leg?'

'Please, madam. I'm a professional.'

In fact, Siri wasn't at all certain. His experience was exclusively with human bones in human bodies. The context rather gave it away. He'd never studied the difference between human and animal bones and never performed surgery on anything with four legs. There might have been a course entitled 'Études Ancienne Comparée et Méthodique des Squelettes de Caprinés et Vertébrés Humains, 101', but, if so, he had long forgotten it. For all he knew, the human humerus might have been identical to the hind leg of a goat.

He rubbed his eyes to get them to focus. He'd slept poorly. Another nightmare had awakened him at two a.m. It was her: the ugly pregnant woman with the worms and the dead dog. He woke with such a heavy weight on his chest it was as if she had been sleeping on top of him. He could almost smell her sweat. His lungs wheezed. Daeng had awakened too and asked him if he was all right. He'd considered telling her the truth but there were times when the truth didn't help anybody.

He looked up as a man in a postal worker's uniform pedalled up on a bicycle whose parts were clearly held together by string and wishes.

'You're open then?' the man said, stepping from the precarious machine.

He arrived at the shop at the same time every morning and said the selfsame thing every time. Normally he'd settle on a table near the entrance without waiting for a response, but today he surprised Siri by handing him an envelope.

'What's this?' Siri asked.

In most places, a postman handing over a letter would not prompt such a question. But Lao postmen had recently ceased their habit of delivering letters. As the populace and the government cultivated their respective paranoias, fewer people were prepared to hand over their secrets to anyone in a uniform. Notes would be delivered by bus drivers or friends allowed to travel up-country or relatives going off to 're-education' camps.

Almost everything from outside the country passed through a Bureau de Poste department known as the Sensitive Issues Section. There mail was opened, read, censored with black ink, and put in large wooden crates for collection. Anything in a foreign language was deemed too sensitive for the Sensitive Issues Section largely because there was nobody on staff who could read it. These letters were filed and never seen again.

'It's a letter,' said the postman. 'I recognized your name so I thought I'd bring it along. Sorry it's open.'

Siri took it. 'Thank you, Comrade. 'Has it been …?'

'I think they looked at it and realized it was from a child so there aren't any marks on it.'

The postman went into the shop where he was greeted warmly by Madame Daeng. Other customers were arriving on foot. The aroma must have worked its way around the downtown area already. Siri took a moment to appreciate the large Lao farm implement dedication stamp that took up a quarter of the envelope then pulled out the single sheet of lined notepaper. At first glance, it did appear to be written in a child's hand, but he noted that it was just a little too careful and too deliberate.

> Dear Uncle Siri,
> How are you? We went to the Buddha Park on the weekend. It was such Fun. There were big animals and a giant pumpkin. I think your little twins would really like it. We're going again on March 30.
> If you take them I can show them around.
> With love, Your niece,
> Bao

Siri smiled, looked up at the blue sky, and said a thank you to the various gods he'd recruited to make this message possible. Bao was a Hmong girl Siri had met a few months earlier when he was in the north-east. The villagers had been about to join the long march to Thailand. Many were escaping repercussions from the Pathet Lao administration and their Vietnamese allies for siding with the Americans during the war. One of the girls in the village had just given birth to twins, and they had asked Siri to transport them to Vientiane with him and take care of them. Travelling with babies was a danger. Many Hmong had been exposed to the enemy by the crying of young children. This letter meant they had survived the journey and were ready to reclaim their young ones.

It changed his mood completely. He walked through the shop with his letter and his cardboard box and greeted the early diners. He walked over to Daeng and kissed her cheek. The gesture drew jeers and snickers from the men in the room who probably wished they had that kind of relationship with a woman.

'What?' Siri asked them. 'You've never seen a man kiss his lovely wife before?'

'I didn't even kiss mine when she was eighteen and beautiful,' called one middle-aged man.

'More fool you, brother.'

'Thank you,' said Daeng. 'But what specifically was that for?'

He whispered in her ear, 'The twins will be leaving us at the end of the month.'

She squealed her delight. 'Your Hmong friends?'

'It looks like they made it. Some of them at least.'

'Your little general?'

He held up the letter and smiled.

'Bao wrote.'

'Siri, I'm so happy for you. See what a little faith can do? Go get yourself ready for work, and I'll bring you up a number two. Oh, what a good start to the morning.'

Naturally, that had been the high point of Siri's day. The boulder of happiness began to roll down the hill of inevitable disappointment almost as soon as he reached the morgue. Ngam's father, Boonhee, was waiting for him in the office. The man had come to claim his daughter's remains and take her home. He hadn't yet worked out how he was going to achieve that feat given that he had no money and no vehicle. After some deliberation, Siri sent Dtui to the clerk's office to make a phone call to the Cooperative Development Works.

She asked to speak to the driver who worked the Vang Vieng to Ban Xon route. They were in luck. He was still at the yard and scheduled to leave with an empty truck after breakfast. Dtui reminded him about his behaviour at the morgue the previous day. Sober, he was a humble and sensible man who was happy to accept this opportunity to put back the pieces of his 'broken' face in the eyes of Dr Siri and his nurse. He agreed to take Mr Boonhee and the body of the invisible woman home.

Boonhee thanked everyone at the morgue for their help. While they wrapped and loaded the body, Siri sat with him in the office.

'How is Mongaew taking it?' he asked.

'Don't think she'll ever get over it,' the farmer said. 'This was all her doing. She thinks that because of her, Ngam never had a normal life. And just when it finally starts to go right . . .'

'I know.' Siri was tempted to say she shouldn't blame herself, but deep down he knew she should. What she had put her daughter through was inexcusable. So, instead, he nodded.

'Comrade Boonhee, we, I mean the police, have been in touch with the Highways Department. They do have a Phan or two but not one who was away in your district on the dates you gave me. In fact, they don't have any projects in progress or planned for Ban Xon.'

'Well, that don't make sense.' Boonhee was still trying to work it all out. 'Phan stayed at the headman's place. He had a letter and everything.'

'Comrade Boonhee, I took a detour via Vang Vieng on my way back yesterday and I talked to a police sergeant who's investigating this case. He'll be travelling up to talk to your headman very soon. If there was a letter of introduction there should be a name and position on it. That might help us locate him.'

'You think he done it, don't you?'

'It's too early to say, Comrade. But as far as we know he was the last person to see your daughter alive. When I left your farm I stopped by the regional registry office. There was no record of a marriage on March the seventh.'

'No, he...Phan said it was better to register here in Vientiane. He brought all the papers signed and stamped when he turned up for the ceremony. He said Ngam would have more rights here, easier to get a passport, he said. But the ceremony was all proper, brother. We had the local official tie the wrists, and they made their vows. We even had a monk there. In the eyes of heaven it was decent.'

Phosy arrived back from Luang Nam Tha just as the rice truck was pulling out of the hospital grounds. He went straight to the morgue and directly into Siri's office. He was obviously worked up about something.

'Siri, I did it. I met the—'

'Good health, Inspector Phosy.'

'What? Yeah, anyway, I—'

'I'd imagine, as you've been away for a few days, you'd probably want to go directly into the cutting room and say hello to your very pregnant wife.'

Phosy smiled and put his pack on the chair.

'Exactly what I was planning to do,' he said.

It was a brief reunion because three minutes later he was back.

'Now,' said Siri.

'Did I just see a body in the truck going out?'

'You did.'

'Was it …?'

'It was.'

Siri spent the next fifteen minutes going over the details of his trip north. Phosy was scribbling as fast as he could in his already full notepad, stopping Siri now and then to clarify and expand.

'I need to get back to headquarters as soon as I can to find out what's happening,' Phosy decided. 'You know? Most of this country's in an information black hole. People up in Luang Nam Tha get more news from Beijing than they do from Vientiane. Only the military seem to have any operable communication equipment and that's for author- ized personnel only. When I was military intelligence I outranked all those stuffed shirts up there. But out of uniform they treated me like I was a pig farmer. I have a good mind—what are you laughing at?'

Siri swung back onto his favourite two legs of the chair and put his hands behind his head.

'Phosy, I never begrudge a man a good grumble, but I

was rather hoping to hear what transpired in the deep north.'

'You're right.' Phosy flipped back through his notes but started to speak without referring to them. 'I didn't have any trouble finding the lycée student's sister. But I did have a problem getting her to speak. She denied she'd ever heard the story. It wasn't till I told her I'd travelled half the country just to talk to her and I'd arrest her little sister for lying that her memory started to come back. It turns out she'd picked up the story from her boyfriend. He'd heard it from a fellow who used to be in the army. He was the horse's mouth.'

'He'd seen it for himself?'

'And tried to forget. It was early in '69. Chaos everywhere. Most of the fighting was concentrated around Huaphan and the east. But it spilled over into the northernmost provinces from time to time. The Royalists were recruiting younger and younger conscripts to defend key installations. Nobody up there really wanted to fight against their own people, but the RLA was one of the few employers that offered a living wage. The young fellow who told the story was called Sida. He'd only been stationed in Luang Nam Tha town for two months. The local police had already fled the scene for fear they'd be shot in their beds by PL sympathizers. The regional army commander had to do something to convince the locals somebody was keeping the peace. He didn't want all-out anarchy. So, as a token gesture, he sent half a dozen of his young boys to man the police box in town. They weren't qualified to do anything but walk around the streets and look official. Heaven forbid they'd have a crime to investigate.

'Sida's on duty one afternoon when a hunter comes down from the hills and reports he's seen a body. The boy's very first case, not even a drunk and disorderly or littering offence before that. So Sida and his pal follow the hunter up the hill road. They don't expect much of a shock. There's a civil war on. People are getting killed all the time. All they have to do is identify which uniform the victim is wearing and file a report. But twenty metres off the main road they see her.'

'Tied to a tree.'

'Exactly like our girl in Vang Vieng. But this one had been there a little longer. There was significant animal damage so you can imagine the scene. Two young conscripts without any battleground experience . . .'

'I'd guess not even war could have prepared them for a sight like that.'

'After they throw up their lunch, they decide they should tell someone. Our boy Sida stays with the body while his pal runs off to find the army commander. And our boy gets bold. He unties the ribbons that bind her hands, and she falls backwards, and that's when he sees the pestle. If he'd had any more lunch . . .'

'Did anyone report it?'

'It all seemed to vanish. The commander told them he'd handle it and that they shouldn't mention a word of it to anyone. I imagine he didn't want a panic on his hands. While Sida was still on duty in the town, not one person came forward to report a missing girl. Case closed.'

'Did you get this directly from Sida?'

'No. For obvious reasons, he didn't stick around once the PL took over. It appears he was pretty close to the nurse's boyfriend, though. But you're right, it's all hearsay. Nothing we could use in court. There were one or two little details that make it obvious this was the same perpetrator.'

'Like the ribbon?'

'And candles…little temple candles. And the pestle was black stone.'

'That's him all right. Did Sida remember any physical signs? Did he notice whether the girl had been strangled?'

Phosy went through his notes. 'No. I get the impression she was pretty far gone as animal feed by the time they found her. I was surprised what a detailed description Sida was able to give his friend. I'd be surprised if he doesn't still have nightmares about it. He talked about her face being gone and one of her fingers hanging off. There was gore every—'

'Did he say which one?'

'Which one what?'

'Which finger was hanging off?'

'I don't think so. Why?'

'Ngam, our girl from Vang Vieng, had a broken finger.'

'You think it might be significant?'

'Just a thought I've been playing with. If it was the ring finger it could mean he was desperate to retrieve the ring. If the fingers had swollen he'd have to break the joint to get it off. It could be an issue he has about marriage.'

'Dr Siri, this lunatic could be killing women all over the country and we'd be none the wiser.'

'Could you contact all the police stations and get them to check their files?'

'I wish it were that easy, Doctor. Most of the files from the old regime were destroyed before they left. It's taken us this long just to get our own filing system in order. And for the first eighteen months it was a lot like the Royalists in Luang Nam Tha: foot soldiers substituting as policemen. Not all of them could read or write. And even if we did have a system, the thing that scares me is this: in both of these cases the bodies were found quite by chance before they were completely consumed by the forest. If there were other murders we might never learn of them.'

Siri dropped onto all four legs of his chair and pulled out a sheet of blank paper and a pencil from his desk drawer. He made a rough sketch on it. Phosy leaned over the desk to take a look.

'A panda?' he guessed.

'It's supposed to be Laos, inspector. And look! Here is Ban Xon, where Ngam met Phan. Here is Vang Vieng, where her body was found. They're forty kilometres apart. Let's assume that he woos and weds them in place A then removes them to place B, just far enough away so that nobody will recognize the body, and nobody will come forward there to report a missing relative. If we apply the same distance rule to your soldier's corpse in Luang Nam Tha, we should assume she was from Muang Sing or perhaps Na Mo. You're quite right, we may never find other corpses. So what we should be looking for isn't bodies, but reports of country girls who were swept off their feet by smooth city boys and never seen again.'

'Siri, you aren't paying attention. I've just explained that we don't even have a murder data bank. How do you suppose we can get information about missing daughters?'

'By using a network that cares about such things – a network far more efficient than the police force.'

'Oh really? And what would that be exactly?'

Dr Siri arrived at the humble tree-bordered office of the Lao Patriotic Women's Association a little after ten. The group had been established in 1955 to mobilize the untapped resource known as women for the Lao People's Revolutionary Party. Lao women were accorded the right to vote three years later in the first coalition elections. Socialism had re-evaluated the status of females and encouraged them to take an active role in the creation of the new socialist state. That encouragement obviously had its limits, as by 1978 there were still no women on the politburo or holding power in the Central Committee. But the network was vast and the benefits to females at both ends of the economic scale were impressive.

The ladies in their spotless white blouses and carefully folded *phasin*s were filing out of a meeting room with their neatly penned notes and their empty teacups. They looked content, every one of them. Perhaps, Siri thought, it was because they didn't have to work with men. But even when they saw the small smiling doctor standing in the entrance hall they nodded and said, 'Good health' as if his presence hadn't spoiled their day at all. The lady he'd come to meet was one of the last to emerge from the room. She carried a bulky slide projector piled high with study materials.

'Dr Pornsawan?'

'Dr Siri. Well, my word. What a sight for sore eyes.'

Despite the danger of being seen to be a chauvinist, he relieved the doctor of most of her papers and left her with the projector. He walked at her side. She was a tidy, compact woman with no bodily excesses, no unnecessary height, and no eyebrows.

'Still no facial hair, I see.' Siri laughed.

'It seems so silly to draw them on, don't you think? Once the damned things refused to grow back after the nunnery I decided to let them have it their way. Men find it attractive, I'm told.'

'And I'm one of them.'

'You're so sweet. Are you here to see me?'

'If you have a few minutes.'

'Your projects are always worth finding a few minutes for, Comrade. Come up to my office.'

The telling of the whole tale took twenty minutes and Dr Pornsawan's tears flowed for nineteen of them.

'I swear,' she said when he was done, 'in all my years of tending to women in the most wretched conditions, I have never heard of such a filthy aberration. What has happened to our society that such horror could occur, Siri? Something in me prays that this isn't just the beginning of the release of the demons. The wars inured us to atrocities, and the demons grew inside. Are they just now showing themselves?'

'I really don't want to believe so, Comrade. This is one renegade devil.'

'And we have to stop him, by God we have to.' She slapped her desk and all her pencils changed position.

'That's why I'm here.'

'How can we help?'

Siri described the type of man they were looking for. He wanted to hear of families whose daughters had been whisked away and vanished without a trace. He wanted to hear gossip of smooth suitors, of truck owners, of seducers of entire villages. He wanted anecdotes, rumours, and hearsay. He wanted women in the markets to include it in their morning news reports and army wives to make mention of it during village workshops. Missing daughters had to be significant news in the women's networks.

'How soon can you start?' Siri asked.

'Yesterday!'

'That should do it.'

10

DANCING WITH DEATH

When Comrade Civilai arrived at the morgue that lunchtime he was surprised to find everyone busy in the cutting room. It was Saturday – a half day. They should have all been on their way home. But he didn't want to disturb them. As a new retiree he found himself bothering a lot of people. He'd pop by his old office to say hello, and they'd be glad to see him, but busy. He'd offer his advice here and there – his seventy-three years of experience – surely somebody would want some of that? But all he seemed to do was get in the way. So he baked.

He sat at Siri's desk with a dozen lemon meringue tarts on a tin tray. He felt a little foolish. He'd imagined walking into the morgue, everybody free, jumping for joy at the sight of his lemon meringues, Dtui running off to fetch coffee from the canteen. Then sitting around the office cracking egg jokes and eating tarts.

But they were busy.

He decided to give them five – no, ten – minutes, then leave. He'd attach a note to the tarts and go. Or he'd take them with him somewhere else. Somewhere he'd be appreciated. There was no shortage of people in need of lemon meringue. He stretched out his long legs and one foot kicked a large cardboard box on the floor.

Siri removed his rubber gloves and went to the sink to wash his hands.

'Right,' he said. 'If that wasn't the silliest task we've performed here I'd say it ranks in the top three.'

'Come on, Doc,' Dtui said. 'It was a public service.'

'It was a private service, and I feel like an accessory.'

The deputy minister of sport had arrived at the morgue before midday with his mother on a stretcher. The old lady had just passed away, but on her deathbed she'd asked to see the family diamonds for the last time. Reluctantly, the deputy had brought her the seven tiny cut stones that would pass down to him and his wife once his mother was gone.

'Let me touch them,' the old lady had said.

Who could refuse a dying wish? Her son had placed them on her withered palm and seen the expression change on her face. She'd smiled and, according to one of the gardeners who'd helped carry the litter, said something like, 'You've been drooling over these all my life. Now you're really going to have to work for them, you greedy ingrate.' With that she threw the diamonds into her mouth, reached beside the bed for a glass of water, and washed them down. That had been both her final act of defiance and her final act.

So how else would one remove one's inheritance gracefully from a dead mother? The deputy had even written himself an official extraction order on ministry stationery. Siri knew this wasn't the last he'd be seeing of the freshly mined lady, and he'd whispered an apology before releasing her body to her son. He hadn't bothered to wash off the stones before handing them over.

Siri was grumbling and wiping his hands when he walked into his office. He'd expected to see worms, so he was pleasantly surprised to find Civilai at his desk rummaging through his bones.

'Hello, old brother,' said Siri.

'Siri, you have a box of ancient relics.'

'I do?'

'Some of this crockery's five hundred years old.'

'And how would you know such a thing?'

'I have skills.'

'I know you do. I just didn't realize they stretched to archaeology.'

'Don't forget they had me showing all those bored foreign dignitaries around the museums. I've had to explain all this stuff a thousand times. It sticks. You can recognize pottery from its glaze and ribbing. This translucent green glaze was typical of the stuff they dug up from the old kilns on Tar Deau Road in 1970. This is valuable.'

Siri took up a sliver of pottery in his left hand and a lemon meringue tart in his right.

'So tell me,' he said, 'why would Crazy Rajid have a box of valuable ancient relics?'

'These are Rajid's? Have you found him yet?'

'No, but I think we must be getting close.' He told Civilai the whole story about the Indian's father and the family disaster and the riddles, pausing only to swallow bites of pastry. Mr Geung went for coffee, and the four of them sat around eating and discussing Rajid.

'The question remains, where else could he have gone?' said Dtui. 'We've been to the edges of his universe. He's never been missing this long. Something must have happened to him.'

Siri looked over her shoulder and saw Saloop amble into the office. The creature walked up to Dtui, managed one pathetic tail wag, and put his head on her lap. Siri was surprised to see his nurse reach for her leg as if she were about to pat Saloop on the head. Instead she scratched her knee. She was, of course, unaware of the dog's presence. Only Siri saw the animal.

Dtui continued. 'It just frightens me that he might be in trouble and we can't help him.'

Saloop looked up at the doctor and raised one side of his brow, and finally Siri came to, crawled from his stupidity like a fly pulling itself free of paint. He excused himself, walked out of the room, out of the morgue, and around to the rear of the building. There was nothing back there but a vacant office and a ladder. Siri walked through the open doorway, stood in the middle of the floor, and danced. He jigged and he polkaed and he Highland flung and he sang some nonsense he'd learned on his travels and then he laughed. Anyone passing at that moment might have assumed he was an old man in the grip of a chronic alcohol binge, but he had never felt more sober or more alive. The omens that had hounded him for the past week, the feeling that death was getting closer, none of this had been directed at Siri. He was not going to die – Rajid was.

He walked back into his office still carrying that wonderful and awful feeling and fought to keep the smile from his lips.

'I've had a premonition,' he said. 'Rajid's in very serious trouble.'

Both Civilai and Dtui knew of Siri's dalliance with the spirits, and Geung didn't really seem to care. Nobody was surprised when he made his announcement.

'How serious?' Civilai asked.

'If we don't find him soon he'll die.'

'Any location or characters attached to this premonition?' Dtui asked.

Siri quickly shuffled through his week of dreams and visions, substituting Rajid for himself.

'A pregnant woman,' he said.

'Dtui,' said Dtui.

'No, the one I mean is ugly, and I think she's buried. Been buried for a long time. There must be a connection here too.' He went to the box of relics and rummaged through them. As soon as he made contact with the bones, a realization swept over him. 'Oh, my word. Of course.'

'What?' asked Dtui, Civilai, and Geung at the same time.

'The pillar of the city: Si Muang Temple. The founding of Vientiane,' said Siri.

'Fifteen …?' Civilai began.

'Fifteen sixty something,' said Siri. 'Could this pottery date from then?'

'Very likely,' said Civilai. 'They dragged an ancient Khmer pillar from somewhere as the heart of the new Vientiane. They dug a huge pit to bury it and threw in valuables and pots and keepsakes that held meaning to the people at the ceremony.'

'They didn't tell us all this in school in the north,' Dtui said.

Siri took over. 'Before they could plant this two tons of stone in its hole, they had to placate the spirits of the land whom they were about to dispossess. The elders called for a sacrifice. They'd left it until a bit late in the day, and there weren't that many volunteers. But then one wronged woman swollen with child ran forward. "Take me, take me," she cried and leaped into the pit. The ropes were cut, the pillar dropped, and the pregnant lady was suddenly lacking a dimension. I didn't make the connection because I'd always imagined the sacrificed girl to have been a gorgeous flaxen-haired beauty. But the vision of a woman I've been having all week was frightening in its ugliness. I can't think how she managed to get herself pregnant in the first place.'

'You've been having these visions all week?' Dtui asked.

'And you're just telling us now?' Civilai chimed in.

'Yes, but you see, I didn't relate the spectres to Rajid. I thought it was…eh, *bo ben nyang*. It doesn't matter what I thought. The important thing is that on the site of the burial of the pillar they built Si Muang Temple, and I have a strong feeling Rajid's there. I think his time's running out.'

11

BROKEN WATER

Civilai's ancient cream Citroën with one hubcap missing sped toward Si Muang. It was less than two kilometres from Mahosot but urgency made the distance more daunting. Civilai drove directly into the temple grounds and stopped only half a metre from the ordination hall that guarded the pillar. Despite all the noise they'd made, there was nobody around to chastise them. They alighted – Dtui, Siri, and Civilai (Geung had been placed in charge of the morgue) – ran through the empty vestibule, and into the pillar sanctum.

If it hadn't been for the patchy gilding and the string of unlit coloured Christmas lights, the pillar of the city might have been mistaken for a lump of rock. It rose from a high platform surrounded by plastic flowers in various stages of bleaching, several guardian Buddhas, and an impressive array of unconnected artefacts, presumably placed there to pick up holy vibrations. Siri walked around to see if there was a way inside the platform but it was a solid block.

'Now what do we do?' Dtui asked.

'I have no idea,' Siri confessed.

'Have another premonition, quick.'

'I can't just conjure them up.'

'Why not?'

'They arrive whenever they're in the mood. I've told you. I'm not the one in control here.'

'Then let's find somebody who is,' said Civilai and went in search of a monk or a curator. He returned a few moments later with a young man who had all the appearances – shaved head, victimized expression – of being a monk, but wore only royal blue soccer shorts.

'This fellow knows Rajid,' said Civilai.

The young man covered his chest with his arm as if he were ashamed of his nipples.

'He used to come often,' said the monk, 'but I didn't know his name. We'd feed him if we had anything to give and let him wander around. He was harmless enough.'

'When was the last time you saw him?' Dtui asked.

'Ooh, I don't know. A few weeks? Three perhaps?'

Siri recalled the worms and the scent of wet earth. 'Do you have any catacombs here, son?' he asked.

The soccer monk laughed. 'We flood here every wet season, uncle. If there were chambers down below they'd be mud by now. That's why they started to put in the pipes.'

'Pipes?' Siri perked up at the mention. 'Where do they run?'

'They don't, uncle. They were supposed to drain out the rainwater. The temple grounds are half a metre lower than the streets in front and back. In the monsoons it's like living in a rice paddy. They were going to lay the pipes from here all the way down to the river, but the project was put on hold when the new people took over.'

'How far did they get?' Civilai asked.

'I don't know. About seven metres? They dug the trench, put in the pipes, then didn't come back. We had to fill in the trench ourselves. They didn't even make it as far as the road.'

'Are there drains?' Siri asked.

'They didn't get around to putting any in.'

'So there's no way down?'

'Wouldn't make any difference if there was.'

'Why not?'

'The pipe's only twenty centimetres in diameter.'

'Why didn't you say so?' Siri was annoyed.

'You didn't ask.'

'The good news,' Dtui said, 'is that we won't have to go burrowing around underground. Heaven knows how much we all enjoy that.'

The three of them were sitting on one of the concrete benches donated to the temple by a follower who had long since fled. A fearful monkey king watched over them. They were shaded by a mango tree but it was still painfully hot. Dtui fanned herself with a handful of calling cards from her purse.

'The bad news,' Civilai continued, 'is that we aren't any closer to finding poor Rajid. Everything here's above ground. Looks like your premonition was a false alarm, little brother.'

'I don't believe that.' Siri shook his head. 'There was all that paraphernalia. He had to get that from somewhere.'

'It could have been any one of fifty temples in a five-kilometre radius.'

'But this one matches: the pregnant woman, the age of the pots. We know he was nosing around underground.'

'But certainly not here,' Civilai decided.

'It must be the pipes,' Siri said. 'They must be bigger than the monk remembers them.'

'Look' – Civilai put his hand on Siri's shoulder – 'we

aren't likely to bring spades and dig up the entire temple grounds, are we now? Why don't we go together to the Land Department on Monday morning and see if they have a record of any tunnels or underground chambers around here.'

'Monday's too late.'

'Well, you were wrong about Si Muang Temple; perhaps you're wrong about his dying too.'

Siri bit his lip.

'I think we should all go home and have a nice rest,' said Dtui. 'I'm sure the solution will come to us in a flash after a little sleep.' She put her hand on her belly. 'I feel like I'm carrying the entire politburo around, and they're starting to give me indigestion.'

'You're right.' Siri nodded. 'I apologize for my over-enthusiasm. Let's go back—'

'Good.'

'After one quick circuit of the temple.' Siri stood. 'Nurse, you may stay here on this shady bench and wait for us. If you feel a birth coming on, just scream and we'll come running.'

After probing around the gardens and the monks' quarters, and a very thorough search of the old Khmer ruins, Siri and Civilai stood on the shady side of the stupa. Apart from one poorly renovated patch halfway up, the *chedi* was a sad structure. The Thais would have cemented it over and painted it gold long ago but here it stood like a stack of charred rusks. To their right a concrete lion sat obediently on a plinth, and sleeping in its shade was Saloop.

'This is the place. He has to be here somewhere,' Siri said. 'We can't—'

He was interrupted by a woman's scream.

'Somebody sounds distressed,' Civilai decided.

Another scream.

'If I didn't know better,' Siri smiled, 'I'd say that was our own Nurse Dtui having a little fun with us.'

The third scream was straight out of *Bride of Frankenstein,* and it didn't end.

Phosy, Siri, and Civilai paced up and down in front of the maternity theatre at Mahosot like three expectant fathers. In front, in this case, meant under the stars and beneath the electric bulb that burned over the door. A cloud of flying ants competed with them for space and forced the men back whenever they dared step forward to listen at the door. The short-lived and very annoying creatures usually appeared as a result of sudden rainstorms, but there hadn't been a drop since November. Civilai put it down to the fact that Dtui's water had broken with such force, the insect kingdom had interpreted it as the coming of the monsoons. Dtui hadn't been in the mood to see the funny side of that. Whatever the reason, the theatre had been forced to close its doors and shutters to keep the insects out.

'You were supposed to be a doctor,' Phosy said angrily.

Siri raised his eyebrows. 'And when did I cease to be?'

'There you were, forcing her to work and having her traipse around hot temples on the day she was giving birth to our baby.'

'Phosy, these things are unpredictable. The baby doesn't have a wall calendar in there. She comes when she's ready. She just happened to be ready a few weeks before we were expecting her. It happens.'

Phosy seemed to be enjoying his bad mood.

'Why does everyone keep assuming the baby's a girl?' he asked.

'Auntie Bpoo, the fortune-teller, told us,' Siri smiled.

'You're all mad,' Phosy decided. 'And who is that clown in there birthing her? Why aren't you doing it?'

'The clown in there is Dr Bountien, the head of gynaecology,' Siri said patiently. 'Although he may know more egg jokes than most, he is probably the best man in the country for this job. The reason I'm not doing it myself is that I'm a coroner, Phosy. The skills don't overlap.'

'It's just not good enough,' Phosy huffed. Neither Siri nor Civilai was certain what 'it' was.

'The world will seem a better place as soon as you see your daughter,' Siri told him.

'Why's it taking so long?'

It occurred to Civilai that he had no cause to pace so he sat cross-legged on the dry grass. 'Honestly, Phosy,' he said. 'You're acting like you've never had children before.'

'I haven't. Not live and in person. My ex always managed to produce when I was far from home.'

'It could have been that you were far from home more often than not,' Siri commented.

'Which in turn might explain why she's his ex,' Civilai added.

'Will you two stop bullying me? Can't you see I'm tense?' They all heard a shrill sound like a whistle being squeezed out of a sparrow. 'What was that?'

'If I'm not mistaken, that was the sound of Dtui Junior making her debut,' Siri smiled.

'Are you sure? Is it supposed to sound like that?'

'If she's got that much wind already, I think you should be very proud of her.'

When the door finally opened, the nurse carrying five-minute-old Malee looked up at the cloud of insects and immediately covered the new arrival's face with the towel. She ran a few metres until she was clear of the plague then turned to ask who the father was. Siri and Civilai both put up their hands but it was Phosy who stepped forward. The nurse unveiled the tiny girl, and Phosy's face lit up like the fairy lights at the That Luang Festival. He looked at his friends with a smile so bright the insects left the lightbulb and started to circle around the inspector.

'I'm a father,' he beamed.

As the theatre and the maternity ward were in different buildings, the nurse hurried away, leaving Phosy by himself. Siri was about to remind him that he was a husband as well as a father, but the policeman had already started for the door. He knocked once and was told to go around the side where Dtui was recovering in an alcove.

'She's all right?' Phosy shouted through the door.

'Fitter than I'll ever be,' replied the doctor.

Phosy punched the air and started for the side door. He paused, turned back, and hugged first Siri then Civilai – then Siri again – before vanishing around the side of the building.

'Funny. I didn't get the impression he was the hugging type,' said Civilai.

'He's a strong lad,' wheezed Siri.

12

IN A STUPA

Madame Daeng always slept as if there were no cares in the world. She smiled in her sleep and chewed the corners of her mouth. At times her eyes would roll inside their lids and the lashes would twitch. Siri thought he wouldn't mind if he never slept again in his life as long as he had her to watch.

When the Saturday night noodle rush had subsided, Daeng had gone to the hospital to sit with Dtui and the baby. She'd stayed there until past ten. When she returned to the shop she'd found her husband going through the items from Rajid's box. Mr Tickoo had stopped by earlier to see whether there had been any progress in the search for his son. He confessed that he'd been having very negative feelings that day. He looked through the box of treasures but they meant nothing to him either. He and Siri parted with a sense of hopelessness. Neither man had the heart to say what he believed: that Rajid was probably no longer of this world.

Siri told Daeng that he would come to bed soon, but he remained at his desk, running his fingers over the dry bones, waiting for a message that didn't come. He was still wide awake when he finally climbed into bed. Although he had no inclination to sleep, he closed his eyes and visualized Si Muang Temple. He pictured Rajid hanging around there, making a nuisance of himself, perhaps flashing at unsuspecting ladies as they made offerings. He could imagine the Indian annoying the abbot by climbing the walls of the prayer chamber and hanging upside down from the eaves. In the wet season he'd . . .

Siri's body became rigid. He opened his eyes. His heart was pounding. He shook Daeng and was surprised at how quickly she came to life, sitting up alert. Siri was already out of bed pulling on his trousers.

'Are we going somewhere?' she asked.

'Do we still have the sledgehammer out back?'

'Unless it walked somewhere.'

'Good. Are you coming?'

'Wouldn't miss it for the world.' She began to throw on her clothes with the same urgency as her husband. 'Where are we going?'

'I'll tell you on the way.'

They stopped first at Mahosot, where Siri retrieved the bamboo stepladder from behind the morgue. He alerted two night orderlies and told them to follow him on their bicycles. It was just as well the police were all tucked up soundly in bed because they might have seen something suspicious in a couple on a motorcycle speeding through Vientiane at two in the morning with a stepladder and a sledgehammer. Siri skidded to a noisy halt on the gravel in front of Si Muang Temple. He hoped he wouldn't find the gate locked. In the old days it was unthinkable that the temple might not be available for troubled souls twenty-four hours a day. But the country had entered a period of suspicion and fear, and even monks slept behind locked gates.

They were in luck. There was a chain wrapped around the two gates giving the impression they were padlocked, but they were not. Siri unwrapped the chain noisily, not caring whom he woke up. The more the merrier. He and Daeng carried the ladder between them while Siri hoisted the hammer, and Daeng held a torch. They went directly to the stupa and set up the ladder against the structure. It barely reached the renovation work.

'You steady me and I'll go up,' Siri said. He knew if this had been anything but a temple stupa, Daeng would have wanted to elephant-mouse-ant him about it, but there were deep-rooted Buddhist taboos against women climbing religious structures. He was on his own and there was no time to lose – perhaps none at all. Daeng tucked the torch into his belt and squeezed his hand.

'There's just a hint of sacrilege in what we're about to do,' she told him as he climbed up the steps with his sledgehammer slung over one shoulder. 'There'd be a lot of explaining to do if we've – heaven forbid – got this wrong.'

Siri wasn't in a talking mood. He saved what little breath he had for the job at hand. He couldn't get into a position to use both hands on the hammer, so he grabbed the ladder top with his left hand and grasped the heavy sledgehammer in his right.

Only four monks and the abbot remained at Si Muang, and they'd all been roused by the sound of the chain being removed. By the time they reached the stupa, Siri had already made an impression on the new brickwork.

'What in the name of all that is sacred are you doing?' shouted the abbot.

Daeng called up to Siri, 'My love, I might be forced to kill a monk or two tonight. I hope you can find it in your heart to forgive me if I'm sent to hell.'

The abbot stopped in his tracks.

'My goodness. They're both mad. Stop them!' he told his acolytes.

He stepped back and let the monks make the advance. They prowled forward. Daeng reached into her shoulder bag and produced an extremely long knife. She brandished it halfheartedly, and the monks froze.

'Look, I'm really sorry about this,' she said. 'I personally have nothing against the temple. In fact, I've been a fairly good Buddhist all my life. But I will be forced to use this if you come any closer.'

She looked up at Siri, who was flagging. He wheezed in counterpoint to the thumps of his hammer on the brickwork. She turned back to the stunned monks and smiled.

'Perhaps I could ask,' Daeng continued, 'exactly when was the renovation here completed?'

'If he has a problem with renovations we could always discuss it like sensible adults,' the abbot said. 'There's really no need to—'

'If you could just answer the question,' Daeng said.

'About three weeks ago,' said the soccer monk.

Daeng heaved a sigh. 'Thank goodness for that. We might be on the right track then. If you'd said three months it would have been one of those embarrassing moments you see in the comics.'

She laughed but nobody joined her.

'Does anyone know what in hell she's talking about?' asked the abbot.

When the two orderlies arrived from Mahosot, wheeling their bicycles, the scene that confronted them defied common sense. Dr Siri was up a ladder battering a hole in one of the city's oldest stupas with a sledgehammer. His wife was holding back five monks with a carving knife.

They looked at each other to be sure they were both seeing the same thing.

Dr Siri had only one last swing left in him. He defied gravity, gripped the hammer in both hands, lifted it above his head, and sent it crashing down onto the seriously wounded brickwork. The sledgehammer bounced out of Siri's hands and passed not four centimetres from his wife's head. Siri clung to the ladder in time to prevent his backward tumble. Seen from the ground, his mission appeared to have failed. The doctor prostrated himself against the stupa, desperately searching for breath.

'Siri, this would be an embarrassing moment to die,' Daeng called up to him.

Siri recovered, put his hands out in front of him, and pushed. What was left of the renovated brickwork caved inward, leaving a jagged triangular window some sixty centimetres by thirty.

'My Thor,' cheered Daeng.

'Oh, my heaven!' said the abbot.

Siri reached to the back of his belt and took out the torch. He pressed the switch and climbed the last step in order to see inside the stupa. The original walls were eighty centimetres thick, which explained why the new brickwork had been so hard to dislodge. He'd put all his effort into weakening the old masonry around the new cement. As he'd hoped, the workers had been too lazy to make the patch any thicker than the eye could see. He pulled himself through the narrow gap and edged forward. There was a narrow chimney of space at the core of the stupa, and he leaned over the precipice so he could look down into the bowels. The ancient bricks crumbled as he progressed. He recognized the earthy, wormy smell that rose to greet him.

'Rajid?' he called. 'Rajid?' Siri's lungs ached, and the mustiness of the air caused him to struggle for breath. He heard his own voice as a whisper. There was a rustle from below, barely audible, perhaps caused by insects. Siri pulled himself forward until he was looking directly down. He shone his light, and there below him on the dirt floor was the crumpled body of Rajid in a space no wider than the inside of a mail box.

'Are you dead, Rajid?'

Siri could see crusted blood on the Indian's head and, from his perch, he couldn't make out any breathing. There was no movement, no sound. Siri grabbed a chunk of brick and tossed it down into the hole. It hit Rajid on the shoulder. There was still no reaction.

'Wake up, damn you,' Siri shouted. He wanted desperately to climb down into the hole but had no more energy. His head was growing woozy. He grabbed another brick and threw it into the pit. This time he hit Rajid on the side of the head. The effort dislodged a shower of brick dust. There were one or two seconds when Rajid vanished in the cloud, then, when the thin air cleared, Siri saw that one of the Indian's eyes was open slightly. The light of the flashlight caught its secret. It was an eye one blink away from death.

Not for the first time, Siri awoke in one of the private patient rooms at Mahosot. An oxygen mask covered his lower face. He wondered what had happened to him this time. His mind travelled back over some of the other disasters he'd awoken from over the past two years: the house that had fallen on him, the maniac's attack, the possession, the electrocution, and of course the drowning. It was a wonder he woke up at all any more. But he was glad he did.

Life really was something to hang on to for as long as possible. It wasn't until you were on the verge of losing it that you appreciated its worth.

Whether it was as a result of the oxygen or the sleep he couldn't say, but he'd honestly never felt better. He took off the mask and looked around the room. The two-year-old Royal Thai Ploughing Ceremony calendar still hung on the wall, and the paint was still Wattay blue like the airport. But the buffaloes looked happier than they had a year earlier and the walls jollier. He gazed down at his own body and he was Johnny Weissmuller, alias Tarzan from the movies. Everything was perfect with the world, and he knew in his heart that Crazy Rajid had survived his ordeal and that it was all due to him.

For a couple of days there was nothing but sunshine and joy. Siri was a hero, albeit with a very small following. Dtui was a mother, albeit with a surprisingly small baby. Rajid was alive, and Civilai had won a prize for his pumpkin pie at the kilometre 6 Lao Patriotic Women's Association cake-making fair.

There had been answers to basic questions. It appeared that while there was still a crack in the side of the Si Muang stupa, Rajid had used his climbing acumen to sneak inside from time to time and dig up relics buried there. Some nights he might have slept inside. The bump on his head suggested he had fallen and knocked himself out at some stage. This was all conjecture, of course, as Rajid was still unconscious and would probably maintain his vow of silence when he came around. But, for whatever reason, he had been bricked inside the Si Muang stupa for three weeks. How he'd survived would remain a mystery. Some of the smaller cracks in the spire must have allowed air to enter. And Rajid was a creature of the earth, a brother to frogs. If there had been water for him to drink it had to have been deep and unpleasant. The only explanation that made any sense was that he'd found nutrients in the insects that abounded inside the old stupa. The spiders and cockroaches and worms had kept Rajid alive.

Siri's overnight stay in the hospital had been just a precaution. His friend Dr Davone informed him that a man with his lung condition probably shouldn't be knocking down stupas with a sledgehammer. She also suggested Siri might find himself blacking out more often in confined spaces or at high altitudes without sufficient oxygen. She forbade him from engaging in scuba diving or mountain climbing in the Himalayas. Siri promised he would avoid both. But there was certainly nothing wrong with him on the day he was released from Mahosot, as Madame Daeng would gladly have testified.

Monday rolled around and the feelings of goodwill and happiness were slowly eroded by memories of the evil that still gripped Laos. Perhaps those involved in the strangled woman case had deliberately blocked the thoughts from their minds and been grateful for a distraction. Perhaps they all needed to believe that the earth was still a safe place on which to live. But it soon became apparent that it was not.

There hadn't been much news from the police investigation. Sergeant Sihot had interviewed everyone in Ban Xon who'd had dealings with Phan. The village headman still had the original letter of introduction from the highways division. It looked very official and had Phan down as Thongphan Ratsakoun. It said that he was surveying for an upcoming road project in the surrounding area and it would be greatly appreciated if the esteemed official at Ban Xon could assist Comrade Thongphan with accommodation during his stay. He had a small budget for food and any cooperation would be 'remembered by the Central Committee'. The letter was authenticated with a circular red stamp and co-signed by the head of the Highways Department, who had his own, even more splendid red stamp.

In this age of mimeograph machines and typewriters with carbon paper, official documents like those in circulation in Laos were not terribly difficult to forge if a man had access to such equipment. Nobody was surprised to learn that there was no Thongphan Ratsakoun at the Highways Department or anywhere else on public file. It would take several months to go through the disparate police record data banks, but there was no point in looking up an obviously fake name.

The villagers who'd mixed socially with Phan at dinners and on the *takraw* court agreed that he was a top fellow: a very friendly and likable person. Nobody had any idea where he went during the day. They had the impression he'd have liked to have told them about his work but wasn't allowed to. He had a truck but no driver, which was interesting. It suggested that he was independent, perhaps a section head. He was clearly someone with the ability to do everything for himself. He had class, some women said. Perhaps he'd come from a well-to-do family. He'd obviously travelled widely. He knew the country very well.

Where did he come from? Nobody knew. He'd moved around a lot when he was young. Army family perhaps? Somewhere in the north, although he had a central accent. He'd given everyone a life history so vague they could barely remember what he'd said. He'd answered most questions with a joke, and they were too awed by his position to embarrass him with an interrogation. Sergeant Sihot had come to the conclusion that this was a very cautious and cunning villain. He'd left no real trace.

Siri, Civilai, and Phosy were seated on the log overlooking the dwindling Mekhong. Civilai had catered all three lunches. It was a new recipe for homemade baguettes with genuine corned beef.

'How do you get hold of all this exotic fair?' Siri asked. He was actually enjoying his lunch. Civilai had hit on the formula. They were washing down the bread rolls with home-squeezed guava juice, courtesy of Mrs Noy. Civilai's wife was slowly coming to terms with the fact that her previously absentee husband had become attached to the house. The kitchen was a place she was allowed to visit but which was no longer hers. Although Civilai still had the general bone structure of a grasshopper, he now had a more substantial body for her to cuddle on a cold night, so she didn't complain.

'I still have friends in high places,' he told his fellow diners. 'You'd be surprised what our American colonists left behind. If you slip me a few bucks I can probably lay my hands on some Spam, canned soup, sardines in tomato sauce, franks and beans, you name it. There's a larder full of the stuff.'

'All that old tin should be rusty by now,' Phosy decided.

'Ah, Inspector' – Civilai wagged his finger – 'they say you can never have too much iron in your diet. And if iron is so beneficial, tin can only be one step below it.'

Siri laughed. 'Just think, Phosy. Before he retired, only

the politburo had access to his brilliance. Now we all get to share.'

'Good, I could use some brilliance,' Phosy admitted and became immediately glum.

'The strangler?' Civilai asked.

'We're not getting anywhere. We're just not cut out to do a nationwide investigation. I don't suppose you've heard anything from your embroidery circle, Doctor?'

'Don't mock the Lao Patriotic Women's Association, Inspector. They'll come up with something. You mark my words.'

'Meanwhile, we've come to a dead end with Phan. Not even anything on the truck. It was a Chinese Jiefang. The road builders in the north are bringing them in and selling them secondhand, cheap. Most government projects have one. Nobody thought to write down the licence number. One Chinese truck is pretty much the same as the next.'

'It looks like the Chinese are invading us one street at a time,' Civilai bemoaned. 'They're doing whatever they want up north in the border provinces. I warned the old fogies on the committee, but nobody listened. It's only because we don't have any money that they're not flooding us with cheap, shoddy goods.'

'To replace the cheap, shoddy goods from Vietnam?' Siri asked.

'Exactly. Some of those Chinese engineers have special dispensation to hop around the country without the inconvenience of applying for a laissez-passer.'

'Like you and me, Siri,' said Phosy.

'Yes, but you two are Lao. It's your country ... at least for a while.'

'That's it.' Phosy tried to click his fingers, but they were slick with mayonnaise. 'Travel. We know Phan travelled across prefectural borders. Even if he was attached to a government project he'd need a laissez-passer. Private citizens can't just pop into the Interior Ministry and say, "I fancy a bit of a drive up to Luang Prabang; could you give me a travel pass?"'

'Even if he had a valid and urgent need, the bureaucracy would delay him for a month or so,' Civilai added.

'So how did Boonhee get down here so fast to claim his daughter's body?' Siri asked.

'Sihot got him a pass,' Phosy said. 'We claimed he was a witness. But for Phan to go to Vang Vieng and then return there two weeks later, he had to be attached to some official project.'

'So you're assuming he was in the region for another purpose but changed his identity and project description in order to fool the people in Ban Xon?'

'What do you think?' Phosy asked.

'It's a stretch, but it's as good as anything else you've got,' Siri agreed.

'So, let's make a list,' said Civilai. He reached into his pack, pulled out three slices of his prize-winning pie, and hunted around for a pen and paper.

'I have a notepad,' said Phosy. 'I'll exchange it for a piece of pie.'

'You'll finish your baguettes, give yourself a few minutes for the first course to digest, then I'll think about letting you have dessert.'

'You're a tough nut.' Phosy laughed. He found his pencil and held it poised to write.

'Number one, "military",' said Civilai.

'I don't know.' Phosy shook his head. 'This fellow doesn't

read like army to me. I get the feeling he's a few pegs above soldier. He seems too polished, too charming. Plus the witnesses said his hair was longish, just over his collar. I know we don't insist on five millimetres like the Thais, but if our Phan's an officer he'd lead by example.'

'I see him as someone who has, or used to have, influence.' Siri thought out loud. 'He knows how to talk. Has some breeding. Now if you'd told me he was a Royalist officer I'd believe that. There were a lot of smooth tin soldiers in that outfit. But not the National People's Liberation Army. They're too country. Too simple.'

'How about the police?' Civilai asked.

Phosy shook his head. 'The only unit that does any travelling is the one I'm in charge of.'

'All right, then let's start the list with politburo members and their aides, members of the Central Committee.' Civilai smiled, happy to finger his old colleagues. 'They get travel passes at the drop of a hat.'

'I don't know about that either,' said Siri, dusting the last of his breadcrumbs from his lap. 'They're too high profile. If anyone with a name was in the region all the local cadres would know.'

'But it's worth a shot,' Phosy said and began the list. 'I'll get Sihot to check whether there were any political meetings in the district at the time Phan was there.'

'But don't forget he had to be there twice,' Siri reminded him. 'Once for the seduction and once for the wedding. There had to be some kind of flexibility in his schedule.'

'Or he picked a location he knew he'd be going back to in a few weeks,' Phosy said.

'All right,' said Siri. 'Let's include all the departments – I'm sorry, I mean ministries – that are likely to have projects up in the Vang Vieng/Ban Xon area. Let's start with forestry. We know it's not roads.'

'Fishery, health, agriculture,' Civilai reeled off.

'Rural development, culture,' Siri added, 'and I'm thinking specifically of the people who go out to hill-tribe villages and convince them they'd be better off as Lao citizens.

'Slow down,' said Phosy.

'Come on, you know which they are,' Civilai told him. 'Virtually every department has a division that goes out into the countryside. You'd have to contact all of them and find out whether they had any projects up there on the dates we've got.'

'And you might want to cross-reference with old projects conducted in Luang Nam Tha in the late sixties,' Siri offered. 'If there are any old-timers who haven't managed to swim across the river, they might recall what was going on up there. Wait, isn't there an office that coordinates all the projects?'

'The National Coordination Directorate: three men and one woman and so much paperwork you need snowshoes to walk from one side of the office to the other,' Civilai told him. 'Forget it. This is going to take legwork, Phosy. Good old-fashioned policing.'

13

A HONEYMOON IN HELL

The letter Phan had been waiting for arrived on the Tuesday lunchtime. He took the truck to the Bureau de Poste and found two envelopes in his box. One was pink and scented and from Thaxi. He didn't even bother to read it. He ripped it in half and threw it into the large plastic waste basket that stood by the door. She'd failed, this smelly perfume girl. In her last letter, wracked with remorse, she'd admitted that she'd lied to him at their last meeting. She confessed to a small sexual encounter when she was fifteen. She hoped he'd appreciate her honesty as she didn't want there to be any secrets between them. She hoped it wouldn't interfere with the plans for their marriage.

'No, dearie. It didn't interfere with them. It obliterated them. You are a slut!' The only thing he wanted from her she no longer possessed.

This second letter, this was what he needed. It had arrived in his box without a stamp through the magic of acquaintanceships. He sat beneath a large Mangifera on the grounds and unfolded the lined school paper. A tiny delicate green caterpillar abseiled down a fine silk thread and landed on the open page. It was an omen. He didn't need omens. He crushed it with his thumb and wiped his hand on the side of his navy blue trousers.

He read her neat handwriting.

Dearest Phan,

I can't tell you how special your letter was for me. I'd prayed at our temple that you would take me to your world. I've seen and learned everything I can here in mine. Now it's time for me to grow and improve myself. We have planned the wedding ceremony for the evening of the 26th. I hope that's convenient for you and your work. It means we can leave directly on the morning of the 27th.

Phan, there are so many thoughts and words in my heart that I am too shy to write. Like you I have never written a love letter. I hope you'll be able to teach me how to express myself so I don't embarrass you in front of the Lords and Ladies of Europe.

From Wei to Phan

Five days away. That was more like it. To the point. No mushy sentiment or scents or last-second confessions. No poetry or bad grammar. She really was perfect, this school-teacher. He climbed back into his truck and sat behind the wheel. He turned the key and pulled the ignition knob. His beast roared. People on the post office steps turned to stare. 'Yes, yes, morons. It's me. Notice me! You'll all hear about me soon enough.' He let his foot growl on the accelerator. This was it. This was the feeling. A woman and a truck. What else could a real man want? He pulled out onto Lan Xang Avenue without bothering to look. If anyone on the road was so deaf they couldn't hear his engine they deserved to be mowed down. He drove twenty metres on the wrong side of the street before crossing to the far lane. It rarely

mattered in Vientiane. He allowed himself a gratuitous honk
of the horn. He was a very merry misogynist.

Siri had ridden to the Morning Market after lunch and bought
some chicken wire. The hornbill wasn't getting along too well
with the ducks and chickens in Madame Daeng's backyard so
he was planning to divide the garden like East and West
Berlin. He hoped he wouldn't have to resort to machine-gun
turrets and barbed wire. On his way back, some idiot in a
truck almost wiped him out in front of the post office. Siri's
heart was still pounding when he arrived at the morgue. Mr
Geung was standing waiting for him on the front step with a
note in each hand. He held them up in front of Siri's face.

'M ...messages,' he said.

'What do they say?' Siri asked, walking past him and into
the office.

'I...I don't know. They're in ...in writing.'

After many hundred hours of earth-staggering patience,
Dtui and Siri had succeeded in teaching Geung some of the
mechanics of reading. He had what Dtui called a 'learn-
two-forget-three letter system'. He finally recognized words
more from their overall shape than their spelling.
Handwriting was noodles to Mr Geung.

Siri read the notes aloud for Geung's benefit. The first
was from the Lao Patriotic Women's Association.

> Siri, how are you?
> I'm sure you're very busy, but it would be
> wonderful if you could come and see me as soon
> as possible.
>
> > Very best wishes, your friend,
> > Pornsawan

The second note was from Justice.

> Siri, I expect you here at 1:30, my office.
> Don't be late. Haeng

Siri smiled. 'Now, Mr Geung, did you notice any difference in style between these two notes?'

Geung shook his head.

'Perhaps I read them badly. Here!' He read them again using his soft and fluffy voice on the first and his Judge Haeng impersonation on the second.

'Now did you see any difference?'

'This one,' Geung pointed, 'is …is nice. This one is bad.'

'That's quite right, Geung. So which one do you think I'm going to respond to first?'

'The nice one.'

'Correct. See? You'll be reading in no time.'

'Judge H…Haeng is going to be, to be p…pissed off.'

'You might be right.'

Dr Pornsawan was working with a group of rural medical interns when Siri arrived at the Women's Association. As soon as she saw him outside the room she excused herself and went to greet him. She swung his hand from side to side and squeezed his fingers.

'Hello, Siri. Thank you so much for coming. My office?'

He followed her to the simple doorless booth she called her own and they both sat. She opened her desk drawer and pulled out a thick wad of notes.

'You'd be surprised how small our country can be, Dr Siri.'

'This is all in response to our strangling?'

'Some of it's dross – some fantasy and myths,' she said. 'But there are one or two reports in there I think could be relevant.'

'But it's only been three days,' Siri reminded her. 'And one of those was a Sunday.'

'We don't mess about, Doctor. We had ladies coming here from the provinces for training and girls going out for workshops. The word got around very quickly. An angry bunch of women actually knows no bounds.'

'You're telling me.'

'I've taken the liberty of singling out two stories. One was from a lady's personal experience. The other was anecdotal. Would you like some tea?'

'Thank you.'

Pornsawan poured and related the first tale.

'A girl in Champasak, in the south,' she began. 'It was in September of last year. Her parents had sent her off to work on a logging concession in the neighbouring province: Attapeu. It appears one of the foremen had taken a shine to her when he was on leave and saw her around Pakse town. He convinced her parents she'd make a good secretary for the projects in the hills. She'd only completed grade three and had never seen a typewriter, so obviously the foreman was a master at recognizing potential.'

'Obviously.'

She sat and let her tea cool on the desk beneath the ceiling fan. Siri sipped at his right away.

'The foreman arranged her travel documents and drove her up into the hills. On her first night there he made his inevitable advances, and the girl, a virgin, ran to the house of the local headman and his family to complain and seek refuge. Staying at the house was a gentleman attached to the Department of Agriculture. He was shocked by the girl's story and went to the logging foreman's house and thumped him one. Some rumours would have it that he beat him half to death, but we all know what rumours are like, brother Siri. We're doctors so we aren't allowed to say things like, "He had it coming." The girl stayed at the headman's house for a few days, and she and the gentleman from Agriculture fell in love. They were parted for two weeks, but as soon as they reunited they were married.'

'That was quick.'

'One of our policies here is to return to the old tradition of getting to know the person you marry. It sounds funda-mental but what with all the upheavals – troops relocating, men dying, and roads being built through remote villages – there are families only too willing to put their daughters into the hands of a stranger who is better off than themselves. Our peasantry is getting poorer and more desperate.

'But I digress. On the night of the wedding at the girl's home in Champasak, the groom announced that he had to return to Vientiane in two days. Given the state of the road, that seemed like an insurmountable task. So he left with his bride directly after the ceremony. He had a truck, but our witness couldn't say what type it was, just that the village boys were all gathered around it oohing and aahing. That was the last the parents saw of their daughter. They didn't hear from her again.'

'And that was the anecdote?'

'No, it came directly from the wife of the headman in Attapeu. She hadn't been able to get a laissez-passer in time for the wedding, but the next time she went to Champasak on Women's Association business she looked up the family and discovered they hadn't heard from their daughter.'

'Did she remember the man's name?'

'Yes, it was the same as her eldest son's. Khamphan.'

Siri whistled. 'Another Phan. Anything else?'

'That's all she could remember. She's going back south tomorrow, and she's promised to look for the man's letter of introduction to her husband.'

'I'm sure it'll be as fake as the last one. Doctor, I'd like to put the lady in touch with Inspector Phosy before she travels. Did she happen to say what the man looked like?'

'Tall, muscular, mid to late thirties, hair a little too long. Sound familiar?'

'Much too familiar, I'm afraid.'

'It is all thoroughly depressing, isn't it?'

'Just the thought that he's out there killing innocent girls and we can't do anything to stop him makes me sick. You said there was another story?'

'Much more sketchy, this one. One of our members heard about a woman who attended a wedding just outside Pakxan. Country girl, sophisticated city man. He lived in Vientiane and planned to take her overseas.'

'That's it?'

'Only that they left for a secret romantic honeymoon directly after the ceremony and vanished.'

'Any time frame?'

'No, we're checking up on it.'

'Did she recall when she heard the story or from whom?'

Pornsawan consulted her copious notes. 'She said it was early last year – when she heard the story, I mean. I'll let you know what comes of this one.'

'Excellent. You're sure the other reports—?'

'I'll give you the lot. If you think there might be anything else, you can get back to me and I'll follow it up.'

'You're doing a marvellous job, Comrade.'

'I'm sure there'll be more.'

'Thank you.'

'*Bo ben nyang.*'

He stood to leave and she walked him to the door.

'I must say you're looking good, considering your exploits at Si Muang Temple,' she said.

Siri rolled his eyes. 'How on earth could you have …? All right. Silly question. Yes, thank you. I'm fine.'

'How's your Indian friend?'

'Doing well. Very soon he'll be well enough to roll about in mud, eat worms, and walk aimlessly around Nam Poo Fountain again.'

'I'm sure he doesn't see it as aimless. We all have different goals. His are achievable.'

'You're so right,' Siri smiled.

'Oh, and Doctor, I have to let you know you have a growing fan club here at the Lao Patriotic Women's Association.'

Siri blushed and headed out into the sunshine.

It was a little past one thirty when Siri arrived at Justice. One hour and fifteen minutes past, to be exact. His visit to police headquarters had taken longer than he'd anticipated. Manivone hurried him along the corridor.

'He's spewing fire, Doctor,' she said, scurrying ahead. 'I swear if he knew which end of a gun was forward, he'd shoot you.'

'What did I do?'

'He was expecting you over an hour ago.'

'I was expecting a comfortable retirement on full pay.

You don't always get what you expect on this planet, Comrade Manivone.'

'Well, I don't think he'll buy an argument like that right now. If you don't want a lecture, you're going to have to come up with a good excuse.'

Siri briefly considered using 'Mr Geung ate my note', but settled on an excuse that better suited his personality. Manivone knocked on the judge's door and said, 'Judge, Dr Siri is here.'

She stepped back to let the doctor go past her only to find him gone. She went outside and looked around but saw neither hide nor hair of him.

'I'm sorry, Judge,' she said. 'He was right beside me. Honestly.'

The judge was too enraged to speak. The pencil snapped between his fingers and half of it jumped up and hit him in the eye. He couldn't even get ire right. A minute later Manivone returned, this time pushing Siri in front of her. She heaved him into the room and closed the door behind him.

It only took Siri a few seconds to take in the scene and understand the reason for his summons. Judge Haeng and Vietnamese adviser Phat were sitting at their respective desks. But to one side, seated on the sticky vinyl guest sofa, were three upright gentlemen in grey, pale blue, and brown safari suits respectively. In front of them on the slightly inclining coffee table were several used cups and glasses, hard evidence of the amount of time they'd been there waiting for him. Siri recognized one of the men, Comrade Koomki from Housing.

Comrade Phat performed an 'I did my best' shrug and grinned at the papers in front of him.

'Siri,' said Haeng in a much deeper voice than Siri had

ever heard him use, 'where the hell have you been?'

'To the toilet,' Siri answered honestly. As was custom, he went along the line of sofa sitters and shook their hands. Though his own hand was damp, they had no choice but to respond.

'For two hours?' Haeng yelled at Siri's back.

'No, just now. I was taken short and happened to pass the WC, so I—'

'I called you here for one thirty.'

'Right. I had something more important to do.'

'You...?' The judge looked and half smiled at the visitors. 'These comrades have been here since one fifteen.'

'They refused to leave until you got here,' said the Vietnamese with the slightest of smiles pencilled across the bottom of his face.

'It's good to see there's one government department with sufficient time on its hands that it can waste it doing nothing,' Siri said and sat in front of Haeng's desk. 'Not many of us have that luxury.'

'Siri, this is a serious matter,' growled the judge. 'Comrade Koomki here is accusing you of—'

'I know what he's accusing me of: charity and kindness. Goodness knows we don't want any of that kind of behaviour in the new republic.'

'Judge Haeng,' said the little man, 'if I may.'

'Go ahead,' said the judge.

'Although we have reservations as to the type of person staying at Dr Siri's house,' Koomki began, 'that is not the matter at hand. We have evidential proof that you, Dr Siri Paiboun, are not resident at government housing unit 22B742.'

'Let's see it,' said Siri.

Koomki stood and walked to Haeng's desk. He carried a large grey envelope.

'My colleagues and I performed five days of surveillance on both unit 22B742 and the commercial property on Fa Ngum Street owned by the doctor's wife, Madame Daeng.'

'Good grief,' said Siri, slumping back in the chair. 'We have foreigners stealing great chunks of our ancient temple at Wat Poo because the government can't spring for a couple of guards to look after it, and here we have three grade-two public officials spending a week watching a noodle shop? Surely our nation has better ways to harness your rapacious enthusiasm?'

'Firstly, I am a grade-three official,' said Koomki. 'And secondly, on the contrary, I consider the honesty and transparency of the actions of our high-ranking officials to be a priority in these troubled times.'

'Really? Then let's bring in an opposition party,' Siri hissed. 'That'll straighten all of us out.'

'Siri,' Judge Haeng interrupted, 'can we just see what evidence the comrade has, please?'

'Judge, surely you can't—?'

'Siri! Thank you.'

Siri held up his hands in submission, and the small man sneered. He produced a wad of documents from the envelope and fanned them back and forth.

'Your Honour, here—'

'You aren't in court, Comrade,' Haeng said. '"Judge" will be sufficient.'

'Yes, Comrade.' Koomki nodded. 'Here we have five days of surveillance records. They clearly show that Dr Siri was not at unit 22B742 for that period but was unlawfully residing at his wife's shop.'

'For the entire time?' Haeng asked.

'What?'

'Was Dr Siri at his wife's establishment for the entire period of the surveillance?'

'Yes, well, no. There were some gaps.'

'How many?'

'Three. Either we saw him leave but not arrive, or vice versa.'

'Three out of five?' The judge raised his eyebrows. 'Not a very impressive statistic.'

Siri looked up in surprise.

'He probably slipped in through the back,' Koomki said with confidence.

'I'm a judge, Comrade. I don't deal with probabilities, only evidence.'

Siri turned to Phat, who was buried in his work.

'Do you have proof that it was actually Dr Siri your man saw at the noodle shop?' Haeng asked.

'Yes, Judge. We have a photograph of him sneaking in at night. Our camera has a gadget that records the date and time.'

'Which is adjustable?'

'Yes, Judge.'

'Meaning you can change the time and date at will.'

Siri leaned forward to make sure the judge hadn't been replaced while nobody was looking.

'Well, technically.' Koomki was getting flustered. 'But of course we wouldn't falsify evidence.'

'Of course not. Show me the picture.'

Koomki handed him a large coloured zoom shot. In it, a short brown-faced man in goggles and a backward-facing baseball cap was being allowed entrance to the shop by Madame Daeng. Not even Siri could recognize himself.

'And who is this man?' Haeng asked.

'Why, it's Dr Siri.'

'All I see is a dark-skinned person with glasses.'

'They're goggles, Judge. He'd just arrived on his motorcycle.'

'Which doesn't appear in the photograph. Nor does the street address of the shop.' Haeng was at his most belligerent, and Siri had a sudden urge to lean over the desk and kiss him on the nose.

'The fact remains—' Koomki attempted.

'The fact remains,' Haeng interrupted, 'that you haven't a shred of evidence that would stand up in any court in the land. I'm offended that you even brought this matter before me. Where was your man stationed at unit 22B...whatever?'

'The tree opposite,' called the man in question.

'Then, Dr Siri, can you give me a good reason why this man might not have seen you leave or arrive at your house?'

Siri took the judge's lead.

'Certainly.' He thought for a moment. Haeng tapped his half pencil on the desk. 'I park my motorcycle in the unfinished project behind my house and leave and enter through the hole in the back fence. That way I don't wake up the children when I arrive late.'

'There you have it,' said Haeng.

'That doesn't make any sense,' said Koomki.

Judge Haeng stood and put one knuckle on the desk. 'What doesn't make any sense,' he said, 'is you petty bureaucrats with your silly rules wasting the time of hardworking forty-year members of the Communist Party. I've humoured you, looked at your evidence, and it is ridiculous. I'd like you to go back to your department and re-evaluate your roles in our society. Remember…'

'Motto time,' thought Siri.

'…the washerwoman takes her laundry to the line and shakes out the creases before hanging out the clothes. Does she look around for those shaken-out creases when she's finished? No. A good Party member understands that not everything has an explanation and knows when to give up. I would like you to deliberate on that thought on your way out, Comrades. Good afternoon.'

The laughter was raucous enough for the nurse to come in from the next ward and tell them not to get Comrade Rajid too excited. He was still weak, she told them, but she couldn't help noticing a broad smile on his face. Two of the three beds in the dingy Mahosot ward were unoccupied. The third was surrounded by people on plastic stools. There was Mr Tickoo, whose sleeping bag was rolled up beneath his son's bed, then Siri, Dtui, with Malee at her breast; Civilai, Geung, and Phosy. They'd just heard Siri's rendition of the previous day's meeting at Justice.

'See?' said Dtui. 'Judge Haeng's secretly liked you all along.'

'I was beginning to think so,' Siri agreed. 'He let me thank him a few times, accepted my gratitude humbly, then limped out leaning on his cane. But it was soon explained to me what was going on. You'll recall, I'd enlisted the aid of the Vietnamese adviser to help me overcome Housing. It turned out he had access to information that not many others knew. It transpires, for example, that Judge Haeng as a government employee has housing allocated to him. But recently, the honourable judge completed the building of a very fine two-storey villa on the way to Dong Dok Institute. It was rumoured that a certain young lady chanteuse at the Anou Hotel is currently residing in his official residence in town. Comrade Phat, as an adviser, merely pointed out to Haeng what an unfortunate precedent it would set to allow Housing to successfully evict the lodgers at my bungalow and sully my name. Haeng obviously agreed.'

They laughed again.

'Darn it,' said Civilai. 'And here I was thinking the tin man had found his heart.'

'And here I am thinking it's time to shake out the creases from Rajid's sheets and let him get some rest,' Dtui announced with a laugh. She stood with her baby and let everyone have a little hand squeeze and cheek sniff of Malee before stepping out. Geung followed her. Mr Tickoo stacked the stools and bowed a goodbye to his son's guests.

Phosy cornered Siri and Civilai and told them he wanted a word with them. They went to the canteen and ordered three glasses of Mahosot coffee, a gooey brew rumoured to have polished off a number of patients who might have pulled through otherwise. They sat by an open window where the scent from the hairy jasmine bushes over-whelmed the general antiseptic atmosphere of the hospital. A fan above their heads kept off the evening mosquitoes.

'All right, boys. Here's the latest,' Phosy said. 'First, we've had no luck at all with the ministries, the Central Committee, or any of the aid programmes. No projects planned or executed in or around Vang Vieng on the dates our villain was there.'

'Damn,' said Siri.

'Doctor, as soon as I got your information yesterday, I

contacted the police station in Pakse. It's one of the few places you can get a phone call through to these days. They're a bit behind in submitting their case ledgers. They still had the last two years' books down there. I thought it might take a few days for them to go through them, but one of the officers remembered a complaint filed by the parents of a missing girl. It rang a bell with the sergeant when I mentioned the logging concession incident.'

'I know the officers in Pakse,' said Siri. 'There wasn't a lot of bell ringing going on down there.'

'I imagine the complaint wouldn't have been remembered, and perhaps not even filed at all, if it hadn't been for the peculiar events that surrounded it,' Phosy continued. 'The mother was still upset about what happened, or almost happened, to her daughter at the concession. The girl had promised solemnly that she'd phone her at the Bureau de Poste on a certain day at a certain time. The mother and father travelled overnight to be there. She didn't call. The parents waited there for five hours. They tried to get through to the Vientiane number the groom had given them for emergencies but the post office clerk told them there was no such code. That's when they went to file with the police.

'It was while they were telling their story that the sergeant tied it together with another case being looked into. And this sounds very much like our villain. There'd been a complaint about a false laissez-passer. You both know how it works – when you travel between provinces you have to report at a police box.'

'Do they take down licence plate numbers?' Siri asked excitedly.

'I'm afraid not.'

'Typical. Something that might have been useful . . .'

'There are army barricades that take down plate numbers, but they tend to ignore anything that isn't privately owned. We're checking with the military posts down there anyway. All they do at the migration checkpoints is slowly and painfully copy down all the information on the laissez-passer and write the date in an exercise book. That information goes to the central registry in Pakse, where somebody else copies it out of the exercise book and into a bigger book—'

'So on ad infinitum,' said Civilai.

'Well, it turns out that the registrar who noted the information was out drinking one night with a couple of mates from the Champasak Forestry Department—'

'Which I believe is now officially known as the Champasak Deforestry Department,' Civilai cut in again.

'Are you going to let me finish, Comrade?'

'Sorry.'

'He told his drinking friends that he'd noticed Forestry had a bigwig from Vientiane in town. They said they hadn't heard about it. They mentioned it to their regional boss, and he confirmed there weren't any visitors from anywhere around the date noted in the book, hence the fake laissez-passer complaint. After further investigation they found that the impostor had checked out of the province at the same checkpoint two days later. Don't forget it takes a while for the checkpoint information to reach the city. These were exactly the dates the parents of the missing girl claimed her suitor was in town. He was calling himself Khamphan this time, by the way. There aren't that many non-military strangers hanging around so the Pakse police put two and two together.'

'Brilliant,' Siri said. 'And what did they do about it?'

'Nothing,' Phosy confessed. He stirred the coffee and condensed milk together in the glass. It was barely liquid. 'They thought it was just a lover's tryst, that the fellow faked the pass so that he could marry his fiancée. They didn't see it as very important.'

'That's more like the police force we know and love,' Siri decided. 'So the story ends there?'

'Yes. We're gathering information about any ongoing projects within a day's drive of Attapeu town over that period. We're going back to all the same ministries. You see, Phan told the parents he was heading north to Vientiane on the night of the wedding. But he didn't cross the northern border. He crossed back into Attapeu. He'd told the parents he'd arranged a laissez-passer for his new bride but there was no mention of her in the ledger at the police checkpoint.'

Civilai whistled. 'So he killed her in Champasak because it was easier than getting her across the border.'

'Either that or he just snuck her across after dark when the police were partying or fast asleep. He could have bribed his way through the barrier with her.'

'I'd go with the first theory myself,' said Siri.

'Me too,' Phosy agreed.

Despite its heat, Siri cradled his glass between his palms, putting off the drinking for as long as possible.

'So,' he said, 'what we have here is a nasty piece of work who's travelling around the country on some official business. It's work that involves returning after two weeks to – I don't know – to follow up or something. He has influence because he's able to falsify documents that pass cursory inspection. He has a truck, which suggests he's at least the head of a section or department.'

'With a very generous gas allowance, judging from all the

travelling he's been doing,' Phosy added.

'Quite. So it's a project that's far more important than the usual road measuring or rice testing – 'Let's look like we've actually done something' – mission. He goes out to the countryside some way from his actual project site and assumes a false identity. He woos a country girl, takes advantage of her naïveté, and she falls in love with him. He promises to come back and marry her. Two weeks later he's in the village bamboozling everyone with all the paperwork he's put together. He convinces them he's registered the marriage and arranged travel documents, and he whisks her off on their wedding night.'

'To a honeymoon in hell.' Civilai sighed.

'You aren't wrong, brother.'

'Then why would somebody so smart be so sloppy?' Civilai asked.

'How do you mean?'

'Well, he was clever enough to fool the regional cadres, and parents and village elders, and then he left the bodies no more than twenty metres from a main road where anyone might stumble across them.'

'I think that's the point,' said Phosy. 'He wants the bodies to be found.'

'Exactly,' Siri agreed. 'It completes the humiliation of the women.'

'Who is he, Doctor?' Phosy asked. 'I mean what's going on in his head? What are we looking for exactly?'

Siri stood his spoon in his coffee and let it go. It didn't fall to the edge, just stood there, trapped.

'Well,' he said, 'my psychology training was two semesters, fifty-odd years ago, and it leaned rather heavily towards Freud. And Freud would probably have suggested that our strangler had problems with his mother, or at least a woman in his past. The symbolism of the pestle doesn't take a great deal of imagination to work out. I wouldn't be surprised if he was impotent. All I can be certain of is this: for him to go to so much trouble, something happened to make our Phan hate women with a vengeance.'

14

COMING TO ONE'S CENSUS

Siri and Daeng sat across from the closed noodle shop on the high bank of the river. They were perched on two old rattan chairs that creaked more than they did. They were well down a bottle of rice whisky, and they both agreed it was pretty damned good stuff. They held their glasses in their outside hands while their inside hands were clasped together. They stared across the tar black Mekhong, which reflected the little lights on the Thai side. The breezes that skipped off the water suggested the rains might come on time this year and spare the earth any more suffering.

'Dr Siri...?' Daeng began.

'You know I'm always tempted to call you Noodle-seller Daeng whenever you say that?'

By this time of night even their slurring was compatible.

'I wasn't referring to you.'

'There's another Dr Siri?'

'That handsome young fellow I met in the south. I was a peanut in those days.'

'You were never a peanut.'

'I was. You just don't understand. You know how peanuts live in their own little shell chambers, and they can see the peanut next door every day, but the gap between them's too narrow to crawl through?'

'I have to confess I've never really thought about peanuts like that.'

'Well, I was that peanut. There you were with Boua, and you were in love then, and you were perfect together. And I was so close every day…but I couldn't touch you. I couldn't get through the gap. And once you both left, I never got over how close we'd been. Eventually I found myself a husband. He was a good man, a rebel like us. And we were content. But every time I saw a peanut it made me sad.'

Siri laughed. 'Daeng, you're starting to sound like Judge Haeng.'

'Don't laugh at me. You know I have trouble expressing myself when I've had a drink or ten. I'm serious.'

'How can you be serious about a peanut?'

'Siri!'

'I'm sorry.'

'All I want to say is, even if you hadn't been with Boua then, we were too important, too big for our own lives. If we'd tried to be together it wouldn't have worked. It could never have been like this. But over the years we got smaller, and I crawled through to your chamber, and now we are . . .'

'The happy peanuts.'

'Exactly.'

'My love, you're so poetic when you've had a few drinks I should keep you sloshed all day.'

'And all day I'd tell you how happy I am with you and thank you for taking me in.'

They leaned their heads together.

'Your turn,' she said.

'To what?'

'To say something nice about me.'

'Shouldn't it be spontaneous?'

'Not necessarily.'

Daeng poured them another drink and Siri considered what story might suit the occasion. He didn't have any fruit or cereal analogies so he resorted to something he knew.

'All right,' he said. 'You know I told you about the visions I was having?'

'The wormy lady and the dog?'

'Yes, well, I told you they were spectres warning me that Rajid was in danger. But at the time I actually thought they were omens about me and the end of my life.'

'I knew that.'

'You did?'

'Absolutely.'

He wasn't really surprised. Daeng had a far better understanding of Siri Paiboun than he did.

'Anyway, once I got it into my head that I was on my way out, all I could think was how unfair it was that we'd had so little time together. If it had happened a year ago before our reunion I would have held out my wrists for the deathly shackles and gone happily. Now you've given me a reason to fight. I don't want either of us popping off into the ether.'

'That's lovely.'

They looked up at the clear, starry sky and grinned at the Great Bear, who always seemed to be falling on his backside.

'The census,' she said.

'You've just changed the subject, haven't you?'

'Not really. It's an ongoing subject. It's what you asked me on Wednesday, about a department that's high profile, has a reasonable budget, whose employees might go back to the same location twice. It just came to me.'

Siri sat up in his seat and glared at his wife.

'To distribute and collect questionnaires,' Siri said.

'Right.'

'You're brilliant.'

'I know. Don't tell Phosy yet.'

'Why not?'

'Because he's a policeman. He's not very subtle. He'd go strutting into their office with his police bell ringing and alert everyone that he's on to them and, if he's there, your maniac would go to ground.'

'What then?'

'Just wander in there. Have a look around. Just some old fellow interested in the census. No danger. You get your information and if you see anything fishy you tell Phosy. That way you can nail the bastard.'

'And you came up with this plan while you were staring at the moon, billing and cooing with me?'

'The woman's brain has two hemispheres,' she slurred. 'One for loving, one for hating. They can operate quite competently at the same time.'

The Minorities Census of '77–'78 was one that the government officially knew nothing about. Despite all the recent posturing on the rights of the non-lowland Lao, it was apparent that nobody actually had a clue as to how many different ethnic groups there were. The prime minister in his annual address put the number at over a hundred, but the Ministry of Culture quoted a figure of sixty-eight. And within those groups, nobody knew how many had survived the war and how many had fled. Before anyone in power was prepared to put his name to a bill to protect the rights and culture of minorities, the

Central Committee needed to know just how many people were involved and what slice of the budget it might eat up. Some sceptics, Siri included, suggested that this might just be a subtle plot to seek out and remove groups still opposed to the PL, but nobody was prepared to admit to such subterfuge.

The collection of data had commenced in early '77. The logistics were daunting, especially considering the fact that most ethnic groups lived in remote locations specifically so they wouldn't be bothered by the government. The census was organized by the Ministry of Interior but operated independently out of a two-storey building on Koovieng Road. There was a director, Comrade Kummai, a clerical staff of six who collated data, three drivers, three mobile teams of survey collectors, and a woman who cleaned and made tea. Of the mobile teams, two flew to remote sites, hired a four-wheel-drive vehicle at the location, and headed off into the hills. The other team operated within convenient driving distance of Vientiane and paid local lowland Lao officials to conduct the surveys among isolated communities in their districts.

When Siri arrived that morning, the cleaning lady showed him directly upstairs to Comrade Kummai's office without asking who he was. The director's door was open, and Kummai was facing an enormous wall chart, making 'Pshh, pshh' sounds, and scratching his head. He seemed to be searching for something in the tangle of lines and figures. The maid left Siri there without saying a word to the director, so he had no choice but to introduce himself.

'Excuse me, Comrade.'

Kummai turned. He was a portly man not much taller than Siri. He wore a white shirt tucked into his belt only where it was in the mood to be. He wore no socks and his trousers were rolled up his shins.

'You're Dr Siri,' he said.

'I am.'

Siri tried to place the director but he was nowhere to be found in Siri's memory.

'Kummai, northern zone 3 regiment,' said the man. 'It's me, Captain Kummai. You were attached to us for a few months. Hot season – '65, I think it was.'

'You've got a good memory, Comrade.'

'Names and dates stick. That's why I ended up here, I suppose. Not surprised you don't remember me, though. I was a slim fellow back then.'

Siri couldn't place him at all but he'd seen so many soldiers. Now if he'd died, that would be a different matter entirely. To Siri's surprise, the head of the Census Department began to unbutton his shirt. Siri took a step back towards the door.

'Remember this?' asked Kummai. He lifted a roll of fat to reveal an appendix scar. Not surprisingly, to Siri it looked like any other appendix scar.

'It's very neat,' Siri decided.

'Of course it is. This is your handiwork. I'd wager half the men in our section have scars courtesy of Dr Siri. Wouldn't be surprised if they boasted to their loved ones about having Siri originals.'

'I should have signed them.'

Kummai laughed uproariously. He crossed to Siri and shook his hand and patted his back.

'Well, well,' he said. 'Dr Siri still alive. What are you now? Eighty? Ninety?'

Siri laughed. 'It feels that way sometimes.'

'I bet it does. I bet it does. Well now, Dr Siri. Let me show you around my domain.'

'I don't want to be a nuisance,' Siri said.

'Nonsense.' Kummai took the doctor's arm and led him out of the office. Siri and Daeng had put together an elaborate ruse to get a look at the inside of the building but the director didn't even ask what he'd come for. The tour began with the upstairs clerical section.

'This is old Dr Siri,' Kummai told the girls. 'Saved my life in the war. Still alive, both of us. Ha ha.'

The clerks seemed mentally exhausted by their director's unending joy. While Kummai went into detail about his burst appendix, Siri noted that the walls were lined with samples of every type of official document there was. As they were leaving the room, he asked the director what they were doing there.

'Checks, Siri. Checks. We often have to verify that documents are authentic. Our lasses in there just compare an original with the sample. If it looks suspicious they call in the heavy brigade. That's me.'

He was still laughing when he reached the bottom of the stairs. In one of the main rooms, two men sat at one desk poring over a large map draped over the desktop like an oversized tablecloth. One of the men was tall and slim with eyes dark and deep enough to dip a fountain pen into. The other was stocky with a broken nose and a scar on his cheek. He could have been nothing other than a boxer.

'Comrades,' said Kummai. The two men looked up. 'This is Siri, my old doctor from the war. I still have his handiwork on my gut.'

Siri and the men shook hands and wished each other good health. Both men had impressive grips.

'These brave men are leaving for the wilds of the Thon River.'

'To interview?' Siri asked.

'To collect the data,' said the boxer. 'We gather a team of locals and train them. They go off into the remote areas with our forms and fill them out. Two weeks later we collect the paperwork and pay off the workers.'

Siri noticed that the slim man was staring at him. It was a look of distrust. A fear of strangers perhaps? Siri felt a tingle the length of his spine.

'Two weeks exactly?' he asked.

'That's how long it usually takes,' said the deep-eyed man.

'And it's just the two of you?'

'These two plus the head of the unit, Comrade Buaphan,' said Kummai. The tingle became a shudder.

Deep Eyes seemed to notice the doctor's change of mood. He raised his brow. 'Are you all right, Doctor?' he asked.

'Of course he's all right,' Kummai cut in. 'In fact he's remarkable for a man his age. I doubt I'll be able to stand up when I'm ninety.'

'Well,' said Siri, 'I've seen everyone else on the project. I suppose I should meet Comrade Buaphan too.'

'Quite right,' said the director. 'I want all my boys and girls to meet the great Dr Siri.' The two men returned Siri's nod and he followed Kummai out of the room. There was a closed door on the far side of the entrance hall and Kummai entered without knocking. Sitting on an armchair reading a Thai magazine was a tall, elegant man with high cheekbones and thick ebony hair that curled at his collar. He was at the opposite end of the best-dressed spectrum from Kummai: light brown stay-press slacks, white shirt buttoned to the collar, and, despite the heat, navy blue socks. This was exactly the identikit picture of the strangler that Siri had drawn in his mind's eye. The man looked up slowly from his article.

'Ah, Buaphan, nothing to do?' asked the director with uncomfortable levity.

'No,' the man replied. His voice was deep and authoritative.

'I thought you might be in a last-minute panic.'

'I'm not.'

Kummai laughed as if it were a joke.

'Right, then,' he said. 'This is Dr Siri, our old bush surgeon.'

Buaphan didn't let go of his magazine or proffer his large hand. He gave a slight nod. 'Doctor.'

'Comrade Buaphan,' said Siri, returning the nod. 'I hear you're taking your team to the Thon River district today.'

'That's right.'

'I didn't see a truck in the yard.'

'Probably because it's not there,' Buaphan said drily then returned to his story. Siri and Kummai looked at one another.

'It's off getting all its bits checked,' said the director. 'And oil and water and all that. Make it fit for the road, you know?'

'Do you drive, Comrade?' Siri asked the top of the tall man's head.

'Yes,' he replied. 'If I had my way.'

'Comrade Buaphan has a problem with our drivers,' the director told Siri.

Buaphan slapped his magazine shut.

'Actually, Doctor, I don't have a problem with the

drivers,' he said. 'I have a problem with inefficiency and waste. The three of us on the team are perfectly capable of driving the truck. Hiring a halfwit to take the wheel seems to me a perfect example of the departure from thrift that our Central Committee is so adamantly against.'

'Comrade Buaphan is a little upset that the ministry insists there be a designated driver on the mission.' Kummai smiled at Siri. The doctor was starting to wonder which of these two was the director of the Census Department and how they'd ever be able to communicate without someone else in the room. The section chief showed a remarkable lack of respect for Kummai, and the old soldier seemed to be in awe of his subordinate.

'I wouldn't mind so much if he could drive,' Buaphan mumbled to himself.

'Comrade Buaphan is a jack-of-all-trades, Doctor,' said the director. 'He wants to drive and coordinate the project at the same—'

Kummai was interrupted by a crunch of gears outside the window. All three men looked out as a large green truck lurched into the yard and screeched to a halt. The driver was bald as a bubble and hunched over the wheel, almost clutching it to his chest. He took his foot off the clutch before taking it out of gear and the vehicle hopped half a metre forward and stalled.

'See what I mean, Doctor?' said Buaphan. 'He always does that. He thinks it's how you're supposed to stop a truck. He has no respect for his engine.'

'Dr Siri,' said Kummai, 'I'm sure you understand you can't just throw somebody out of a job. The driver's a political appointee just as I am. You could no sooner get rid of him than you could me.'

Siri saw Buaphan look away with a 'would that I could' expression. He wondered what kind of appointee the bad-mannered section head might have been. He had the type of arrogance that the doctor had seen before in the children of influential men. Perhaps he was the relative of one of the rich business families bankrolling underground military projects. He certainly had breeding, albeit with an absence of manners. Was he one of the advantaged who could buy his way into a position of authority? And if so, why this job? What was there about regular trips into the country-side to appeal to a man like Buaphan?

'Have you been involved in this project long, Comrade Buaphan?' he asked.

'If I didn't know better, Doctor, I'd say you'd left medicine and gone to work for the secret police,' answered the man. He stood and tossed his magazine onto the chair.

'Buaphan has been with the project since the beginning,' said Kummai.

The section head took a pile of documents and his briefcase from the desk and walked past the two men without saying another word. His footsteps creaked on the parquet floorboards.

'Friendly chap,' Siri said.

'He's a bit brusque but he's very good at his job,' said Kummai.

'And you've worked with him for over a year?'

'Almost two.'

'I would have thumped him long ago.'

Kummai's laugh was genuine but his eyes seemed to agree. They watched through the open window as Buaphan climbed into the passenger seat beside the smiling driver. Deep Eyes and Broken Nose made themselves comfortable among the bags on the flatbed. They put on large straw hats and rolled down their sleeves. It would be a long journey for them.

'Nice truck,' said Siri.

'It's sturdy enough,' Kummai told him. 'It belonged to the Chinese military. We converted it.'

The driver started her up and crunched the gears before finding first. They saw Buaphan raise his eyes to the heavens and yell at the poor man behind the wheel, probably not for the first or last time. Siri stared at the section head. He was an objectionable man, but was he capable of murder? Was he a sadist? As the truck pulled out of the yard, the two men on the back gazed at Siri and exchanged a word or two.

There were other questions that needed to be asked of the men who had just begun the six-hour journey to the Thon. But Siri was a coroner, not a policeman. Phosy was the man to take over from here. He could use his clout to look at the transport records of the Census Department and compare them with the dates of the abductions of the brides. He was almost certain he had his man. His instincts had been on edge since he'd first arrived there. Everything fitted: the access to documentation, the two-week hiatus between distribution and collection, and the truck. There was only one point that didn't mesh with the facts. Champasak, the home of the missing girl they'd most recently learned of, was way down south. It was hardly a comfortable driving distance from Vientiane. Siri turned to Kummai.

'What's their radius?' he asked. 'I mean, how far from Vientiane do they travel?'

'Usually no more than two hundred kilometres.'

'I see.'

'There was too much wear and tear on the trucks. Petrol costs were too high. That's why we started sending two of the teams off on scheduled aircraft flights.'

'But before that they all drove?'

'That's right.'

'When did that system change?'

'A little over a year ago.'

'Did anyone drive to Attapeu before that?'

'Yes, Buaphan's team, in fact. They were away for a couple of months.'

'That's it! Kummai, I have to go.' Siri gave the director's hand a quick shake. 'Good to see you again.'

He turned on his heel and was out of the door and across the yard in seconds. Kummai watched him climb onto his bike, kick it into life, and fly out through the open gates.

'At his age, unbelievable,' said the director, scratching at his appendix scar.

15

A LACK OF POLICE INTELLIGENCE

Central Police Headquarters wasn't a very imposing or secure compound of buildings. There was a fence with no gate and a dirt quadrangle. The main building was a horseshoe with all its doors opening onto the yard. If a visitor didn't bother to stop at the police box in front or go to the little reception desk tucked up on the veranda, nobody would call him back. They'd assume he knew what he was doing. They hoped that with all the uniforms around, nobody would be foolish enough to try anything silly.

Siri drove into the yard like a bull from hell, scattering young officers out of his way, and skidded to a stop directly in front of Phosy's office. The sign over the door read POLICE INTELLIGENCE. All the jokes had already been used up over that one. He ran up the three steps and in through the open doorway. The five desks were of different shapes and sizes. The only thing they had in common was that they were all deserted.

'Shit!' he said aloud. He asked around outside and in the surrounding offices, but all he learned was that two of the staff of Intelligence were at a seminar in the north and the others hadn't left messages to say where they were off to. All anyone knew for sure was that their jeep wasn't parked in the police lot.

Siri found one pen on Phosy's desk that hadn't been dried up by the March heat and wrote, 'Urgent! Call Siri!!!!'

He taped the note to the typewriter and left.

By midday, Phosy still hadn't been in touch, and a cauldron of fears and apprehensions was bubbling inside Siri. He'd just allowed a maniac to head off into the countryside. He should have stopped him. How? Not important. The fact remained that he should have found a way. Twice he'd hurried to the clerical office to phone police headquarters. The receptionist had told him to stop phoning. They had the message and they'd get Phosy to call as soon as he came back. The police telephonist had even gone to the trouble to tell him they weren't stupid. Siri knew when to hold his tongue. He knew also that the responsibility had fallen firmly on his own shoulders. With Dtui nursing a new baby, there were only Siri and Geung at the morgue with nothing to do. Siri put Geung in charge and told the administration clerk that if anyone called they should go to see Madame Daeng immediately.

It was the lunchtime rush at the noodle shop. Daeng had a happy sweat on her brow. The small fan on the post beside her kitchen had its work cut out for it. Siri knew his wife could cook noodles in her sleep; so he stood at her shoulder while she worked and told her everything about his visit to the Census Department that morning. She nodded at the right times, asked for clarification once or twice, and, when he was finished, she reached into her handbag, which hung beneath the spirit table, and handed him all the money she had in there.

'Drive carefully,' she said.

Siri hurried upstairs to fill his day pack, and when he came back down she was there waiting for him with food for the trip. 'Don't forget your lungs don't work so well,' she said.

'I'm just going as a scout,' he told her. 'As soon as Phosy gets there I'm through. But I want to be sure I haven't condemned another girl to death by letting the strangler out of my sight.'

'I know. I trust you.' She squeezed his hand and watched him drive away. Siri looked back and waved. It occurred to him that there was no longer a Siri and a Daeng. They'd become one.

The reason the Intelligence unit had been empty that morning was that Sergeant Sihot had gone down to Champasak to make inquiries about the missing girl, and Phosy and his most senior investigator, Tham, were at the scene of a murder, an old murder.

Once he was certain there had been more than one abduction, Phosy had dispatched the Lao equivalent of an APB. This involved sending wires to the larger cities and towns, then relying on the passing along of documents through police couriers to the more remote stations. It might be up to a month before he could be sure everyone had received a copy of the memo. That's why he'd been surprised to receive the call at eight that morning.

'I'd like to speak to Inspector Phosy,' the voice had said.

'I'm Phosy.'

'I got your note about the girls.'

'And who are you?'

'I'm Sergeant Oudi from the police box at Kilometre 38 on the Bolikham Road intersection. But I'm calling from the bank in Pakxan. The manager lets us use—'

'I'm listening, Sergeant.'

'All right. Well, they were fixing the bridge down at kilo-metre 10 last year, and one of the workers went to take a leak in the bushes, and he ran across these bones.'

'Just bones?'

'Yes, Comrade. And no particular order to them, all scattered around this tree. I went to take a look, just for curiosity's sake. They could have been an animal for all I knew, but I found this long human hair. So I figured it was a dead woman, and the beasts had laid into her. Nothing to suggest there'd been foul play, and there hadn't been any reports of missing persons. So I buried the remains just to keep her spirit happy, you know? And I wrote out the report and sent it in with the ledger. Didn't hear anything more about it.'

Phosy hadn't been surprised there was no follow-up. They barely had enough staff to stack the ledgers, let alone read them.

'All right,' he said. 'So what makes you think this could be connected to our case?'

'The ribbon, Inspector. There was pink ribbon around one of the bones.'

While Sergeant Oudi and his colleague dug up the bones he'd so lovingly buried six months earlier, Phosy and Tham rummaged around the tree.

'You're sure this is the right place?' Phosy called to the local policeman.

Oudi held his hand against the amulet at his neck for the tenth time. Spirits didn't take too kindly to having their bones dug up.

'Yes, Comrade,' he said. 'All around there, they were.'

'And apart from the hair and the ribbon, you didn't find anything else out of the ordinary?'

Phosy had withheld the most awful component of the murders from his memo. He believed it would be beneficial to have that one vital piece of evidence held in reserve in case they had a suspect.

'I mean anything at all,' Phosy pushed. 'No matter how irrelevant you think it might be.'

'Yes, Comrade. Oh, wait. There was something.'

'Yes?'

'A pestle.' Phosy's heart clenched. 'I found this pestle while I was gathering up the bones.'

'And what did you do with it?'

'It was a good one, Comrade. I took it home for my wife.'

Police headquarters had found it in its heart to provide Phosy's department with a jeep. It was a 1950 Willys, and Phosy liked the solid feel of it around him. It had a limited petrol ration, so it spent much of its time sitting idle under the corrugated tin carport. But this trip to Pakxan had been so urgent the inspector hadn't thought twice about filling the tank and putting two spare containers in the back. The cans stood either side of the remains of the poor woman now wrapped in a green groundsheet: the strangler's fourth suspected victim. The pestle, removed amid a scene of consternation from the kitchen of the sergeant's wife, was wrapped in the package along with the ribbon and hair. It was Phosy's intention to take all of it directly to the morgue and go through it with Siri.

Investigator Tham was driving. He was in his fifties, somewhat sedentary but a good soldier, more of a follower than a leader. Phosy took the opportunity to thumb through the notes he'd received from the ladies at the Lao Patriotic Women's Association. He was looking for the anecdotal account of the wedding he'd heard about from Siri. He needed to confirm the location. If it was within driving distance from Pakxan he might be able to tie the two together.

'Here,' he said.

'What's that, sir?' Tham looked to his right and saw his boss pawing through all the junk in the flapless glove compartment.

'Any idea if there's a map in h…? Ah, yes.'

'Want me to stop?'

'No, keep going. I'll manage.'

Phosy unfolded the map and quickly homed in on the location where they'd just found the bones. He then traced his finger along the highway until he found the village he was looking for.

'Damn! It all fits,' he said. Tham turned to him again and plummeted into a deep pothole. 'Don't feel obliged to look at me, Tham. You concentrate on the road and I'll work the map.'

'OK.'

'The wedding was held at Paknyun. It's forty kilometres from the intersection. Given the state of the road, he was probably able to drive there in a couple of hours. It's just far enough away to be under the jurisdiction of another police force. So if the parents did make a complaint about a missing daughter, the news probably wouldn't make it to our Sergeant Oudi. He's very smart, our strangler. He's got it all worked out. Tham, I want you to stop at the next village on the main road and wait for the bus going back out to Bolikham.'

'That'll take me away from Vientiane,' Tham said.

'That's right. Any problem with that?'

'I promised my wife I'd pick up some big head catfish on the way home.'

'Right. And I promised the parents of a beautiful girl in Ban Xon that I'd catch the maniac who killed their daughter. See any difference in priority there?'

'Yes, sir. Sorry.'

'You'll stay on the bus till you get to Paknyun. I need all the information I can get from the people who attended the wedding. Don't tell them we might have found the missing daughter. It's possible we won't be able to identify these bones. I don't want to upset them unduly.'

'But you think it's her?'

'Yes, Tham. I do.'

When the police jeep pulled up outside Daeng's noodle shop, it was already three p.m., and Madame Daeng was sitting outside on a rattan chair. She was dressed in her thick gabardine workers' trousers, a loose-fitting blue shirt, and boots. Since her move to Vientiane she'd worn her hair short and wild. Now she'd greased it back, and at first glance Phosy thought she was a man. He jumped from the jeep and looked behind Daeng to see a CLOSED UNTIL FURTHER NOTICE sign on the shop shutter.

'Madame Daeng, what's so urgent?'

'What on earth kept you, Phosy? I've been waiting for hours.' She threw a pack into the back of the jeep.

'I just got back,' he said, eyeing the bag. 'I dropped some bones off at the morgue. I didn't get the message till I met the clerk.'

'Are you alone?'

'I dropped Tham off at a bus stop. Why?'

'I think you're going to need to pick up one or two officers on the way.'

'On the way where?'

'To the Thon River.' She walked past him and climbed up to the passenger seat.

'What are you talking about? I've just driven all the way from Pakxan. What's at the Thon River?'

'Your murderer, Inspector. Siri left already. He has a three-hour start on us.'

'What's all this "us"? If you're serious about the murderer being at Thon, I'm certainly not going to take an elderly lady with me. It would be more than my job's worth.'

'Well, Phosy, that would be a terrible shame, because then you wouldn't get to hear about it. Dr Siri will be massacred, the killer will claim his next victim, and you will have – dare I say it – egg on your face.'

'Madame Daeng, listen! Withholding evidence is a serious offence. It's not a game.'

'I'm not withholding anything. I'm just planning to tell you on the journey.'

Phosy slapped the fender of the jeep and hurt his hand.

'You aren't going to bully me into this. Besides, you can't go to the Thon River. You don't have a laissez-passer to leave Vientiane Prefecture.'

'But you have one. Nobody's going to notice a frail old lady. I'll scrunch down on the floor under a blanket. They won't search your vehicle. You're a policeman. Now come on. It's getting late.'

'Madame Daeng, I—'

'You're wasting valuable time.'

Phosy was still fuming as they neared the intersection at

Sangkam. The road was in an awful state. Daeng sat beside him on the passenger seat and the two young officers he'd requisitioned from HQ sat in the back. She'd told him the entire story as Siri had told it to her, and he didn't like it one tiny bit.

'How could you let Siri go after him?' Phosy asked.

Daeng laughed. 'How could I stop him? You know Siri as well as I do. I could say, "Siri, please don't go" and he'd go anyway, and we'd both feel bad. Or I could give him my blessing and a bag of noodles for the journey, and only I'd feel bad.'

'You're each as ornery and obstinate as the other,' he yelled above the drone of the engine. 'When you first suspected it might have something to do with the Census Department you should have contacted me straight away. I'm sick of you two playing detective.'

'You weren't here. Your office was empty. Somebody had to play policeman.'

'There were other officers around.'

'Like them?' Daeng nodded to the rear-view mirror. Phosy looked at the hairless faces of the two young men he'd snatched from headquarters. They were still twenty kilometres from their destination, and they already looked as if they might wet themselves with fear. 'What would they have done?'

'And what, tell me, is a seventy-three-year-old man going to do?'

'You have a short memory, Phosy. Just how many of your cases have been solved by the doctor?'

Phosy didn't answer. He sulked all the way past the intersection. The window wipers smeared an omelette of insects across the thick glass. The jeep listed left and right as it negotiated the deep truck furrows. Eventually the policeman deigned to speak.

'I think he's got this one wrong,' he said.

'Why so?'

'The girl up in the north – the case I went up there to investigate – it happened way back in '69. The Census Department was run by the old regime in those days. There's nobody left from that era.'

'I've been thinking about that too, Phosy. Siri placed this man Buaphan's accent as from the central region, and cultured. I can't work out what someone like that is doing working for the Republic on an official project. The doctor suggested he might be from an influential family that had bought him a position. If that's so, he might well have spent time up north with the Royalists during the war. He might have been an engineer or something. Plus she might have been his first victim. If he started his killing spree back then he wouldn't have needed the Census Department job as a pretext to move around and attack these girls. There was chaos. He would have had ample opportunity. He liked it so much he got a job with the new regime so he could continue his hobby.'

'You think somebody high profile would take such a gamble?'

'Why not, Phosy? You've seen how arrogant he is. He believes he's better than all of us. He's planned it all so care-fully. He can't imagine anyone catching him. In his mind, he's God.'

16

SWIMMING THROUGH ROCKS

Phan sat naked and cross-legged beneath the tree he'd selected on his previous visit. He welcomed the ravenous red ants and vampiric mosquitoes that chewed at his flesh. Eventually they too would learn he was invincible. By the light of the candles he looked through the documents one last time: the registration of marriage, the housing certificate, the laissez-passers, permission from the Social Relations office, bank statements, a police letter verifying that he was unmarried and not wanted for any crimes, birth certificate, Party membership record, and, just for icing on the cake, a full curriculum vitae.

He lay back on the itchy grass and sighed. How wonderful it was to live in a state where the actual person was no longer important. Everything existed only on paper, including him. A man who merely walked the earth with nothing but breath and a strong beating heart was no longer a man in the Democratic Republic of Laos. God had been replaced by an earthbound bookkeeper.

'I carry identification, therefore I am,' he said. And in this incarnation he was Phumphan Bourom of the Irrigation Department: a senior engineer with a degree from East Germany. He would overwhelm the village with his paperwork, let them mull over it, knowing there was no

way for them to verify its authenticity before the wedding. It was all signed and stamped by respected cadres in the capital. The village heads would co-sign the forms and give the go-ahead for a ceremony that had already been planned. It was inevitable because the responsibility had been removed from their shoulders. There was nothing a local administrator liked more than having someone else make decisions for him.

Phan sat up on his elbows and looked for the eleven billionth time at the celestial error between his legs, hoping that overnight it might have made up its mind. This way or that? One or the other?

His mother had made that call early on in his life. She'd thought the little dresses and pink ribbons from the missionary's sewing box might prod her son/daughter off the fence.

'But she's getting so tall,' dumb Father had said. 'The face isn't a girl's at all.'

Mother ignored him. She persevered. She even coached her only child in the arts of womanhood.

A mockery at school.

Every single waking day a nightmarish humiliation.

Swimming through rocks.

The word 'Miss' was on his national identity card so this gawky, hairy-chinned female, still in his mother's pink ribbons, waded uncomfortably through life to the age of fourteen. And then, all at once, the strings snapped.

There was a war on. Neighbours were shocked but not particularly surprised to find the husband and wife hacked to death in their own home with a machete. The odd daughter was missing, presumed violated and dead. And Phan's life began. It was an awful, violent period in Laos, but his country wasn't unused to such brutality. There were unnecessary deaths and, in the confusion, identities became vacant. Phan began his metamorphosis, stepping out of one skin and into the next and the next, becoming more confident with each shedding. He tried on other men's lives as if he were trying on shirts at the market. He was a patriot fleeing the Royalists, a deserter escaping from the Reds, a pacifist seeking refuge from aggression. With each stage he deliberately became more of a man in his own mind. And to complete the transition – to prove that he had been meant to be male all along – he decided to take a wife.

He knew how to talk to girls. He'd been one. He'd heard them gossip and understood what they expected. He was in Luang Nam Tha in the north, living the life of a man whose papers he'd taken: a man who lay wounded on a battlefield. After learning a little about his family and history Phan had finished him off with a bayonet. In the skin of this man, Phan had met a girl. She was beautiful and innocent and so in love with him he could sense the warmth emanate from her body when they were close. He felt something for her too, although he wasn't sure what to call it. He believed, somewhere in his confusing emotional spin drier of a soul that this was the solution to the puzzle. Everything would find its true place once he became a husband.

The ceremony had been simple: sweet, and low-key with only her close friends and relations. He'd charmed them all. They loved him. They'd set aside a room for the newly married couple behind the family house. It was a simple thatched building. As sound travelled unimpaired through bamboo the parents had arranged to be discreetly absent.

Phan had planned it in his head. It was to be a slow,

romantic night. As they held each other in the lamplight he would explain his circumstances. She might be a little surprised, but she would hear him out. After a moment of thought she would tell him that she loved him for himself – that everything else was unimportant.

But the drink had turned her mind. As soon as they were alone, she tore at his clothing like some wild beast. He held her off, tried to engage her in conversation, but she seemed unnaturally obsessed with his body. 'Very well,' he thought, 'let her see me. That might work just as well.' But first she touched him between the legs, then she sat back to look, and her mouth fell open. She ceased her attack and fell backwards against the wall of the building. The posts and beams shuddered. It was the mocking expression on her face, not the subsequent laughter that left a scar branded on his soul and closed down his heart. It was a look of disgust – one that he would see in the eyes of every woman he met from that day forward.

He'd strangled her to death that night there in her parents' back room. He'd driven his medical supply truck a hundred kilometres south to the outskirts of Nam Tha, parked beside the highway, and carried her body into the undergrowth. It was all over. But as he headed into the town in search of a new battlefront and a new identity, thoughts of his untouched bride flooded his mind. She was his. In the eyes of the Lord Buddha and the Royalist government, she belonged to him. She'd sworn her devotion. He had the paperwork to prove it. The fact that she was dead didn't terminate that contract. He could still have the honeymoon he'd imagined in his dreams.

It took him most of the day to put together the equipment and supplies he needed. When he found her again he was dismayed to discover her body so ravaged by nature in such a short time. But it didn't matter. He wined and dined her, told her his secret, and at last, he gave her the pleasure she'd so obviously craved. He tied her to a tree with ribbon and, as he sat naked admiring his new bride, he became aware of a powerful joy that had welled up inside him. He had never experienced such elation. The feeling was deep in his groin, exactly as he'd always imagined it to be. He had experienced some kind of sexual pleasure. He was complete.

That seemed far in the past to him now. There had been so many disruptions since then. Political changes were being made all around him. After the ceasefire in '72 he moved to Vientiane and adopted an identity nobody could question. A lot of new people were arriving and leaving each day. The Royalists could see the inevitable Red sun dawning on their empire and, one by one, they slipped across the river, unannounced, under cover of darkness. Phan had merely stepped into the shadow one of them left behind. He found work, did well, and as good men were hard to find in the empty city, he was offered a position with the Census Department. It was ideal: travel, anonymity, a veritable factory of documentation. Everything was set for him to prove his masculinity again and again without fear of discovery.

He had wrested possession of the truck from the imbecile and left him doing some inane, unnecessary task. Phan would spend this night here in the bridal suite remembering each detail of the honeymoons he'd enjoyed with his five wives and the pleasure he'd given them. He'd dream of tomorrow's wedding and the seduction of the bright and *beautiful teacher, Wei, and he'd sleep the sleep of a man – a real man.*

Phosy drove into Natan at nine p.m. He stopped once or twice to ask directions to the house of the resident government cadre, but it wasn't really that difficult to spot: the largest wooden building on the main street. They parked opposite and stepped down from the jeep to stretch like waking cats. It had been a bone-jarring ride, and they were exhausted. For Phosy it had been a day of particularly slow hours. The administrator came out of his house before they could knock or shout hello. He was a young man relying on one or two chin hairs to lend him an air of authority.

'Can I help you, Comrades?' he asked. Phosy and the policemen showed him their identification papers.

'We are here on a very serious police investigation,' Phosy told him. 'We need to contact the team collating the census data immediately.'

'You mean immediately now?' the cadre asked.

'Unless you know of any other type of immediately.'

'Well, that might be a problem.'

'Why?' asked Phosy.

'The census people did pass by earlier, and they presented their credentials. But after they left here they were due to split up. They said they've got data to collect from twenty districts in two days. The only way they can do that is to set up three bases to make it more convenient for the collectors to get to.'

'Presumably they told you where they'd be based?'

'My deputy, Comrade Sounthon, organized it for them. But he's off on a night hunt with the locals. You know? Headlamps, shooting lorises and other nocturnal game.'

'Animals too drowsy to run away,' Daeng remarked.

'Does anyone else have any idea where we can find the census collators?' Phosy asked.

'One or two people, Comrade Inspector, but they're all out on the hunt.'

'Damn.'

'Have you had an old fellow on a motorcycle here this evening asking the same question?' Daeng asked.

'Not that I've heard, Auntie, and I hear most things.'

Daeng involuntarily squeezed Phosy's arm.

'What time are you expecting your deputy back?' the policeman asked.

'Sun-up usually.'

Phosy looked at his weary passengers.

'All right. Then we could use a few hours' sleep. Can I trouble you for accommodation?'

'Guesthouse is just around the corner, Comrade. Turn left at the tyre repairers.'

What the cadre had described to be the cheapest rooms in the province had every right to be. The kapok mattresses smelled of sweat and worse, and the stuffing had coagulated into lumps. The patter of tiny feet on the tin roof hinted at an all-night squirrel hoedown. Phosy had long since given up the thought of sleep. He sat on the veranda steps drinking weak tea from the communal thermos and waited for the sun. He hadn't said anything to Daeng but he was worried about Siri. Out here they weren't far from the Thai border. Rebels occupied the hills and insurgents crossed the river to create havoc. Bandit gangs and renegade gunmen often hijacked lone vehicles. A Triumph motorcycle in good condition would be quite a catch. He hadn't thought to ask at the police boxes they'd passed whether they'd sighted the doctor, and now, deprived of sleep and mad at everyone, he imagined all the fates that might have befallen his friend.

'Can't sleep, Inspector?' Phosy turned his stiff neck to see Daeng behind him in the candlelight. She came to sit beside him on the step, and he poured her tea.

'The kids up too?' she asked.

'No, they're made of putty. They could sleep on a pile of jackfruit.'

'Jackfruit sounds quite comfortable compared to the beds in there.'

The indigo sky had begun to pass through less depressing hues on its journey to blue, and the sounds of happy voices hummed in the distance.

'I wonder if that's our hunting party returning,' Phosy said.

'I do hope so. I would like to get away early.'

Phosy smiled. 'Oh, no, Madame Daeng. You blackmailed your way onto the jeep yesterday. You aren't going to get away with that again.'

'Inspector, you wouldn't leave a girl alone in the wilds?'

'There's a good restaurant on the main street. You can swap noodle stories with the owner. This is a police inquiry, not a tour. You'll stay in town and we'll pick you up on our way back.'

'You're sure you can't use an extra gun?' She patted her fat handbag.

'If I thought for a second you'd brought a weapon with you, I'd have you in handcuffs right now.'

'Why didn't I get offers like that before I got married?'

'Madame Daeng!'

'All right. I'm joking. I'll swap recipes and crochet while you're away doing manly things.'

'Good.'

The voices had become louder now, and a small posse of happy hunters loomed through the morning mist along the unlit street. At first it appeared they were dressed in large animal suits, but it was merely that they were festooned with carcasses. If there was a more frightening gallery of rare, beautiful, and bleeding creatures, Daeng hadn't seen it.

'Have a successful night, boys?' she called.

'Fantastic, auntie,' said one.

'Half of them just fell out of the trees from the shock of hearing gunshots,' said another. They all laughed.

'Bravo,' she clapped.

'Which one of you is Sounthon?' Phosy asked.

A short, plump man wearing a lei of big-eyed lorises stepped forward. 'I am.'

'Well, I'm Inspector Phosy from National Police Headquarters, and I need the locations of the three census takers.'

'Comrade,' the man laughed, 'I've just come back from—'

'Look! I don't care whether you're just back from the northern front full of bullet holes. I want the locations and I want them ten minutes ago.'

Sounthon had arranged accommodation for the visitors in three villages that were central to the collection zones. They were thirty kilometres apart and formed a perfect triangle on the map. But the deputy had no information as to which collector was staying at which location. They'd have to go and see for themselves. Phosy and the two young officers were nine kilometres from the first site, a village called Ban Noo. It was only the absence of vegetation and a thin layer of sand that distinguished the road from the surrounding landscape. The journey had been more rock than roll.

'What do we do if he's there?' asked one of the fearful officers.

'We talk to him,' Phosy said, concentrating on keeping the jeep on the track. 'We ask a few pertinent questions. We check out his attitude. We say we're just making a few inquiries and we'd like his cooperation. We start with things like work, his routines, marital status, family – the usual. Then we hit him with something direct like, "Have you ever met a woman called Ngam in Ban Xon?" We look into his eyes and see if there's a reaction. And we take it from there.'

'Then we shoot him,' came a voice. Madame Daeng's smiling face loomed in the rear-view mirror as she rose from behind the back seat. Phosy slammed on the brakes and ran into a tall clump of swollen-finger grass. All three men turned to see her, large as life, clutching the roof.

'Madame Daeng? What the ...?' Phosy yelled.

'I told you I could scrunch up to almost nothing,' she smiled.

'But where were you?'

'Under the tarpaulin behind the back seat.'

'There's barely ten centimetres down there.'

'I'm pliable.'

Phosy was furious. 'Get out!' he said.

She laughed. 'What, here?'

'I told you to stay at Natan.'

'You want me to walk all the way back there on my arthritic legs?'

Phosy hammered his fists against the steering wheel.

'Madame Daeng, if you were a man I'd punch you on the nose, I swear I would.'

'If you did, even if I weren't a man, I'd punch you back.'

The young officers laughed.

'You two can wipe those smiles off, right now.'

'Listen, son,' she said, 'believe me, I can help. If I thought I'd hamper your investigation I wouldn't have come. Really I wouldn't.'

'I know your history. But that was . . .'

'Then you know I can only be an asset. Siri's up here somewhere and, brave as he is, I want to be around to ...to support him. That's what couples do. And, Phosy, a steering wheel can only take so much abuse.'

Phosy gave one last punch then put his hands on his head. He knew when he was beaten.

'Let this be a lesson to you boys,' he said to the policemen. He left it there, and they didn't ever learn what the lesson was. Phosy reversed out of the grass and drove in silence to Ban Noo.

Comrade Ying Dali, the one-time North Vietnam region 6 boxing champion, now gone to seed, sat beneath a camouflaged tarpaulin receiving piles of paper from two colourful characters: one with a cheroot hanging from her lip, the other with a crossbow strapped to his back. Phosy killed the overheated engine and watched.

'According to Siri's description, he's one of the two junior officials,' Daeng said. Phosy kept quiet.

They waited until the boxer was alone before strolling across to him. They were in a village so basic the main house was a thatch of twigs. They were well-plaited twigs but really nothing to stop a good wolf puff. It was a picturesque place with a stream, like an illustration for a month on a calendar: heaven, unless you had to live in such an isolated place with no power or sanitation or medicines. The boxer stood when the strangers reached his lean-to.

'Comrades?' he said.

Phosy introduced himself and his men, ignoring Daeng completely. He announced that they were investigating a murder in the district. It was a small untruth only in that the offence had not yet taken place. He hoped he wasn't tempting fate.

'Can you tell us exactly how your system here works?' he asked Ying.

'Well, it's quite simple,' Ying began. 'We draw up an area into grids. We come in and identify literate people. We pay them a few *kip*, and they take our questionnaires off to the surrounding minority villages. We come back two weeks later, and they bring us the results. We check that everything's in order, pay them the rest of their fees, and give the documents to the section head to collate.'

'Comrade Buaphan?' Phosy asked, consulting an imaginary list in his notebook.

'That's right.'

'How do you get them to him?'

'Depends. If he's busy he sends the driver. But he prefers to drive himself. He's a bit touchy about his truck.'

'And is that the only communication you have – the truck? I mean you don't have walkie-talkies or such?'

'No, they don't work over these distances, and the mountains block shortwave signals as well. So we rely on the truck to ferry messages back and forth.'

'So for long periods you wouldn't know what the other two men are up to, whether they're at their bases or not?'

'Well, that's true. But I mean, we can tell. If the work's not done we know who's been slacking off. Comrade Buaphan's always efficient.'

'Do you know anything about Comrade Buaphan's personal life?' Phosy asked.

'No. He's a bit of a loner. When we aren't on the road – I mean, outside office hours – we never see him.'

'Does he have family?' Daeng asked from her rearguard position out in the sun. Phosy turned and glared at her.

'He had a wife once, I believe,' the boxer replied. 'Somewhere up in the north. She passed away.'

Phosy took a step to his left to eclipse Madame Daeng. 'Have you seen him with any women? Girlfriends? Doing any socializing on these trips?'

'No, but like I say, apart from the journey out and back we don't see each other that much. Why? What's he done?'

Phosy ignored the question. 'How do you get along with him?'

'He's all right. He can be really charming at times. He knows some funny stories when he's in the mood. But I don't get the feeling he's in this type of work for the social contact. I think it's the isolation he likes, being up here in the hills. It can be addictive, I have to admit.'

Madame Daeng had sidled around to get shade from a cow's-earring tree. She was biding her time until Phosy ran out of questions. Her chance came sooner than she'd expected.

'Well, thank you…' Phosy began. Daeng put up her hand. 'What?'

'One last question,' she said and smiled too sweetly for him to refuse.

Phosy waved her on.

'There are women at your office?'

'Yes, about half a dozen.'

'How does Buaphan act around them?'

'Act?'

'Yes, is he friendly? Does he flirt?'

Ying laughed. 'One thing I could never imagine is Comrade Buaphan flirting with the women at the office. If you wanted a playboy you couldn't go past my office mate, Nouphet. He's the charmer. But Buaphan, no ma'am. He's really not that type.'

'What type is he?' Phosy asked.

'Well, he's...don't get me wrong. I get along with him OK. But Buaphan can be a bit...self-important. It's as if he thinks he's better than other people. It doesn't worry me, but I know the clerks and the cleaner and the drivers complain about him treating them like servants. They gossip about him a lot.'

From Ying, the boxer, they learned at which of the three locations Buaphan was based. In order to get there they had to return along the track they'd just taken and go all the way back to the intersection with the main road. There they were to head north, away from Natan, until they arrived at the small village of Nahoi, where Comrade Nouphet, the playboy, was billeted. The village was at a second turn-off that led up into the mountains to the remote outpost where Buaphan had chosen to spend his time.

Phosy had yielded the driving to one of his men, who had his nose up against the windscreen studying the rocks ahead. Phosy sat in silence, riding the bumps.

'I could drive if you get tired,' Daeng said.

'No!' snapped Phosy, still deep in his huff.

'You know?' Daeng said. 'It doesn't make sense. Something worries me about all this.'

'And something's worrying me,' said the policeman, with a finger pointed at her nose. 'And do you know what that is? It's you. I swear, old lady, if I have to tie you up and duct tape your mouth to keep you quiet, I will have no hesitation.'

She wasn't offended. He was a nice boy who had commanded men in the jungle. He was just a little too fixated on authority. She knew he'd get over it. She smiled serenely and watched the birds that fluttered from the bushes as the noisy jeep approached.

The main road was only marginally better than the track. At the first intersection they were only five kilometres from Natan and Phosy considered making that detour to drop off the heavy weight that had attached herself to their party. But the drive to and from the first base had taken four hours and he couldn't afford to waste any more time. He reassumed the role of driver on the way to Nahoi and decided it would be wise to stop off there to check as to whether Comrade Nouphet had seen Buaphan or the truck. While Daeng and the two officers went to the small road-side market to buy food and drink for the next leg of their journey, Phosy walked into the village to find the second census collator.

It was an untidy place decked out all in brown, courtesy of the road dust. He was given directions by a six-year-old girl who had a two-year-old at her hip. She walked him up the dirt path to the headman's house, where the man from Vientiane was staying. The headman was sitting on a home-made rocker on his porch. He was dark and bony like leather stretched over spare washing-machine parts. He waved as Phosy approached.

'Good health,' the man said in very strongly accented Lao. 'You looking for the boy?'

'Good health,' Phosy replied. 'The census collector, yes.'

'He's up there someplace.' He pointed over his shoulder in the direction of the range of hills behind the village.'

'Far?' Phosy asked.

'Could be by now. He left at midday. Said there was some problem with forms or something. Somebody took the wrong ones, I believe. Same thing happened last time.'

'He walked up?'

'Took the truck. There's a piddling little track goes up there.'

Phosy considered this for a moment.

'He took the census truck?'

'No, he took mine.'

Phosy looked at the poor surroundings. 'You have a truck?'

'Some Royalist coward abandoned it here when he was fleeing the PL. I don't get to use it much, what with petrol being the price it is. It was just sitting growing weeds. When the boy was here last time he fixed it up. He gave us a few *kip* for petrol and said he'd have it back by tomorrow. He's good with motors, that boy – wasted on paperwork. He could make a nice living as a mechanic, I reckon.'

The conversation on the way up to Buaphan's encampment was exclusively about Nouphet and his truck. Phosy had allowed Daeng into the discussion only to recap Siri's comments about the boy.

'The doctor said he was keen eyed, seemed to notice things,' she recalled. 'He might have mentioned he was good-looking.'

'Might have?'

'I was cooking lunch at the time. But you do know what this means?'

'You'll probably enlighten me.'

'I see we have not one but two suspects. Young Nouphet is good at fixing motors, and I'd guess every decent-sized village has at least one old truck lying around in need of repairs. He seems just as likely a suspect as Buaphan. I think you need to—'

'I know what my responsibilities are.'

'Of course you do, I'm sorry.'

'I'll question Buaphan. If he's our strangler, I'll know.'

'Policeman's intuition?' Daeng smiled.

'It's a little like doctor's intuition. I remind you we're here following up on a guess by your husband.'

'It's certainly more than a guess, Inspector. And I remind you your policeman's intuition hasn't done you much good so far in this case. Siri has a sixth sense about these things.'

'Then let's hope his sixth sense hasn't put him in a grave somewhere.'

He sucked air through his teeth as if to vacuum the words back, but it was too late. A veil had dropped over his passenger's face. Phosy hadn't meant to say it. She'd goaded him. Her constant interference had forced him to it. Her smile had become pinched and her glazed eyes stared at the sky. In an attempt to right his mistake, Phosy tacked on, 'Of course, we all know how indestructible Siri is.'

But the damage was done. For the rest of the journey up the winding mountain road, Daeng had nothing to say.

17

THERE GOES THE BRIDE

Phan drove slowly along the main street, beeping his horn at people he recognized. They waved back or held up a thumb as he passed: the returning hero. He went directly to see the headman and his wife. The old woman came running out to meet him and opened the truck door so he could step down. She squeezed his hand and told him how handsome he looked. He asked if she and her husband were well. He told her he was excited but joked that he was marrying the second most beautiful girl in the village. The headman had married the prettiest. She giggled and punched his arm and led him inside.

It was all so formulaic. People were boringly predictable. Once they'd worked themselves up into a lather of enthusiasm, they'd believe any shit you cared to toss their way. He handed a pile of papers to the headman, who didn't even bother to read them. He just asked where he should sign. He said he'd invited the district political cadre from Natan and his wife, but it was far, and the wedding was late. The headman doubted they'd come. They'd done up the school very nicely for the reception, he was told. There should be a good turnout. They hoped he had a strong constitution because there was plenty of liquor. All the women had been cooking since sun-up.

*The children had learned a dance, et cetera...la-di-da
...blah-de-blah.*

*'All right,' Phan thought, 'just get on with it. The sooner
it starts, the sooner it'll all be over.'*

*But nothing was due to begin until six so Phan asked if
he could take a nap. He'd driven directly from Vientiane,
he told them, and needed to rest. He lay shirtless on the
thin mat that covered the bamboo floor. His jacket was on
a hook. Thirty-six degrees celsius, hot as hell, but he
always gave them a jacket show. They'd remember the
jacket long after he'd taken it off and rolled up his sleeves.
There might be a camera. Someone probably took the bus
to the town and used the money they'd all saved up to buy
film to record the happy event. It was no problem. He'd
insist on taking a picture of the guests. While they were
lining up he'd briefly flip open the back of the camera and
let in the light just long enough to leave them with twenty-
four exposures of snow. Not a shred of actual evidence that
he ever existed.*

*He waved the banana-leaf fan in front of his face. What
a place. They lived beside a main road and didn't even have
electricity. How could anybody exist like this? How awful
it was that somebody as special as he was had to mix with
such people. So much had gone wrong already that day. He
needed some good fortune. Never mind. A few more hours
and he'd be driving back along that road to the honeymoon
supper. Before midnight, he'd have his sex and be whole
again. Not so long now. Not so long.*

The sun's glare filled up the windscreen. The dust-jacketed
jeep pulled into the clearing that marked the end of the
track. There were a few unloved houses around its rim. It

had the mood of a village that had seen bigger and brighter days. The clearing had two crude soccer posts at either end, but Phosy knew that the labour invested in preparing that land hadn't merely been to give the children somewhere to play. He'd seen its like before.

'I wonder how many helicopter drops this place saw in its heyday,' Madame Daeng said to nobody in particular.

Phosy parked on the halfway line, and they all climbed from the jeep, slowly unknotting their joints. They carried a different type of tension with them also. They'd begun to feel it when the odometre announced they were two kilometres from their destination. They all knew what it was. There's a gland somewhere in the human body whose sole purpose is to allow pessimism an outlet. It is particularly active when you're on the doorstep of danger, when you know a homicidal maniac is somewhere ahead of you, one who is capable of unthinkable acts of cruelty. Real-life evil couldn't begin to match the horrors the pessimism gland secreted.

Nobody was in a rush to come and greet the new arrivals.

'Anybody else not see what I don't see?' asked Daeng.

'We're missing a truck,' said Phosy.

'We didn't see it on our way up,' Daeng agreed. 'So, unless there's another way out of here, and I don't see that either, the truck had to leave over three hours ago.'

Phosy thought about it. 'We've come from the two other collection points and nothing passed us going in the opposite direction. The only way it could have gone was north at the Ban Nahoi intersection, away from the census bases.'

'That is a very bad sign,' Daeng decided.

'And where the hell is everybody from this place?'

'Twelve o'clock,' said Daeng, pointing north. The

policemen turned to see a bedraggled couple in their fifties coming toward them. Given the ghost-town feel of the surroundings, they could easily have been the curators of a haunted historical site. They had all the attributes.

'Good health,' the man said, although he obviously hadn't been blessed with it. He was pitted with childhood smallpox scars and had a yellowish sheen to his skin. His anorexic wife made him look like a paragon of health by comparison.

'Good health,' said Phosy, reluctantly shaking the man's hand. 'We were hoping to see Comrade Buaphan.'

'He left,' said the host.

Phosy thought, 'damn' but said, 'When?'

'Around midday. Went off in the truck. Left me in a pickle, he did. We've had census collection volunteers coming down from the hills all afternoon to hand in their papers and get their fees. I didn't know what to tell them.'

'Did he do anything like that the last time he was here?' Phosy asked.

'He did take the truck a few times, but he was usually back in time to talk to the collectors.'

'Where does he sleep when he's here?'

'Up there,' said the man, pointing to a solitary hut on a hill. 'We told him he could stay with us in the main house but he preferred it up there by himself.'

'How many of you live up here?' Daeng asked. Phosy didn't bother to reprimand her.

'Just us and our kids,' the man said. 'One house. This used to be a busy community during the war. But after the ceasefire there wasn't much of a reason to be here. We're a long way from running water, you see. This settlement was always more strategic than natural.'

'So why are you still here?' she asked.

'Got nowhere else to go,' he told her honestly. 'The government wants to relocate all us hill tribes to the plains but we wouldn't know how to survive down there growing paddy rice. This is where we're comfortable, up in the clouds.'

They started up the hill to the lone hut, all but the wife, who stood like a solitary stalk of rice in the clearing.

'Does the truck spend a lot of time up here?' Phosy asked as they walked.

'Well, they only just came today, but when they were here two weeks ago it was in and out all the time. We got the idea it was supposed to be collecting forms from the other bases. When Comrade Buaphan took it out, the driver used to sit with us and have a laugh about him. The boss had the poor fellow counting papers and loading stacks of questionnaires in cement sacks. They weren't often here at the same time.'

'But the truck wasn't here that often at night?'

'Hardly at all.'

'And you're certain you saw Comrade Buaphan and the driver leave at midday together?'

'No, Comrade. I didn't see that at all.'

'You said . . .'

'I saw Comrade Buaphan leave by himself. There was no driver with him.'

'So where's the driver?' asked Daeng.

'I don't know.' The man seemed to think about it for the first time. 'Haven't seen him since this morning. I suppose he could be up in the hut. There aren't many places to hide.'

They were surrounded by bush, so Daeng noted that that statement wasn't true at all. They arrived on top of the butte. The hut was a thatched box with door and window shapes sliced out of the front like a child's drawing. The five of them filled the room. There was a military sleeping bag rolled up against the rear rattan wall and an empty American-issue knapsack standing beside it. Buaphan's few possessions were laid out on top of a bamboo bench.

'The simple life,' said Daeng. 'I'd say he didn't have too many parties up here.'

There were two white shirts folded the way the Chinese laundries preferred, one pair of black trousers rolled to keep out creases, a small heap of underwear and socks, an expensive-looking watch, an English language novel book-marked halfway through, a Thai handbook of local birds, a pair of binoculars, and a small stack of *kip*.

'Wherever he was going he didn't need his watch or his money,' Phosy said, looking at the engraving on the back of the watch. 'From your loving parents,' he read.

'Rich family by the look of it,' said one of the police officers.

'So it is possible he bought his way into the job,' Daeng said, recalling Siri's theory.

'And there's only one reason a man with money would want to go off into the wilderness,' Phosy said.

'He might just have wanted peace and quiet,' Daeng suggested.

'No, he put himself out here in this isolated spot and worked out a regimen where nobody knew where he was at any one time. It's why he was so annoyed about having a driver attached to the project. He wanted the truck to himself. And look, he's right out here at the end of the chain. Logically, the project coordinator would be based in the centre, down at the Nahoi intersection. But that was too busy. There were too many witnesses to his comings and goings. This place is ideal.'

Everything fitted in Phosy's mind. The only thing missing was the driver.

'You're absolutely certain the driver wasn't in the truck?' he asked again. 'I mean, he might have been asleep in the back or hunched down on the seat.'

'There's nothing wrong with my eyes,' the man said. 'I was up on the other butte. I saw Comrade Buaphan walk down from his hut large as life, climb in the truck and drive off. There was nobody else with him.'

'Perhaps he ran off,' said the other officer.

'Why would he do that?' Phosy asked. 'He's got a cushy government job. He doesn't have to do a lot of work.'

'But he didn't get along with the section head,' one policeman reminded him.

'We all of us have to work with people we don't like, Officer. You don't just run away in the middle of nowhere like this. You wait till you're in a city where there are options.'

'He could be out hunting, though,' Daeng said.

'Good point,' Phosy said. 'In which case he'll be back soon. It'll be getting dark. On the other hand, he could be dead.'

They all turned to look at him.

'Why?' Daeng asked.

'Assume Comrade Buaphan has set up his next victim. He was here two weeks ago working it all out, laying the foundations. All he needs to do is drive to the next victim's village. But, as usual, there's one person in the way. He tried again to get the driver kicked off the project but failed. He's the only one who can verify when Buaphan took the truck.

He's the only witness. There's conflict between them and Buaphan knows the driver would gladly give evidence against him if news of the murders got out. He's a liability, so the comrade makes him disappear. He goes off in the truck, kills his next victim, and at the end of the mission he puts in a report that the driver ran off. Nobody could question it. It's a logical next step. He might have even done away with other project drivers. We could check with—'

He was interrupted by a woman's scream. It was the type of scream used in the mountains to alert rather than to alarm. They rushed out of the hut. The ailing sun had bled the sky crimson and in its glow they could see the jeep in the clearing and the man's wife standing beside it. She was pointing to the top of the track where three undernourished children stood beside the road like marker stakes.

'Who are they?' Phosy asked.

'Our kids,' the man answered proudly. The children were jumping up and down and pointing and beckoning for the policemen to come down.

'It looks like they've found something,' said Daeng.

'And if it isn't the body of the driver I'll eat the truck, starting at the wheels,' Phosy told her.

They walked down the hill and across the clearing. They arrived at the top of the road where the children stood. In front of them some of the thick wayside plants had been flattened, leaving a narrow cave of leaves.

'Bom was taking a pee,' said the oldest boy. He was about ten. 'She found it.'

Bom was half his age. She waved at Daeng and smiled. Phosy decided that if she'd found a body she was being very relaxed about it. He pushed his way into the bushes before Madame Daeng could take the lead. Only four metres in, he found a mound of branches. He knelt and cleared them carefully. Daeng and the two officers had followed him in and were staring over his shoulders. Even before all the leaves had been removed it was evident what had been hidden there.

Daeng put her hands to her mouth and gasped, 'Oh shit. Oh shit.' She turned and pushed her way out of the vegetation past the young policemen.

'Isn't that the doctor's Triumph?' said one of them.

The bike lay on its side beneath the broken branches. Its left-side mirror was smashed.

'Yes, it is,' Phosy replied, running his finger over a dark stain on the saddle.

'That's not gasoline, is it, sir?'

'No, boy. It's blood.'

The happy couple drove towards the honeymoon supper. It was ten p.m., and the interminable wedding ceremony was over. They'd made an awful to-do of it. They'd had the villagers march along the track to the school carrying Phan on one litter and the bride on the other. There was nothing traditional about it. It was some ridiculous idea of the headman. There were lanterns along the route and people singing and ramwong *dancing. The school had been done up like the damned presidential palace. Phan could think of better ways for the idiots to waste the little money they had.*

Visions of the feast kept haunting him: farmers who had nothing else to look forward to fattening up their favourite pigs for strangers to eat, sacrificing their hens' precious eggs. Out comes Mother's best phasin *wrapped in tissue paper. Father gets his hair washed in rice water and has a shave for the first time in his worthless life. Teenaged girls experiment with cheap Chinese make-up that turns them into whorish circus performers. Granny, bent double from a lifetime of bowing to the rice stalks, finds a few dance moves to entertain the crowd. And, oh yes, the booze. The deeper you ventured into the countryside, the more reliant the peasants were on rice whisky for a good time. Heaven forbid the thought they might just possibly be able to have fun without being paralyzed with alcohol. And they didn't offer it, they forced it on you. God help the man with cirrhosis of the liver at a village wedding.*

He sighed at the thought of it all.

Wei used her teacher's voice to be heard above the growl of the engine.

'What are you thinking about?' Wei asked.

That damned stupid question again. Surely, if a person was thinking something, wasn't it because he chose not to speak it? 'Be patient,' Phan told himself. He turned to his bride with the same smile that had won her.

'You,' he lied. 'Imagining what it will be like when we're together.'

He reached for the gear knob to drop the old truck into second and, before he realized it, she had leaned forward and squeezed his hand. The fine hairs on his arm bristled and bile rose in his throat. He switched back to third gear, throwing off her hand as if by accident. There certainly wouldn't be any of that. If there was contact it would be when he was good and ready. Nothing would happen until its allotted time.

'Are you nervous?' he yelled to his bride: his possession in the passenger seat. She was only a shadow, but he could tell she was smiling.

'Not really nervous,' she shouted. 'More excited. If I

hadn't had so much to drink I'd be scared to death, I'm sure.'

'Really!' he mumbled beneath the angry engine noise. 'You don't know yet just how scared you'll be, my little darling.'

His mind wandered again. The day hadn't gone the way he'd planned it. He'd killed two men that afternoon. Killing was nothing new to him. It didn't trouble his soul at all, didn't make a dent on his conscience. But it had disoriented him. The sense of control, so important on his wedding days, had been sent into a spin. He'd lost his calm. They'd asked for it. There was no question about that, the imbecile especially. Phan had caught him tinkering with the engine, threatening to take parts out and clean them. He'd said the truck would have to stay at the camp overnight. This was Phan's wedding night, for God's sake. Weddings only came around two or three times a year. He wasn't going to let the idiot spoil this day for him. It was easier to kill him than argue about it. He'd slit him with a bayonet. He'd had it coming for a long time. There would be no more discussions over who was in charge of the truck.

But for some reason that didn't make him feel any better and as if he wasn't already disoriented enough, then came the old man: nosy little blighter. He wouldn't shut up with his questions. He saw the blood on Phan's hands so there'd been no choice but to slit him too. Being forced to gut two men on your wedding day had to be a bad omen. It was as if he could feel a warning drape itself across his shoulders. He'd dragged the second body over beside the first, blood and entrails everywhere. He wasn't worried about being caught. They were in bandit territory. All Phan had to do was shrug, 'I wasn't there, Comrade. I just drove up to the *base and there they were – dead.' They'd blame the Hmong. They blamed everything on the Hmong.*

He should have been able to get it out of his mind but he'd been irritable all evening. Not even the thought of defiling the woman he owned could settle his mind. He just wanted it over and done with. All through the ceremony he'd been unable to summon his charming self. He was curt and insulting. He'd looked at his wristwatch more times than he'd looked at his bride. If they'd been sober, the guests might have put his mood down to nerves. But nobody seemed to care and it no longer mattered. He had his prize.

An hour on the road and they hadn't passed another vehicle. They were only ten kilometres from the Ban Nahoi turn-off. The moon nudged its way between two large clouds. Soon the rains would come, and all these roads would be impassable, even with a four-wheel drive. He slowed as he approached a withered tree that stretched its desperate branches across the road like the spines of a windblown umbrella. This was his marker. He stopped in the middle of the road. When he turned off the engine the silence hit them like a sigh of relief. Apart from the clicks and hisses of the cooling motor the sounds of nature all around were as soothing as a swim in a warm water stream.

'Why have we stopped?' Wei asked.

'I have a surprise for you,' he said. 'But I need to prepare everything. Promise me you'll stay here in the truck till it's ready?'

She laughed. 'Phan, you really are a special man.'

It was as if he couldn't pretend any more. Urgency had taken him over.

'Do you promise?'

'Yes, I promise.'

He climbed from the cab and ran around to the flatbed. He used the metal stirrup as a step and clambered up. One feature of the old Jiefang army trucks was a fixed tool chest that could be locked. It was nestled up against the back of the cab and had the dimensions of a good-sized coffin. He took out his padlock key, unfastened the lid, and retrieved his holdall. There were other tools of his trade in the chest but this was all he needed for now. He jumped off the truck, called, 'Don't go anywhere,' and vanished into the under- growth beside the road.

Wei sat enjoying the buzz of the whisky and the silence and the thrill of being a wife. She'd imagined all the wonders the position might bring into her life. She couldn't believe her luck. This was no ordinary man and this was an extraordi- nary day. He hadn't really been himself this evening but who could be themselves on such an occasion? Goodness knows she hadn't behaved naturally since she'd first met him.

Ten minutes later her husband was back, running around the front of the truck. He waved at her through the wind- screen and climbed into the driver's seat. He seemed so happy.

'I have to park off the road,' he said. 'We don't want to be disturbed.'

She started to speak but her words were overwhelmed by the restarting of the engine. He didn't put on the lights. He reversed across the road, bumped heavily into a bank of dirt behind them, then aimed at a small gap between an old dead tree and a younger version to its left. There hardly seemed enough room to get through. The side mirror grazed the dead trunk. Wei laughed. It was all part of her fairy-tale adventure. The truck forged through the thick undergrowth, leaves and twigs caressing the windows, branches twanging from the mirrors.

A little way ahead, a pale aura of light beckoned them on. She leaned forward in her seat excitedly to get a better look. They arrived at a sandy clearing barely twice the length and breadth of the truck and he switched off the engine. At the centre of the clear patch of ground was a beautifully embroidered double quilt. It was surrounded by a ring of flat temple candles. Their flames were untroubled by the breeze. At the head of the forest marriage bed was a tray with a bottle of champagne and real champagne glasses and small snacks on a plate. To one side, pink ribbons were tied around a tree trunk.

Wei looked at it all with her mouth open. She had never seen or imagined anything so beautiful. It was a scene from a mythical tale that perhaps she might tell her students: of handsome princes and poor country maids. A lump formed in her throat and tears began to flow from her eyes.

'You don't like it?' he asked.

She finally found words, 'Oh, Phan, it's…it's so lovely.'

The cheap make-up was smeared around her eyes. She leaned across to kiss him but he was too fast for her. He was out of the door and standing in front of the truck, signalling for her to get down. Her legs wobbled as she walked into the circle. Her posture was bad. He'd already started to notice her failings. He was anxious. He couldn't rush this but he didn't want it to take for ever.

'There's a bucket over there with soapy water,' he said. 'And a mirror.'

'You want me to wash?' she asked.

'Just your face for now. They make brides put on so

much junk at their weddings. You're beautiful. I want to see the girl behind the mask. Just take off the make-up.'

She shrugged and giggled and knelt by the bucket.

'Have you had champagne before?' he asked.

'No.'

He kicked off his shoes and sat cross-legged on the quilt. He started to peel off the foil from around the cork.

'There's a shop in Vientiane,' he said. It was as if he were just reading his lines but not investing any emotion into their delivery. 'They have imported luxury items for foreign dignitaries. You can get a lot of exo—'

His eyes had wandered to his bride. She had unbuttoned the top of her blouse and rolled down the collar so she could wash. Her long neck was exposed and, at last, the feeling came to him. It was like a powerful drug that coursed through his veins and made him feel twice the man he was.

'Enough,' he said. 'Come over here.' He fought to keep the anxiety out of his voice. She walked to the edge of the quilt and stepped out of her shoes. She reached for the silver belt that held up her phasin.

'Should I …?'

'No,' he said. 'I mean, not yet. We have all the time in the world and I want this to be special. Come and sit here.'

He patted a spot beside him and quickly put the glasses there as a barrier. She knelt, then eased herself into a polite sitting position with her legs out to one side. He could see that her hands were shaking. It wasn't a cold night. He knew she wanted him, like they all did. He closed his eyes briefly and took a deep breath to calm himself.

'One, two …' he began in English.

'Three,' she said, and the champagne cork exploded high into the starry sky. He heard it land somewhere at the rear

of the truck. He was quick enough to have the sparkling wine in the first glass before it spilled.

'You've done this before,' she said and reached for the glass.

'No, wait,' he told her. He poured his own drink then put down the bottle before reaching for the small plate of hors d'oeuvres. 'There are customs in Europe about how to do this. You'll have to get used to all this when we move there. This is caviar – real Russian caviar. You have to . . .'

'I've heard of it,' she said. 'They say it's very expensive. You really shouldn't sp—'

'All right, and one of the customs is that you listen to the customs. There'll be time to talk later.' He smiled, embarrassed by his lack of control. 'To drink champagne after taking a mouthful of caviar is an experience like no other. You'll think you're in heaven. But the rule is that you have to close your eyes when you eat it.'

'So many rules. I'm surprised the Russians—'

'Here,' he said, holding out a spoon piled high with small dark pearls of sturgeon roe. 'Close your eyes and imagine we're sitting on a balcony overlooking the Black Sea.'

She giggled again. He wanted to slap her.

'Go on. Close them.'

She closed her eyes.

'Now open your mouth but keep your eyes closed. You have to promise to keep them closed until it's all melted in your mouth.'

She opened her mouth. With his right hand he placed the spoon on her tongue and she closed her lips around it. Meanwhile, his left hand reached into his shirt pocket, took out a small envelope, and held it over her glass.

'What's that?' she asked.

He looked at her face. Her eyes were wide open. Rules! Rules had to be obeyed.

'I told you to shut your eyes.' He was furious. He poured the powder into her glass and swirled it around. He was somehow able to hold his temper. 'It's another surprise,' he said. 'A love potion.'

Her laugh now was less spontaneous, more affected than before. She looked into his angry eyes.

'Where's yours?'

'What?'

'If it's a love potion, shouldn't we both—?'

He grabbed the bottle and hurled it with all his might at the tree. It didn't break, merely bounced back in their direction. The champagne spewed across the quilt. She squirmed backwards.

'Phan, what's happened?'

'Just drink the damned champagne, will you?'

'No, you're scaring me.'

'For Christ's sake! Why is this so difficult?'

He was across the quilt and had his forearm around her neck before she could react. He held her as if she were a calf ready for branding. She tried to pull his arm away but he was fearfully strong. His grip was unbreakable. Still confounded by what was happening, she reached for his hair with her free hand. She tried to yank at it but to her astonishment it just came away from his scalp with a slight tearing sound. She looked up at him, at the candlelight playing off his bald head, at the look of rage in his eyes. She had no idea who this man was.

She kicked and flailed her legs as he dragged her back across the quilt to where the champagne glasses still stood on the small tray. He took hold of her drink and squeezed her neck tightly. He held the glass in front of her mouth, waiting for her to gasp for breath so he could hurl the liquid down her throat.

'Drink it,' he snarled. He was crying with frustration. 'You've spoiled it. There were rules and you broke them. You've ruined the whole thing.'

Her fingernails clawed at his flesh but he seemed not to notice. She clamped her lips shut and he threw the champagne in her face. He kept hold of her glass and smashed it against his. It left him with a stem and a jagged point in his fist. He held his new weapon in front of her face and drew his arm back to get full force. She closed her eyes and gritted her teeth, waiting for the inevitable.

There came an almighty crack. The grip around her neck loosened and her attacker slumped against her. She opened her eyes in time to see the glass drop to the quilt. Phan was still draped over her but without strength – without life. She fought his body off hers and fell back, panting, onto the quilt. Her shirt was ripped almost off. Her hair had broken free of its bun and hung across her face. Phan lay as if asleep on his side of the bed. His face on the pillow wore an angelic smile, but his hairless skull was cracked like an egg. A puddle of red yolk spread beneath him.

Wei swept back her hair and looked up. Standing beside the quilt was an old man with green eyes and snowy white hair. He seemed drugged and woozy. She could hear his breaths like saw cuts on teak. In his right hand he held a fifty-centimetre monkey wrench, the largest you could find in a standard Lao toolbox.

18

THE BUDDHA AMUSEMENT PARK

It was a rare treat. Mr Inthanet had somehow managed to convince his ex-fiancée, Miss Vong, that he didn't actually have a wife in Luang Prabang. Or at least that he hadn't seen her for so long that some sort of statute of limitations was now in place that technically made him single. The engagement was back on, and she'd given him permission to use the teacher training department truck that Sunday. It meant that everyone from Siri's house at That Luang, plus one or two stragglers, could make the trip out to the Buddha Park. The fantasy park at Xiang Khuan had been built in 1958 by an eccentric mystic called Luang Pa Bunleua. It housed a collection of concrete interpretations of various scenes from the *Ramayana* and other mythical tales as well as Buddhist and Hindi deities.

Luang Pa himself had been deported the previous year for antisocial behaviour, which many had taken to mean antisocialist behaviour. The Party was a little overwhelmed by a man so steeped in religious convictions that he would build a theme park to the gods. Luang Pa's first task upon arriving in Thailand had been to build a brand-new Buddha Park in Nong Kai, even grander and weirder than its predecessor. Rather than bulldoze the Lao site, the government declared it a national park and hoped children would grow up believing the huge stone figures were Thai cartoon characters with no religious connections.

It was a busy place on weekends. Goodness knows there was little enough entertainment in the country, and locals gravitated to the ex-deities as if the monuments had some drawing power of their own. There were a few army and government vehicles in the car park and some motorcycles, but most people found their way to the Buddha Park by public bus. The department of road transport had laid on extra buses on weekends to cater to the numbers.

Even though there was a guard on duty specifically to discourage acts of obeisance, Mr Tickoo, Crazy Rajid's father, had smuggled in a dozen jasmine leis and a whole box of incense to give thanks to the Lord Shiva for his son's recovery. He had astounded Siri and Daeng earlier when they cornered him at his room above the Happy Dine. Given his knowledge of foreign languages and his obvious intelligence, Siri had decided the man could make better use of his talents. The *Lao Huksat* newsletter was expanding into English and they needed a writer and editor. Siri knew the publisher and had made a very good presentation on the Indian's behalf. There was a small but livable wage and a free room behind the office. It meant Mr Tickoo could have money rather than curried potatoes in his bank account.

'Oh, sir,' he had said, 'you are far too kind. But, you see, I have promised to look after the owner of this restaurant. I made a vow to his father that I would not allow him to go bankrupt and destitute. I fear without me he would be on the streets. But I am deeply honoured by your offer.'

Mr Tickoo laid a discreet prayer mat down behind a bush at the Lord's left hand and told the others to collect him on their way out.

Mrs Fah's children, Mee and Nounou, were running excited rings around the inside of a giant pumpkin. Dtui and Phosy walked with Malee from statue to statue, explaining who these giants actually were. It was an early step along the little girl's path to becoming a doctor. Tong and Gongjai, the ladies of ill repute, were carrying a twin apiece, and everyone wondered how they'd cope with being separated from their surrogate babies. They had all the appearances of kidnappers about to make off with their button-nosed loot.

Comrade Noo, the renegade Thai monk, had wanted very badly to join the house excursion. Siri had explained that it might be inadvisable for an incommunicado alien member of the Sangha to be seen strolling around Buddha's own Disneyland in robes. Noo had obviously taken the teachings of Siri to heart because, as they were all loading into the truck, he'd appeared in white slacks, a bowling shirt, sunglasses, and a straw hat. He had entered the Buddha Park unnoticed, yet, despite his clever disguise, he still had the walk: head bowed, hands gently clasped, that left nobody in any doubt as to his calling.

'You can take the man out of the saffron, but you can't take the saffron out of the man,' Daeng said as they watched him wander around in the afternoon heat.

There was one more unexpected participant in this Sunday jaunt. Comrade Civilai hadn't come to see the nine drowning victims or the waving naked damsels or the five-headed serpent. Nor could he care less about the five-metre-high reclining Buddha. He'd been forced to attend because for four days he'd been hounding Siri for the facts leading up to the denouement of the strangler case. He had everything clear up until Siri's sudden departure by motorcycle for the Thon River district. He knew that the killer had been cornered and somehow lost his life in a struggle. It was all the stuffing in between that he lacked and it was driving him insane. In the space of four months the old politburo member had been relegated from a man who was told everything to one who didn't even know the name of his next-door neighbour. As his best friend, Siri was obliged to fill his dull life with adventure, and if Civilai had to endure a day at the Buddha Park to get it, so be it.

After the picnic lunch, he cornered the doctor once more.

'It doesn't look like your little Hmong general's going to put in an appearance,' he said.

'She'll come,' Siri told him with confidence. 'I know her.'

'Good, then while we're waiting...'

Siri smiled. He enjoyed the odd occasion when he could keep his older, non-related brother dangling.

'I promised Madame Daeng I'd show her the...' Siri began.

'She's seen it already. Siri!'

'Tsk, tsk. And you used to be such a calm elder statesman.'

'I've been having testosterone injections. You'd better not mess with me, little brother.'

'All right. You win.'

Siri laughed again and led Civilai to a concrete bench overlooking the river. They were shaded by an old-fart bamboo, which seemed appropriate. Siri began by telling him of Phosy's mission to Pakxan and everything leading up to their arrival at Phan's base in Nahoi.

'Which brings me to my contribution,' Siri said at last. 'You wouldn't like to go and get a soft drink or visit the bathroom at this juncture, would you?'

'Just get on with it.'

'Certainly. Here we go. Although I'd hit the road several hours after the census truck, I was on a thunderous machine and I had the spirit of Steve McQueen. You'll recall we saw *The Great Escape* in that illegal back-room cinema in Da Nang? You'll agree that was—'

'Can we dispense with the garnish and go straight to the meat?'

'If you insist. I caught up with the truck just after we passed the Thon tributary turn-off but I decided I could afford to hang back. A truck isn't a helicopter, and it's limited to roads, and there weren't that many to choose from in that part of the world. So I stayed a way back and kept out of sight. The first major intersection was at Natan. I assumed they'd report to the local cadre and drop off the census coordinators at their respective sites. Avoiding police checkpoints isn't really that hard on a motorcycle. I didn't want anyone reporting that there was an old codger asking questions so I steered clear of anyone who looked official.'

'That wouldn't be a bad philosophy for you to adopt in your day-to-day life,' Civilai suggested.

'If you insist on interrupting, you won't get the story.'

Civilai afforded him a polite *nop*. 'My humble apologies.'

'I'd had a lot of time to think about things during the ride. Phan was my prime suspect, but one of the other collectors, young Nouphet, also fitted the bill in some respects. So I wanted to keep my options open. All I knew for certain was that the truck was involved. They'd seen it in Vang Vieng and in the south. I believed if I could keep the truck in sight, or at least in earshot, I'd have a good chance of discovering who was using it for his nefarious deeds.

'I learned from the locals that there was only one track leading to the first base at Ban Noo and there was nothing beyond it. When the truck came back down I was sitting by the road with a group of old fogies eating peanuts so I was fittingly camouflaged. Nobody in the truck noticed me. I could see they'd dropped off the first census collector. They dropped off the second, Nouphet, at base two: the next intersection at Ban Nahoi. That only left Buaphan and the driver on the journey to base three. I decided that was where I should be. Sound carries up there in the hills so when I saw the lamplight up ahead I got off and pushed the bike the last kilometre.'

'I admire your stamina.'

'It killed me. I hid the bike in the bushes at the top of the track. It was dark. I was covering it with branches so they wouldn't know I was there and I managed to skewer my hand on a sharp sprig and bled like a spigot.'

'But you didn't cry out in pain, thus giving away your position?'

'No. By now I was in my undercover mode. I swept around the outskirts of the village like a black moth on a dark night and located the hut of Buaphan. He was sitting out front, reading by the light of a hurricane lamp. There was something…how can I put it? Something serene about him. I talked to Daeng about it after the event and she'd come to the same conclusion in her own way. He didn't match our mental picture of the perpetrator at all. The man we were looking for had to be charming. He had to win hearts. Neither of us could imagine Buaphan switching so drastically. He just didn't like people. His Nirvana was to be alone. That was his motivation for working on the census project.

'And it was while sitting watching Buaphan read that I heard the truck start up. I could see the headlights veer off down the track. I'd adopted a "keep the truck in sight" policy but I wasn't sure how I'd be able to follow it without the driver seeing my lights. I was tired and I knew by the time I'd uncovered the bike he'd be long gone. And I still had my mind set on the census collectors at that point. Nouphet had moved up to take the lead in my suspicions. I planned to go down the track the next day and see what he was up to.

'But as I sat there and meditated, I started to think about the driver. He spent a lot of his time ferrying between the three bases. He was their only form of communication. Who could possibly know where he was at any given time? He could tell base two that he'd spent the night at base one and none of them would be any the wiser. He had plenty of opportunity to disappear. The only thing that made him an unlikely suspect was his looks.'

'Plain – bald?'

'It didn't fit. Then I thought back to the reports. Nobody ever said the man was good-looking. They talked about his healthy hair and his interesting face and his bearing. You tend to use the term "interesting" to describe someone who's average-looking but oozing with sexual charisma. You, for instance – you're quite ugly but women find you irresistible. They see beyond your bald head and your grasshopper features.'

'I take your point.'

'Our perpetrator had to be a clever actor. He was able to lie to his victims credibly. The driver had every reason to hate Buaphan but he also had the opportunity to study him. He could steal his identity: walk like him, talk like him, adopt his mannerisms. All he needed was hair. And, these days, with so much vanity in the world, a convincing wig isn't that hard to find.'

'And all this came to you as you sat in the bushes watching your original suspect fade from your reckoning?'

'Yes, until I fell asleep. It had been a long day. Much as I love Madame Daeng, I sleep much better beside a shrub. Being surrounded by greenery takes me back to my years in the jungle. I slept like a sloth. It was the sound of the truck returning that woke me up.'

Civilai sat entranced with his elbows on his knees and his chin on his fists. 'And what time was this?' he asked.

'From the position of the sun I assumed it was around ten. I should wear a watch. The driver came up to talk to Buaphan in the hut. I took the opportunity to slide back down the butte and sneak a look at the truck. It was parked in the shade to one side of the clearing. But there were children down there playing around. I didn't want them to see me, so I waited. On reflection I have to presume it was around this time that the driver killed Buaphan. Then he had to do away with the old census collector who had the misfortune to turn up asking for his fee. I knew nothing about it.

'After about an hour the children were called to the house for lunch and I had my chance. I can't say for sure what I was looking for in the truck. While I was scratching around in the cab the driver came down. I was sure he'd find me and I had no idea what I was going to tell him. But the banshees were on my side that day. He didn't get in the front. He climbed up on the flatbed and unlocked the metal chest. I heard him rummaging around back there and then the sound of the lid closing. He jumped off the truck and headed back up to the butte. He'd left the chest unlocked. I went to have a look. And that's when I knew I had the killer. There was a holdall in there. It contained some pretty fancy hors d'oeuvres in cans, and dry crackers and a bottle of champagne as well as two rolls of pink ribbon. It was incriminating in itself but there's nothing illegal about drinking champagne. It wasn't solid evidence that he'd killed anyone. What I should have done then was left on my bike and gone to contact Phosy. He could have arrested the driver and had witnesses identify him as the man they knew as Phan.'

'But of course you didn't?'

'It was difficult, Civilai. If I'd left then I didn't know how long it would take me to find Phosy. I had no idea that he was already in the district. I was afraid that if I went to the local police, they wouldn't believe me. They certainly wouldn't arrest a man on my say-so. And in the meantime, I was giving the driver free rein to run off and kill again. So I made my decision. There was a rubber groundsheet in the chest. I wrapped it around myself and waited. I'd left myself breathing room in the chest, just a wedge of daylight under the lid. Through the gap I could see him approach the truck. The driver had completed his transformation already. It was astounding. He *was* Buaphan, complete with hair and clothes and confidence. It was as if he'd taken over the other man's skin.

'To my horror, he climbed onto the bed of the truck, threw something into the chest on top of me, slammed the lid shut, and locked it. As you know, I've had more than my fair share of claustrophobic dices with death since I became coroner, but this was a nightmare. It was midday, and the temperature in there was in the mid thirties, so hot, I needed to do something fast. It was a solid, Chinese-built metal coffin riveted to the bed of the truck. I calmed myself, slowed my breathing, and recalled that there was a toolbox in the chest. I fumbled my way to it and found a hammer and a screwdriver. A metal drill bit would have been handy but fate wasn't that kind.

'The truck started and I used the cover of the noisy engine to hammer myself an airhole. But these Chinese, I tell you. Why use twenty-millimetre metal plate when you can use fifty? I pounded myself into a good old sweat making the tiniest of holes. I was still going at it when I passed out for the first time. And, Civilai, that pinprick of a hole saved my life. When I came round I had no idea where I was. The truck was stopped and it was quiet out. I was afraid someone might hear me but I needed more air. I used the sharp end of a file to gouge out a larger hole. After an hour I had it to the size of a nostril. I could see through it. It was dark out. We were parked beside a road in some sort of village. There was nobody in sight. All I could think about was Phan being with a new victim somewhere and me stuck in the chest.

'I was deciding whether to yell for help and risk him catching me when I heard the music. It was a band of bamboo instruments and a small choir of drunk-sounding singers. The music was getting closer. I wrapped myself up in the groundsheet again in case anyone opened the chest. It wasn't a logical response, but I was suffering from oxygen deficiency by then, so don't expect common sense.'

'I never do. You know? If only we had a campfire and a good bottle of whisky, this would be one of your most classic Siri tales of the improbable.'

'We can still do that sometime. Trust me. This story will get better every time I tell it. Where was I?'

'Wrapped in a groundsheet.'

'Right. I have the groundsheet over my head, and I am blocked from the airhole, so I pass out for a second time. On this occasion I absolutely believe I'm a goner. As I'm fighting off the black moths, I try to summon my resident spirits: my mother, my dead dog, even the pregnant lady with worms, anybody to get me through it. But I was alone. When you need a good spirit there's never one around. But next thing I know, the lid of the chest is open, and I can see actual stars. I can see Phan's face looking down at me. I'm drowsy from the lack of air, and he's a blur, but I'm sure he must be able to see me if I can see him. Yet he didn't. It was dark in the chest and he was in a hurry. He reached beside me for something – the holdall, it must have been – yanked it out, and he was gone.

'I was disoriented, nauseous. My breathing was awful, but the rush of night air cleared my head a little. Sounds and images were passing in and out of my consciousness: footsteps, the truck starting, driving through thick under-growth, silence, a distant conversation. I tried to climb out of the chest, but I couldn't summon the energy.'

'Where was he going?'

'He'd pulled off the road and gone a little way into the trees. I knew in my heart that this was where he'd be killing his next victim, but all I could see was white spots in front of my eyes. I might have even passed out again if it hadn't been for the pop. I know now it was the sound of the cham-pagne cork, but in my fuzzy state I imagined it to be a bone snapping. That small rush of adrenalin was enough to get me out of the chest and off the truck. I was sure he must have heard me, but no. I don't remember when I picked it up, but I had a large wrench in my hand. I staggered towards a light. He'd set up a space like a sort of open-air love ring with a quilt and candles. I saw them there. I really didn't believe I could make it, but he was on her, forcing her to drink, and he smashed a glass and held a shard in front of her face. I knew he'd use it.'

'So you whacked him over the head with the wrench and killed the bastard,' Civilai yelled and let out a loud, 'Woohoo!' It frightened a small whiskery-nosed otter out of the tall grass beside them. Siri cast his eyes downward, not sharing his friend's glee. Murder was nothing to be proud of.

'Come on, you have to be pleased about it,' Civilai told him.

'Of course I'm pleased that he's not free any longer to kill. But what kind of world are we living in where something like this can happen?'

'I'd prefer to see it as a one-off. I don't want to believe there are maniacs crawling out of the woodwork. You have to admit this was a special case, Siri. I heard a rumour your strangler was a bit confused in the gender department.'

'He was a hermaphrodite.'

'That'd be enough to throw anyone off-kilter. It doesn't pardon him but it does explain what happened. Even I'd go nuts if I didn't have a willy.'

Siri looked into his friend's eyes and smiled.

'Mrs Noy tells me…'

'Don't even think about saying it.'

'How do you know…?'

'Whatever it is, keep it to yourself. I recognize that mischievous glint. Finish the story. How did the girl come through it all?'

'She was in shock, of course, but unharmed. We spent the

night asleep in the truck. I wasn't in any state to drive. I caught up with Daeng and the police the next day. By then they'd discovered the bodies of Buaphan and the census collector and put two and two together. Daeng was in a terrible state. She'd expected the next body they found would be mine. I'm afraid I'd rather set her up for that by telling her about my premonitions of death.'

Young Nounou came skipping along the path to the two old men.

'Grandpa,' she said. 'Granny Daeng says your friend's looking for you.'

'Ah, at last,' Siri smiled. 'I suppose it's time for the handover. You coming, old brother?'

'No,' said Civilai. 'Give me a few minutes. I want to bask in the afterglow of your adventure. I need to work out the few changes I'd have to make to turn it into a story about me for the next cake party.'

Siri laughed and thumped his friend on the cranium with his fist. He took Nounou's hand and she led him back towards the giant pumpkin. Daeng was standing talking to a small man in a floppy Burmese bush hat. As they got closer, he saw that it wasn't a man at all. The figure looked up with a beaming smile.

'General Bao?' Siri laughed and switched to Hmong language. 'Is that you inside that ridiculous disguise?'

He didn't know whether to hug her or kiss her so he settled for a long, lingering handshake. It had concerned him during their time together in the north that he had fallen in love with this beautiful, brave little warrior. But once they were apart, it began to make sense. She was the daughter he'd wanted so badly all his life – the daughter his wife claimed would distract them from the fight for political

THE BUDDHA AMUSEMENT PARK

freedom. She was the girl upon whom he could bestow all his paternal pride and joy. When they'd parted a few months earlier it had been harder than he could understand. And now, at their reunion, he felt he could cry. He wanted to boast to the world that his brave girl had survived.

'Who is that?' Nounou asked.

'A very special lady and a very good friend,' he said. 'Do you want to go and find your auntie Tong and auntie Gongjai and tell them to bring the twins?'

'OK.' She ran off.

'How did you two...?' Siri began.

'Instinct,' said Madame Daeng. 'We sort of gravitated to one another.'

'That's nice. Do you mind...?'

'Of course not.' Daeng smiled at Bao and went to sit on a bench. Siri realized he was still holding the Hmong's hand.

'Is everybody safe?' he asked.

'We lost Chia.'

Siri felt a pain in his heart at the matter-of-fact way she reported her sister's death. But the tribe had lost many before her and the departed were best grieved for in private.

'We walked for three weeks,' Bao said, smiling proudly. 'A few kilometres every night. We hid from the PL and the Vietnamese during the day. And it was true. The twins would have given us away with their crying. You saved our lives.'

Siri blushed. 'And Chia?'

'She went to find us water and was shot by a lone guard. She didn't suffer. How are the babies?'

'They're enormous. You won't recognize them. How did you get across the river?'

'It was easy. The uncle who made this garden has another garden on the Thai side. He has a little boat and he travels back and forth bringing his Buddhas and amulets. The guards don't dare stop him because they believe he has very strong magic. He sometimes lets people hide on his boat.'

Siri laughed. 'That's marvellous. I bet he doesn't have too many passengers coming in this direction.'

'He said I was the first.'

Siri introduced Bao to his friends. It was time for the surrogate mothers to hand over the babies. Tong and Gongjai watched teary eyed as Bao cooed and snuggled her nose into the babies' bellies. They seemed to recognize her scent or her language because they glowed pink as if their batteries had been recharged.

'Very well, ladies,' Siri said. 'It's time to let Bao take her relatives home.'

The two women looked at each other. It was Tong who said, 'Uncle Siri, we're going too.'

A shocked mumble rolled around the crowd.

'The twins have a family,' Siri said. 'A whole tribe even.'

'It's not about the babies,' said Gongjai. 'We know we can't keep them. That's not why we're going.'

Siri understood immediately. He'd heard the officials at Housing describe the women. They'd served their sentences but he knew they would never be free of the stigma. He turned to their aunt.

'Are you all right about this?'

'It's for the best, Dr Siri,' she said.

'Life won't be easy on the Thai side,' Siri told them.

'We know girls who have gone over,' Gongjai told him. 'They're earning a living wage. We might even get a little respect over there. Who knows?'

Siri doubted that, but he knew they'd weighed the odds. 'So be it,' he said.

They all kissed the babies, then the women, and it was time to part company. General Bao took Siri to one side.

'Yeh Ming,' she said, using his shaman name, 'none of us will ever forget you.' She squeezed his hands in hers and kissed his cheek. For good measure, she said in Lao, 'Thank you.'

She turned and joined the twins and the ladies of ill repute and walked jauntily off toward the workers' huts and the little pier. He knew in his heart he would never see them again. With a catch in his voice he whispered, '*Bo ben nyang*.'